Also by Laurence Anholt

*Art of Death*

# Festival of Death

## A Mindful Detective book

Laurence Anholt

CONSTABLE

First published in Great Britain in 2020 by Constable

This paperback edition published in 2021 by Constable

1 3 5 7 9 10 8 6 4 2



*All characters and events in this publication, other than those clearly in the public domain, are fictitious and any resemblance to real persons, living or dead, is purely coincidental.*



A CIP catalogue record for this book is available from the British Library.

ISBN: 978-1-47213-003-7

Typeset in Adobe Caslon Pro by Initial Typesetting Service, Edinburgh
Printed and bound in Great Britain by Clays Ltd, Elcograf S.p.A.

Papers used by Constable are from well-managed forests and other responsible sources.

Constable
An imprint of
Little, Brown Book Group
Carmelite House
50 Victoria Embankment
London EC4Y 0DZ

An Hachette UK Company
www.hachette.co.uk

www.littlebrown.co.uk

*For my lovely daughter, Maddy,*
*who dances at the Festival of Life*

## *Chapter 1*

# While My Guitar Gently Kills

In the days leading up to the Glastonbury Festival, a raggle-taggle army of revellers hauled backpacks and tents through the leafy lanes of Somerset, towards the mythical valleys of Worthy Farm.

To pass through those turnstiles was to enter another world – a carefree utopia in which the air was thick with hypnotic rhythms, the spicy aroma of a thousand and one food stalls, and the sticky scent of ganja.

Discarding their packs, the festival-goers hunkered down for five days of sun-baked, blissed-out music and mayhem in that kaleidoscopic canvas city.

This was a special year. For the first time since the seventies, the headline act would open the festival, instead of closing it on the Sunday night. The reason was simple – the biggest band in the world could choose their own slot.

And so it was that on the Wednesday afternoon, as if guided by an invisible force, the multitude converged towards the beating heart of the festival: the Pyramid Stage, which thrust like an intergalactic chariot into the sky. Over the years, the likes of Amy Winehouse, Stevie Wonder, Baaba Maal, David Bowie, Adele, Dolly Parton and The Rolling Stones had strutted their stuff on those hallowed boards. Pity the B-listers on the outlying stages; tonight they would play to empty fields, as the rapt eyes of 175,000 festival-goers and a TV audience of gazillions were fixed on the band called Stigma.

Unless you lived on Mars, you could not have avoided the lurid stories of the Flynn twins, Ethan and Tyrone – the arguments, the bust-ups, the court cases. But now, following an acrimonious seven-year split, Stigma had reunited. Of course they would headline the festival. Of course they could choose their own time slot, no matter how inconvenient for the festival organisers and the rival stars of the music world.

Twins they might be, but the Flynns could not have been more different. Legend had it that they were even born in different years: Ethereal Ethan, first and favoured in everything, arriving a few minutes before midnight; Tyrannical Tyrone, angry and late for the proceedings, in the dawn of the new year.

What Stigma fans – or Stigs – knew was that the animosity rarely came from Ethan. His was a gentle, almost feminine presence. The bitterness belonged to his dangerous brother, who emanated resentment towards everyone, and especially his beautiful and talented twin. This was their thing. This rivalry was their identity. The Flynn twins were the Beauty and the Beast of the music world.

Despite Tyrone's hostility, or maybe because of it, Stigma's YouTube videos had clocked up a staggering numbers of views. Their songs were endlessly streamed and downloaded. There was something mesmeric about the incongruous pair. Androgynous Ethan was a virtuoso on any instrument, his voice a crystal river, his lyrics like mystical poems. With flowing curls, a wisp of a beard and delicate features, he had been likened to Marc Bolan, and even Jesus Christ. By contrast, snarling, spitting, shaven-headed Tyrone, whilst a competent bass guitarist, lacked his sibling's divine talent, and having lost out in the looks department had compensated by building bulging muscles, adorned with terrifying tattoos. Tyrone was also an amateur boxer with past convictions for GBH.

By early evening, the huge bowl of Worthy valley was a churning ocean of Stigs, waving flags and jostling for position. Like antelopes to a watering hole, their numbers grew. Only the bravest or most inebriated elbowed towards the mosh pit in front of the stage, where the noise would be deafening and the crush almost unbearable. On the hillsides, families picnicked in the sunshine while teenagers snaffled cider and spliffs.

The dark stage lay unoccupied but for a few technicians in skinny jeans and Stigma T-shirts, making last-minute adjustments to the array of stringed instruments that lined the back of the platform – autoharps, dulcimers, lutes, mandolins, sitars, zithers. Yes, Ethan could play all of these and many more besides.

Now even the techies melted into the shadows, and for ten long minutes, the stage lay silent, empty and brooding. The anticipation was palpable. Would Stigma show up at all? It was not unknown for Tyrone to throw a last-minute tantrum and refuse to perform.

Slow handclaps rose and subsided. Loud yells, followed by laughter. A leaking beer can was hurled in the air.

And then at long last, a single spotlight picked out a solitary figure who entered from the wings. It was the ubiquitous Canadian radio presenter and MC, Vula Plenty. She appeared tiny on that vast stage, but she was grinning from ear to ear. Everything was all right. Stigma were here. They were going to play.

Vula raised the microphone, her velvety tones welcoming the many viewers at Worthy Farm and around the world. At last she stepped backwards, urging the crowd to give 'an enormous Glastonbury welcome to . . . THE MIGHTY . . . STIGMA!'

A deep-throated roar of joy echoed around the valley. Pyrotechnics ejaculated into the sky. The stage erupted into incandescent brightness. And now Exquisite Ethan glided barefoot like a ballet dancer across the boards. Delicate, slender, draped in flowing clothes. On the vast screens, those emerald eyes twinkled with kindness and intelligence.

The roar did not diminish for one second as his brother entered stage right – swearing, swaggering Tyrone, swigging from a beer bottle and wrenching ugly notes from his bass guitar.

Any Stigma show was a spectacle in itself. Tonight the Flynn twins were supported by eight musicians on drums, keyboards and brass, backing singers and an exotic troupe of dancers, dressed for the occasion as sinister characters from Tarot cards – the Fool, the Magician, the Priestess, the Hermit, the Devil, the Sun and the Moon.

Taking the mic, Ethan spoke for a few minutes about how young the brothers had been the last time they played this stage, and about someone special who had come into his life and made him rethink everything. He was not a natural speaker – he mumbled and stuttered shyly – but when he began to sing, those awkward, childish tones melted into liquid silver, like the song of a fabulous bird.

The performance kicked off with Stigma standards: 'Legend of You', 'Tiger in the Subway', 'Heathen Child', 'And For You a Love Song' – in which Tyrone plucked moodily at his strings, while Ethan coaxed enchanted rhythms from mandolin and lute, his tremulous voice floating into the evening air, where countless iPhones and cigarette lighters swayed.

In one extraordinary piece of theatre, the fragile man stopped playing abruptly. He raised a thin finger to his lips. As the world fell silent, he pointed across the stage, over the festival site, beyond fields and woods towards a distant hilltop where the sun was sinking in a melodramatic blaze behind the ancient tor of Glastonbury. Even the most cynical viewer felt the skin-crawling magic of the moment.

As lasers and strobes lacerated the sky, Stigma launched into several classics from their best-selling album, *GlobalEyes*, which had scooped nearly every award the fawning music industry had to offer. The years of separation had done nothing to diminish their genius. The multitude swayed and dissolved in a communal orgasm of bliss . . . Ethan Flynn was on fire!

At the midpoint of the concert, Ethan turned to raise his legendary vintage Stratocaster – a gleaming marvel of craftsmanship known to Stigs as Excalibur. The audience went wild; St John Ambulance crews worked frantically, tending to over-excited fans who had simply passed out with rapture. Ethan slung the strap around his neck and gazed tenderly at the instrument like the father of a newborn child. The world knew what was coming, and they prepared to sing along to Stigma's all-time greatest hit, 'While My Guitar Gently Kills'.

Ethan's pale face turned towards his sweating brother, and in the faint smile that illuminated a billion screens, the love he had for Tyrone and every one of his doting fans was plain to see. Ethan so loved the world that he gave this unforgettable song . . .

But as his fingers shaped the first complex chord, something appalling happened. Something momentous.

Something shocking in every sense of the word.

## *Chapter 2*

# Shock and Awe

DI Shanti Joyce was working late at her cluttered desk at Yeovil HQ when she took the call.

'Seen the news, boss?'

'What do you think I'm doing, Benno? Relaxing in front of the TV?'

'Take a look at the Stigma gig at Glastonbury.'

Shanti had heard of Stigma, of course – all those trancey-dancey numbers like 'Heathen Child' – but it wasn't really her thing. She didn't think it was Sergeant 'Benno' Bennett's thing either.

As a rule, she didn't bother much with Glastonbury, although she'd make an exception for soul legend Sista Tremble on Sunday night. That was real music. Shanti had an evening planned in front of the TV with Mum and a bottle of Chardonnay. Maybe Paul could stay up late if he behaved.

Prodding her iPad into life, she quickly realised that the internet was alight, like a sparkler in a firework box. On every news channel and social media platform, an extraordinary image was playing again and again – a Stigma performance on the Pyramid Stage. Ethan Flynn, slim-limbed, mesmeric and barefoot beneath the spotlights.

The rock god turned and raised his guitar, Excalibur. Tossing the strap around his neck, he paused and smiled. But at the very first chord of the song, an ear-splitting wail surged from every amp, and a searing flash of electricity burst from his fingers.

In front of the astonished multitude, his long hair leapt outwards. Eyeballs bulged. Smoke streamed from fingers and toes. And then, with a ghastly rictus snarl on his face, he began to dance. Not the usual Ethan Flynn girlie-whirly gyrations. This was jerky, spasmodic St Vitus dancing that was painful to watch. He twisted. He shimmied. He jived. Thin limbs thrashed like a houseplant in a hurricane.

Ethan Flynn was quite literally on fire.

At last someone cut the power, and he fell. As the music died, brother Tyrone and the backing singers were left gawping dumbly like goldfish. The throaty roar of the crowd disintegrated into chaotic wails and screams as a weirdly costumed troupe of dancers rushed towards the smoking body, which enfolded the guitar like a giant mantis around its prey.

Shanti stared at her screen in disbelief. What had she just watched? Was that part of the act, or had the world's media livestreamed a demonic dance of death?

On the stage, MC Vula Plenty pleaded for calm, but without a working mic, her words were swallowed in the jeers and wails and boos of the crowd.

At the back of the stage, a surreal tableau was taking place as the strangely costumed dancers bore Ethan's charred and twisted body into the wings.

'Holy moly, Benno! I'm watching it now. That's Ethan Flynn. Is he . . .?'

'Dead, boss.'

'Well I'm truly sorry. But why are you telling me?'

'The festival is policed by the Keynsham squad and they've put in an urgent request for you to attend.'

'I'm flattered. I think. But why me?'

'They're stretched to their limits with the demands of the festival.'

'I see that. But there must be other DIs closer to hand.'

'It's you they want, boss. And Caine too. Since the two of you cracked the Havfruen case, it seems you're the "go-to team for weird shit in the West Country". Their words, not mine.'

'Jeez, Benno. I won't be putting that on my CV. But Caine's on leave, isn't he?'

'Shall I track him down?'

'I'll handle it. What I want you to do is seal the area – I need screens around everything and a cordon across the stage. Gather every millisecond of footage you can lay your hands on. And Benno . . . don't let a soul within a hundred metres of that smouldering superstar.'

As she threw a few items into her shoulder bag, Shanti reflected on something odd that Benno had mentioned just before he hung up:

'By the way, boss, you may as well know that the rumour mills have started to turn.'

'What kind of rumours?'

'People are speculating that this wasn't an accident. That Ethan's death was . . .'

'Deliberate?'

'Yeah. Deliberate.'

She ran the footage one last time, noting the way in which Tyrone Flynn responded to his sibling's demise. You'd expect astonishment. Horror. Disbelief. But from what she could tell, the bellicose brother simply tossed down his guitar, drained his beer and stormed off the stage in disgust.

Hurrying along the flickering corridors, Shanti experienced a familiar mix of sensations: distress at what she had just seen – this was a human being after all, a talented young man microwaved in his prime – but alongside that a surge of adrenaline more thrilling than any drug. *She* had got the call. *She*, DI Shanti Joyce, was on the job. Whatever the hell had taken place, just twenty-five miles from here, was her responsibility. She alone would solve the case.

Alone? The Keynsham Kops had asked for Caine too. She liked to think of herself as a lone wolf, but she had to admit that her long-haired colleague knew stuff that she did not. The local geography for a start, and Caine probably had all kinds of irritating facts at his fingertips about music and the effects of high voltage on the nervous system. Come to think of it, he was bound to be a Stigma fan. He probably collected their albums in alphabetical order.

Hurrying across the car park, Shanti made two calls. The first was to her mother – 'No, Mum, I won't be home any time soon. Go to bed and don't worry. How long? One night at least. Maybe more. How's Paul? Well give him a kiss for me. Thanks, Mum. Love you . . .'

The second call was to Vincent Caine – 'Veggie Cop' as he was known to the Yeovil Yoof. The chances of him answering were virtually zero. He seemed to spend most of his time 'in retreat' at his cabin, deep in the Undercliff outside Lyme Regis. It was virtually the only place on earth that had no network coverage whatsoever, and Caine liked it that way. He wanted to be 'at one with nature'. He wanted to meditate in silence. She decided to give him one chance and then go it alone. So she was astonished when, after a few rings, Caine answered her call.

# Chapter 3

# The Dancing Detective

'Good grief. You answered.'

'You'll have to speak up, Shanti. It's very noisy here.'

'I can hear that, Caine. Where the hell are you? Feelings workshop at the men's group?'

'Can't hear you, Shant . . .'

'I said . . . Oh never mind. Listen, there's been a death. A weird one. On the Pyramid Stage at Glastonbury.'

'I saw it.'

'Yeah. Half the world saw it. You at a seance? What's all the wailing?'

'No, I mean I *saw* it. Right in front of my eyes. Twenty minutes ago . . . I'm at the festival. I was dancing.'

'You what? You hate noise and crowds . . . and there are probably beef burgers too.'

'I'm keeping someone company. Anyway, I like Glasto, Shant. There's a lot of love . . . At least there was until just now.'

'OK, well we got the case. So sit tight, I'm on my way.'

'Shanti, I'm on leave. I took a week out for the festival. I'm sorry.'

'Tell me when I get there. I'll meet you directly in front of the Pyramid Stage in an hour.'

'There are a hundred thousand people in front of the Pyramid Stage. Text me when you arrive and I'll find you. But I'm telling you, you're on your own with this one.'

As she shovelled a pile of rubbish from the front seats of her Saab – bundles of files, a Lego space station, a weeping can of Fanta and a useful-looking half-eaten Mars bar – Shanti considered her reluctant partner. He was a Buddhist, for God's sake; why of all professions had he chosen the law? Then she recalled his uncanny ability to solve crimes. Slow, alert, intuitive, like an Apache tracker . . . an Apache tracker working out of the concrete edifice of Yeovil Police HQ.

The satnav told her that the festival was situated at Worthy Farm in the village of Kilton, just outside Glastonbury. Under normal circumstances, that was less than thirty-five minutes up the A37, but she knew traffic would be heavy around the festival site. Benno had arranged for her to leave the car as close as possible to the Five Heads pub in Kilton. From there, one of the Keynsham Kops would collect her in a 4x4, and blue-light her to the scene.

Jeez, this was exciting! There was nothing she loved more than an off-road adventure.

In the dying light of the day, she passed ancient farmyards and apple orchards; a converted van by the roadside where a tie-dyed family sold chainsawed toadstools. She saw signs for yoga retreats and shamanic healers – everywhere an incongruous blend of the bucolic and the bohemian.

As she entered the pretty village of Kilton, she realised the traffic was almost at a standstill; in and out of the gridlocked vehicles, a stream of pedestrians wove like fish – many staggeringly stoned or inebriated, some weeping at what they had seen.

It was a hot night, and to her right, the door of the ancient Five Heads was propped open. Within the gloomy interior she made out a huddle of locals sitting around tables sipping pints. She watched a dreadlocked couple enter with backpacks and two skinny lurchers on strings. Even from inside her car she could sense the hostility with which they were received. A moment later they emerged empty-handed and went on their way.

The lanes were lined with hundreds of traffic cones, but Shanti spotted a space just beyond the pub. Expertly nudging a couple of cones aside with the front of the Saab, she parked tight against a stone wall.

Within seconds, an angry cop in a high-vis jacket came rushing to her side. 'What the fuck d'you think you're doing?' he snapped.

Shanti stepped calmly onto the warm tarmac and flashed her warrant card.

'I'm doing my job, Constable. There's been a major incident on site and I'm leading the case. And don't you dare swear when you're on duty, or I'll have you on a fucking charge. I've clocked your collar number.'

'I . . . er, sorry, ma'am. It's been a long day.'

'Right, well see this car?'

'Yes, ma'am.'

'I love this Saab. You guard it with your life, all right?'

'Yes, ma'am.'

She pulled the cones back into place. 'Now please excuse me . . . my carriage awaits.'

A blinking neon Land Rover glided towards them. Shanti pulled open the passenger door, and as the embarrassed plod held up the traffic, the driver executed a swift U-turn and, with sirens wailing, returned in the direction of the festival site, swerving frequently up the steep banks of the lane to circumnavigate vehicles.

'DI Shanti Joyce?' asked the outrageously young female driver. 'I'm a big fan of your work. I followed every detail of the Havfruen case. This is awesome!'

Christ! thought Shanti. I've got a fan club. Just wait till I tell Mum.

As they slalomed between the crowds, she gathered a little background. The on-site force had a base to the north of the festival site, with spill-over cells at Keynsham HQ. Up until now they had considered themselves prepared for almost any eventuality at the world's largest green-field festival. After all, Glastonbury had been running successfully for nearly fifty years. In the early days it had been overdoses, drug dealers and unlicensed vehicles. Lost children, several births and a few heart attacks. Thefts from tents, the occasional brawl or sexual assault. In recent years they had introduced an armed unit and upped the helicopter presence to counter the terrifying threat of terrorism. But the outrageously theatrical death of music legend Ethan Flynn was in a different league. A kind of mass bereavement had swept over Worthy Farm, and the police were having a hell of a time keeping distraught fans from the body.

'The Pyramid Stage and backstage VIP area are being sealed, and I've just heard that the SOCO team have arrived.'

'Who's the festival coordinator?' asked Shanti.

'Best person to talk to is MC Vula Plenty. Vula knows everybody.'

They were heading through boundless car parks, across rutted fields towards the towering eight-mile fence that encircled the 1,100-acre site.

As they paused behind a reversing tractor, the young cop asked to borrow Shanti's phone. 'I'm downloading an interactive map of the festival site for you. Here we go . . . This is where we are now . . . and the Pyramid Stage is down there.'

'Thanks,' said Shanti. 'That's really useful.'

The Land Rover passed through a heavily guarded gateway set aside for emergency vehicles, and as they entered the site, it felt to Shanti that they were crossing a border into a strange country with its own set of laws. The vehicle inched through the almost impenetrable crowds, avoiding a tundra of tents and the occasional horizontal figure in the grass. Didn't these people ever go to bed? Shanti wondered. It was Wednesday night, for Christ's sake. Didn't they have jobs in the morning?

The youthful driver was still talking, more loudly now because of the incessant dance music. 'Could you give me, like, your top tip? You know, for investigating a crime?'

'Well . . . I suppose you need to be constantly vigilant – there may be hidden clues in every detail you see and every phrase you hear.'

'I like that. But I guess they're just as likely to be red herrings?'

'That's the skill, telling one from the other . . . And by the way, we don't yet know if a crime has been committed.'

'That's true. But when a celebrity like Ethan dies, everyone is quick to draw conclusions. I mean, it's well known that there was no love lost between the Flynn twins – at least from Tyrone's point of view.'

The fresh-faced cop reminded Shanti of a younger version of herself – keen as mustard but with very little actual experience. 'Yeah, well the thing I've learnt is not to jump to conclusions. You're young, but here's a little wisdom: a good detective is prepared to embrace uncertainty.'

'Oh, I love that phrase. Isn't that's what Vincent Caine always says?'

'You know Caine?'

'I've never actually met him, but like I say, I studied every detail of the Havfruen case, and Vincent Caine is my idol. I believe he's known as the Mindful Detective.' The young driver had that annoying upturned inflection that made every sentence into a question.

'You know, you should get out more . . . and talking of getting out, why don't you drop me here? Thanks for your help, but I can see the Pyramid Stage in the distance and it's got to be quicker on foot.'

'It's been awesome meeting you. Listen, there's a copy of *POLICE* magazine in the glove compartment – it's the Havfruen edition. You wouldn't . . .?'

'You want me to sign it?'

'Well, if you like. But I was really hoping that you would get Inspector Caine to sign . . .'

Shanti threw her bag over her shoulder and jostled along the walkways between multicoloured stalls selling everything from

Bob Marley wigs to fairy wings. My God, there were youths openly smoking drugs . . . If she wasn't on a case she would . . .

The surging throng left her completely befuddled, so she was almost relieved when she finally made contact with Caine.

The tall detective was dressed in loose trousers, walking boots and a white T-shirt, looking very much at home. Shanti noticed that he was in the company of an attractive flame-haired woman at least five years his junior. To her annoyance, she felt a frisson of jealousy, which she swiftly booted to the backwoods of her mind. She was here for one thing only. Emotion was a tool she did not need.

## *Chapter 4*

# The Passing of the Pale Prodigy

'All right, Caine. Let's do this.'

'Shanti, I'd like you to meet Misty. She's—'

'We'll socialise later, shall we? Is this the entrance to the backstage area?'

She turned in time to see Caine kissing the girl tenderly on each cheek whilst gazing deeply into her eyes.

'Caine. Get over here.'

'Shanti, I'll say it again – I'm on leave. I don't want to get involved . . .'

Deaf to his protests, Shanti flashed her ID at the beefy security guards and strode into the screened VIP zone, where musicians and festival crew stood shell-shocked amidst an array of vehicles: tinted tour buses, Winnebagos, full-sized articulated trucks loaded with equipment; even a couple of vintage double-decker buses. She noticed various temporary structures – yurts and marquees, equipped with bars and catering facilities to suit the demands of every diva, crooner and starlet – as well as rows of luxurious pods and tents, toilet and shower facilities, and a spacious seating area laid out with picnic tables and sun chairs.

Near the back of the towering Pyramid Stage, two private ambulances were parked haphazardly alongside SOCO vans and a flashing cluster of police vehicles. Dunster, Spalding and a few of the Yeovil crew were questioning tearful technicians and reeling roadies.

Benno came down a flight of black steps from the back of the stage, and she noticed the respectful way in which he and Caine acknowledged each other. Big, burly Benno. A third-generation cop who played by the rules.

'How are you, boss?'

'Unhappy, Benno. Too many people trampling on my crime scene. Who are that lot?'

She nodded at a small crowd gathered around a handsome woman in her early fifties who appeared to be utterly convulsed with grief.

'Queenie Flynn, boss. Mother of the deceased. She's also been Stigma's manager since the early days. The big lads are road crew, and from what I gather most of them were related to Ethan in some way – nieces, nephews, uncles . . . It's a family affair, and the Flynns are very protective.'

'Will the mother talk?'

'No chance. She's completely beside herself, poor woman. The medics gave her something to calm her down, but . . . take a look . . .'

Queenie Flynn had broken away from her minders and was on her knees in the grass, sobbing and crawling towards the stage. Some of the Flynn womenfolk hauled her back, soothing and murmuring and stroking her hair.

'Send them all home, Benno. Where are they staying?'

'The Flynn family home isn't far. Just outside Frome.'

'Tell Queenie we'll visit as soon as she's ready to give a statement.'

'Sorry, boss, but she won't leave until the body has been removed.'

Caine's face was a picture of pained compassion. 'Tell us about Ethan's brother,' he said quietly.

Shanti had seen this before – the way Caine's reluctance gave way to curiosity. He couldn't help but help.

'Tyrone? He's an aggressive sod. He seems more concerned with record sales than his dead twin.'

'He has previous convictions, doesn't he?'

'Three counts of GBH.'

'Nice,' said Shanti. 'Where's he staying?'

'Tyrone and Ethan had rooms at a farmhouse in Kilton village. It's where many of the big names stay. I instructed him not to leave the vicinity and I've stationed a couple of uniforms outside the farm.'

'Good work, Benno,' said Shanti. 'By the way, do the Flynn twins have partners? Or children?'

'Ethan was unmarried, but in and out of relationships according to the tabloids. Tyrone is married and I believe his wife is expecting their first child. That's why she isn't on site.'

'OK, that's all useful. Now Caine and I would like to view the deceased, if we may.'

'Up the steps and left into the wings. You'll find Dawn Knightly and her SOCO team are already there.'

'Of course, the body was moved. Damn it ... when will people learn to leave things alone?'

'I guess it was all too public. The dance troupe carried him offstage, then the paramedics did their thing. Ironically, they even tried to shock him back to life with a defibrillator.'

'I'm assuming no one thought to photograph him *in situ*?'

'Don't think so, boss. It was a bit chaotic and hysterical.'

'Has the stage been screened off?'

'We've made a start.'

'Right, come on, Caine. It's time to meet the legend that was Ethan Flynn.'

'Better on an empty stomach,' said Benno. 'I'm afraid he ain't as pretty as he used to be.'

Shanti headed towards the steps, taking two disposable suits and two pairs of latex gloves from the constable on duty. But Caine did not follow her.

'For Christ's sake, Caine,' she hissed. 'Don't do this to me. What is your issue?'

A long pause.

'I'm sorry, Shant. I'm no good at this. I'm not as tough as you. It's too painful ...'

'This is unbelievable. Right, let me spell it out. You're a serving officer. This is what we do. Don't you realise this is potentially the biggest case of my career? Of *our* careers. Look up there ... Police helicopters! With searchlights. When was the last time you had a job with helicopters?'

'It's just that—'

'I *need* you, Caine. Is that what you want me to say?' My God, his eyes were actually moist. 'OK, well, will you please just examine the body? You're good at that stuff, you know you are. Do it for her . . .' She nodded towards Ethan's genuflecting mother, who was praying wide-eyed to the heavens, then shoved the paper suit firmly in Caine's direction and watched him pull it on, reluctant as a child dressing for school.

At the top of the steps they entered the wings area, where a group of similarly white-clad investigators were at work behind a nylon screen. As they drew closer, they saw the familiar stocky form of senior forensic investigator Dawn Knightly bent over a body. Dawn was a few years older than Shanti, but there was mutual affection between the pair, both tough women.

'What have you got for us, Dawn?'

Knightly's eyes sparkled when she saw Shanti and Caine.

'Ethan Flynn, aged twenty-nine, musician from the band Stigma. Probable cause of death: electrocution. I've got a team on stage hunting for DNA and dusting for prints, and my electrical whizz is on her way. You know the deal – we treat it as homicide until we know different.'

'Quite right, Dawn. Caine and I will examine the body if that's OK.'

Dawn stepped away from the cadaver and Shanti and Caine flinched in unison.

Corpses come in many shapes and sizes. Most are horizontal. Some appear almost asleep, but the blackened rock star was weirdly angular and rigid – like a giant grasshopper caught in a forest fire. That was tolerable. But it was the face that made the Fanta and half a Mars bar lurch in Shanti's belly – a cheap joke-shop imitation of a face, with wild hair extended to its tips, vast bulging eyeballs, and a sharp, blackened tongue protruding from the distorted mouth.

'Whoa!' she gasped.

'May he be at peace,' said Caine.

'Only ever seen one like it before,' said Knightly cheerfully. 'Nineteen ninety-eight I think it was. A cricketer got caught out . . . by a bolt of lightning.'

'Right. Just give me a moment,' said Shanti, backing away a few paces and closing her eyes. As she inhaled gulps of Somerset air, she felt the gentle pressure of Caine's hand on her arm. Remembering his annoyingly pretty companion, she shook him away and steeled herself for action.

'Time of death?'

'Twenty-one forty-four,' said Knightly.

'Witnesses?'

'About twenty-four million, boss,' said Benno, coming alongside.

'Funny, Benno. I mean who was onstage?'

'The other members of the band – drummer, keyboardists, brass section – the fancy-dress dancers, backing singers, a crew of roadies, sound and lighting technicians, MC Vula Plenty, who'll be joining us shortly, brother Tyrone, of course . . . and Ethan's mum out the back. Poor woman watched the whole horror show.'

While they were talking, Caine reverentially approached the cadaver. With gentle fingertips he touched the forehead, muttering some sort of incantation. Then his gloved fingers fell to the gawping eyes, but without lids, they would not close. Pulling a pen torch from a pocket, he knelt and scrutinised each rigid limb within the charred cloth. Next he raised the slim feet and examined the scorched soles.

At last he inspected Ethan's hands, which were clenched into black fists. Prising open the carbonised fingers, he shone the beam within. In the centre of each palm lay a raw wound, from which black blood oozed.

With an expression of wide-eyed amazement, DI Caine turned and looked up at the silent group around him.

'Stigmata,' he said.

# *Chapter 5*

# Beautiful Musical Murder

'Why did you have to say that, Caine?'

They had stepped away from the body, allowing Dawn and her team to resume their work.

'Say what?'

'You know, *stigmata*. You sounded like a fruitcake.'

'Stigmata are marks on the hands or feet that correspond to Christ's crucifixion wounds. But in fact there are mentions of them in Buddhism and other belief systems—'

'I know what they are. I'm not a total idiot. But that creepy thing you did with his hands . . . I'm embarrassed to even say it – you sort of *smelled* them. Everyone was watching.'

'Oh, OK. Well, it's said that stigmata have a particular smell – a sweet aroma like flowers, which is sometimes called the odour of sanctity. But I couldn't detect anything except scorched flesh.'

'Listen, Caine, it doesn't matter about our team, they're used to your weirdness. I mean the Keynsham crew – they're going to think we're a pair of nutjobs. Did you know we're already described as the "go-to pair for weird shit in the West Country"?'

Caine smiled faintly. 'Ah, Shanti, you shouldn't care what people say. You're a first-class DI. The best.'

'I am. I know that. It's you I'm worried about.'

'You're right. I don't have the temperament for this work. I think about handing in my badge every day.'

'Oh boy, why are you always fishing for compliments? OK, listen . . . Benno reckons you're just about the most talented DI he ever knew, and he was literally born in a peaked hat.'

'All right, Shanti. I'm going to show you something I noticed. Then I'll be on my way.'

He led her out of the wings and onto the stage itself, where, behind screens, Dawn's SOCO team were dusting for prints and scrutinising the complicated apparatus: towering stacks of speakers and amps, a huge drum kit on a dais, a plethora of keyboards and a line of antiquated stringed instruments on stands.

To step onto that high stage was a dizzying experience, which only the likes of Ethan Flynn would ever know. As far as the eye could see, the lights of the festival twinkled in the pounding night. On the grassy arena below their feet, a cordon had been established thirty metres back from the stage, where armed and mounted cops patrolled. Beyond that, a multitude of Stigs stared up at the Pyramid Stage, forlornly holding ragged flags, like defeated troops after a battle. Shanti noticed dozens of popping flashes in the half-light.

'Bloody hell,' she said. 'Do you ever feel you're being watched? It's like being an actor in some crazy play.'

'Just ignore it,' said Caine. 'Right, this is where he fell. Don't worry, the power has been shut down.' He led her towards the front of the stage, where microphones on stands stood in front of wedge-shaped amplifiers. He pointed to the deck. 'And this is Excalibur.'

The lethal instrument lay at their feet – lacquered and elegantly curved.

'What do you notice, Shant?'

'Jeez, I don't know . . . It's still connected to the amp. It has a canvas strap. There are scorch marks and . . . oh my God, are those scraps of burnt flesh stuck to the strings?'

'Look carefully at the floor. What do you see?'

'Caine, this isn't the time for party games.'

'There are footprints, Shanti. Wet footprints, left by Ethan Flynn, I should say.'

'Footprints? Where?'

He was touching one of them, and examining his gloved fingertips. The footprints were long and slim and ghostly faint.

'They've almost evaporated in the heat,' said Caine. 'But if you follow them backwards, you'll see that they originated from this damp area by the amp. The guitar stand is right in the middle, so he couldn't have avoided stepping in it as he picked up Excalibur.'

'He probably pissed himself. It happens all the time as people die.'

'But he didn't die here. He died over there at the front of the stage.'

'He spilt something. Maybe he was holding a drink.'

'Tyrone had a bottle of beer, but Ethan never drank on stage. And I'm fairly sure this is water.'

'Excuse me. What is the relevance of this, Caine?'

'Well, as you know, Ethan always performed in bare feet.'

'Yes, but what's that got to do with anything?'

'Conductivity. The combination of electricity, water and bare skin is lethal.'

She stared at him with half-concealed awe. 'All right, Caine, you're a bloody marvel. Another twenty minutes and that water will be gone. I'll order some photos and a sample for analysis.'

He gave her a slow smile.

'But it still doesn't make sense,' continued Shanti. 'They were halfway through the gig, right? So how come Ethan wasn't electrocuted before?

'I wondered about that too. But I'm pretty sure Excalibur was the first and only electrical instrument he played tonight – the others were old-fashioned acoustic instruments, which he used with mics or pick-ups rather than direct leads.'

'So tell me this, Oh Wise One – why wasn't he frazzled the second he picked up the guitar from the stand?'

'It's a good point, but if you study the footage, I'm pretty sure you'll find that he lifted Excalibur by the canvas strap and the wooden body, neither of which is conductive. The first contact he made with any live components – I mean the strings – was when he played that first note.'

Shanti thought for a moment. 'Well, OK, there we have it. Despite the rumours, what we're looking at is an unfortunate accident. Possibly criminal negligence. A wet stage, plus bare feet, plus an electric guitar equals . . . KERPOW! It's tough for Stigma fans, but a disappointingly easy case for us.'

'Not so fast, Shanti. I'm afraid it isn't that simple. The thing is, a guitar doesn't carry a live current.'

'Of course it does. The clue's in the name: *electric guitar*. Get it? Ethan Flynn was electrocuted.'

'The techies will confirm this, but if I remember correctly, it's all about electromagnetism. When you pluck or strum the strings of an electric guitar, it sends a signal to the amp via the jack lead. But no electricity is fed directly to the guitar. Under normal circumstances it would be virtually impossible to receive a shock from an electric guitar, let alone a lethal voltage.'

'That's exactly what I told them,' said a soft Canadian voice from behind.

They both turned to see the famous radio presenter and MC, Vula Plenty, infinitely slender and elegant beside Benno's burly form. She was dressed in loose-fitting harem pants, a short embroidered jacket and a violet headscarf.

'All right, Ms Plenty,' said Benno. 'I'm going to leave you in the capable hands of DIs Shantala Joyce and Vincent Caine, who are leading the investigation.'

Ashen-faced and trembling, Vula Plenty shook hands, and Shanti noticed long ruby nails and multiple bangles on her wrists.

'You'll have to forgive me. Look . . . I can't stop shaking. Ethan was such a dear friend and I guess I'm traumatised. My God, won't they *ever* stop taking photos?'

'Come and step behind the screen,' said Caine gently.

'I want to help, really I do. I'll do anything you ask, except . . . except please don't make me look at that *thing* again. I'll never, ever erase that image from my mind. Ethan was so beautiful, do you understand?'

'It sounds like you've known him for a long time?'

'Years,' she sighed, wiping her big eyes with the back of her hand. 'He was just nineteen when he first appeared on this stage. And let me tell you, I meet rock stars every day of the week and ninety-nine per cent of them are arrogant narcissists – Tyrone is a perfect example. But Ethan was different. He was gentle and modest. He knew he had nothing to prove, because he was a true genius. Everyone fell in love with him. I'm sorry, but I still can't believe this is real. It's like an out-of-body experience. Right now I'm wondering if the festival will even survive . . .'

She dissolved into shuddering sobs, and to Shanti's consternation, Caine stepped swiftly forward and wrapped an arm around her.

'My God, you're the sweetest cop I've ever met,' said Vula, burying her face in his chest.

'Look, I hate to interrupt,' said Shanti. 'But I'm trying to run an investigation here.'

'Sorry . . . sorry,' sighed Vula, fumbling with a leather-bound water bottle and swigging thirstily.

'Could you give us a little background information, Vula? How many people would be involved with setting up a Stigma performance?'

'The size of the crew? Well, Stigma are big,' she said, clearly relieved to discuss practicalities. 'Huge. I guess they employ twenty or more of their own guys, and subcontract many more. Let me think . . . There are two front-of-house sound engineers in the mixing desk halfway up the field, and monitoring engineers at the side of the stage – those are the guys who adjust the sound the artists hear in their earpieces and from these wedges on the deck. Then there's the lighting crew and the pyrotechnics and video team. On top of that, the festival organises grunt labour.'

'Grunt labour?'

'People from the local community who like to get backstage passes and earn a little cash. The football team usually. They unload the trucks and shift stuff around.'

'Is it possible that something went wrong with the wiring? A fault, I mean?'

'It's incredibly unlikely,' said Vula. 'There are all kinds of checks and tests – multiple RCD trips, and of course all the equipment is PAT tested. And as lovely Inspector Caine pointed out, there's no electrical feed to the guitar itself.'

'So who is in charge of the electrics?'

'A man named Mudget, though everyone calls him Sparky. He's an old professional, who lives for his job. He owns a big electrical contractor called Spark1Up. They specialise in large-scale gigs all over the country and in Europe too. You'll see a fleet of Spark1Up vehicles parked under the trees outside. But I can tell you that the festival has never had the slightest problem with him, otherwise we wouldn't use him.'

'No quarrels between Mr Mudget and Ethan?'

'Like I say, everyone loved Ethan.'

'Except his brother, Tyrone . . .'

'Tyrone hates everyone.'

'So can we speak with Mr Mudget?'

'I'm sure you can. Poor Sparky never goes far from the stage. He's a bit of a loner – I feel sorry for him, to tell you the truth. He lives above the cab in the Spark1Up artic out back.'

'You've been most helpful, Ms Plenty. We may have further questions, but that's all for tonight. Could you do us a favour as you leave?'

'Sure.'

'Go over to Mr Mudget's cab and see if he would care to join DIs Joyce and Caine on the main stage.'

They watched her slender frame walk away.

'Damn,' said Shanti. 'I'll be glad when they finish screening off the stage. How can we carry out a forensic investigation in front of an audience? Maybe we should shut down the entire festival. What do you think, Caine?'

'It would be a logistical nightmare. Imagine refunding tickets to all those angry fans. In any case, there would be potential witnesses dispersing in every direction. No, it's impossible. The fact is, we have until Sunday night to solve this case.'

'You said *we*.'

'I meant you; *you've* got until Sunday night.'

'Let me get my head round this. It's nearly Thursday now. That gives us four days to crack this thing. It's outrageously tight.'

Sparky Mudget entered stage left. He was an untidy man who could have been anything from thirty to seventy-five years old. His pallid black-haired belly bulged from a faded Status Quo T-shirt with salt residue beneath each armpit. Locks of greasy shoulder-length hair curtained his balding head. Tiny eyes blinked from behind smeared wire-framed spectacles.

'Sparky Mudget? I'm Detective Inspector Joyce, and this is DI Caine. I understand you were in charge of the electrics for the Stigma gig.'

'This is insanely heavy.'

'We understand it's difficult. But we need to ask a few questions, if you'd be so kind?'

'Maybe tomorrow. Would that be OK?'

'Er, no. That would not be OK. I'm sorry, Mr Mudget, did you have a more important engagement?'

Mudget studied the complicated watch on his wrist.

'Not an engagement exactly, but . . . Look, could we be finished in, like, fifteen minutes?'

'Was there something you wanted to watch? *Cash in the Attic*, maybe? Thing is, we've got a dead superstar out there. He's been electrocuted, Mr Mudget, which makes you what we call in the trade a person of interest. To be clear, we'll speak to you for as long as we need. All night, if necessary.'

'OK, OK . . . but could you talk . . . you know, more kindly?'

'Mr Mudget, were you involved in the death of Ethan Flynn?'

'W-whoa! I can't handle this.'

'Just answer the question, please.'

'Hell, no! I loved the man. Besides, Glasto is the biggest gig on the planet. Why would I kill that? Fourteen minutes, by the way.'

'Hold on. Are you being deliberately obstructive? What's with the countdown?'

'I'm sorry, it's just that . . .'

'Just what, Mr Mudget?'

'I can't say.'

'I suggest you try.'

'All right. You may as well know . . . I dropped something.'

'You dropped something?'

He buried his face in his hands, which were small, hairy and heavily ringed.

'Everything got so stressful, and I . . .'

'I think what Sparky is saying,' said Caine gently, 'is that he dropped some kind of a tab.'

'Like a controlled substance kind of tab?' said Shanti.

'I'm really sorry,' wailed Mudget. 'I was unbelievably strung out. I know it was stupid. But what can I do? In ten minutes it's gonna kick in.'

'You said fourteen minutes.'

'Time is liquid.'

Shanti sighed and folded her arms.

'OK, Sparky,' said Caine. 'Work with me. We're all friends, right?'

'Like brothers, man.'

'So tell me, did you set up Ethan's equipment yourself?'

'Every time.'

'Now what I want you to do is to look over the equipment with me. Can you manage that?'

'Caine,' hissed Shanti. 'This is utterly absurd. Let this man go and let's get on with the job.'

'I agree it's not ideal, but you wanted me to work with you, so let me handle this for a moment.'

Caine turned to Mudget, who was looking increasingly fearful.

'Do you have a screwdriver, Sparky?'

'Always,' said Mudget.

'Good. So let's start with the amp. How are you feeling?'

'A little paranoid, if you want to know the truth. Your friend scares me.'

'Her bark's worse than her bite. Now forget about everything else. What I want you to do is put on these gloves. See, I'm wearing them too.'

'My skin is elastic.'

'Let's get to work, Sparky.'

Sparky Mudget dropped to his knees in front of the large amp, which was still connected to Excalibur, and began expertly removing screws.

'You're doing well,' said Caine. 'I see you've done this before.'

'A million times . . . yet never.'

Shanti stared at the pale hillocks of Mudget's upended buttocks and sighed again. 'Damn it, Caine. In what possible way is this helpful?'

'Bear with me, Shanti.'

As Mudget removed the front casing, he let out a terrible groan. 'Whoa! This is unreal. I can't even look . . .'

'Tell me what you see, Sparky?'

'I see a bummer. A downer. A box of burnt spaghetti.'

'Some of the cables have melted, is that it?'

'My wiring. My beautiful wiring!'

'Why would they be melted, Sparky? Wouldn't there be some kind of trip?'

'A deeply heavy trip.'

'I mean an RCD trip. Take a careful look at the circuit boards and tell me if anything is out of place. But try not to touch anything unless you have to. You're doing great, Sparky. We really appreciate your help.'

'I like you. You're gentle. Like the cop of love.'

'So let's work together.'

'That one . . .'

'The green and white wire? Is it . . .?'

'Disconnected from the earth.'

'What the hell is he talking about?' hissed Shanti. 'Who's disconnected from the earth?'

'Be patient, Shant,' said Caine. 'Sparky, are you saying that the earth lead has become disconnected?'

'The earth is disconnected from the motherboard.'

'OK, Caine. I'm going to wrap up this travesty.'

'Please, Shanti, this could be crucial . . . Sparky, you're saying that the earth lead has become disconnected from the motherboard?'

'Ethan is disconnected from the earth,' said Sparky Mudget, rising to his feet, arms floating outwards like wings.

'Stay with me, Sparky. Are you telling me that someone has tampered with your wiring?'

'Nothing is how it should be.'

'Who would do that? Who would want to hurt Ethan?'

Mudget was attempting to clamber on top of a huge speaker.

'Tire . . . tire . . . own . . .'

'Tyrone? Did he say Tyrone, Caine? Mudget, did you say Tyrone?'

'I'm tired of being alone. You have beautiful eyes, Officer. All twelve of them . . . like dancing candles . . . I worship you . . .'

'Benno,' called Shanti. 'Would you and Dunster escort Mr Mudget back to his lorry? And I'll need someone to watch him. He's not to leave the area under any circumstances. Oh, and maybe you'd better have him checked over by a medic on the way. I think he may have inadvertently ingested a substance.'

As Benno and Dunster gave chase, Mudget leapt from the speaker and orbited the stage. Finally, to the ironic applause of the audience, he crashed amongst the drums, sending cymbals in every direction, before being firmly apprehended.

'I realise that interview was a bit irregular,' said Caine. 'But you heard what he said – he clearly believed that someone had tampered with his wiring.'

'That man is pretty much the definition of an unreliable witness,' said Shanti. 'However, I take your point. Let's get some verification. I'll see if Dawn's electrical expert has arrived.'

As Dawn and the technician huddled around the amplifier, Shanti and Caine sipped tea from cardboard cups.

'If I had my way, I would have banged him up and turned over his artic,' complained Shanti. 'Apart from anything else, he danced on my crime scene and that's a crime in itself.'

'Listen, Shanti, you could search every vehicle and tent on the site. You'd probably find a ton of drugs, but it wouldn't help us catch the killer.'

Dawn and the technician probed, photographed and examined each charred wire. Eventually they rose to their feet with grave expressions.

'What's the verdict?' asked Shanti.

'Well, we'll need to take all this gear back to the lab, but I can tell you that your man Mudget was right. The earth has been disconnected, so there's no cut-out.'

'Could that be accidental?'

'Possible but unlikely,' said the technician. 'However, that's not the only issue . . .'

'Go on,' said Shanti.

'There's an additional lead that shouldn't be here at all. Take a look . . . You see this cable? It seems to be a live feed to the chassis – that's this board inside the amp.'

'Not surprising Sparky was so distressed,' said Caine.

'He was distressed because he was off his tits,' said Shanti.

Caine ignored her. 'So you're saying this was a deliberate act?'

'In simple terms, the system has been rigged,' said Dawn. 'Someone – someone who knew precisely what they were doing – has tampered with the wiring in such a way that the entire amp became live, and two hundred and forty volts were delivered straight down the lead to Excalibur and Ethan Flynn . . .'

'. . . who had walked barefoot through a puddle of water,' added Caine.

There was a long pause punctuated by the pulsing of the festival.

'You know me, Shanti,' said Dawn. 'I'm not one to jump the gun, but unless I'm very much mistaken, what we're looking at here is murder . . . beautiful musical murder.'

# *Chapter 6*

# A Veil of Tears

Side by side under the arc lights, Shanti and Caine watched as the strangely contorted body bag was stretchered reverentially from the stage and into a black-windowed ambulance.

The sombre spectacle was accompanied by the moans of the many Flynns. A phalanx of officers held back the jostling crowd in the backstage area, but Queenie Flynn managed to wriggle through and throw herself, wailing and clawing, at the swathed body of her son.

Once she had been prised away, the ambulance doors were closed and it began to move slowly across the grass and through the heavily guarded gates of the VIP compound. As it entered the main site, a groan like a dirge of didgeridoos went up from the waiting Stigs outside.

Caine touched Shanti's hand. 'This is where I leave you,' he said gently. 'I have to find someone . . .'

'Misty, isn't it?'

'Yes, Misty. I'll see you, Shant. I hope you catch your killer.

Send my love to Paul, and your mum too. It would be great to see them soon.'

He turned and walked away. But just as he reached the gate, his passage was blocked, and he found himself staring into the frantic, tear-stained face of Queenie Flynn.

'Wait. Hold it there. Are you Caine? Are you Vincent Caine?'

'I am. I'm so sorry for your loss. I can't imagine—'

'Life is a veil of tears, Inspector Caine. From beginning to end. But you can help. I know you can. Your man Bennett tells me you're in charge of the investigation . . .'

'Ah, no, you'll want my colleague, DI Joyce.'

Queenie prodded his chest with a finger. 'I believe *you* have been sent to find him . . . the one who killed my son. Don't deny it now. There's something about you. You have a gift, young man.'

'Police work is teamwork, Mrs Flynn.'

She gripped his arm and stared skywards. 'Listen! Do you hear?'

'Hear what?'

'Ethan, of course. I know you hear him like I do. He's begging you to release him – "Find the one who did it, Ma", that's what he's telling us. He's calling us . . . calling . . . calling. Don't tell me you can't hear him, Mr Caine.'

'It's true,' said Shanti. 'Caine has loads of intuition. Did he mention the stigmata, Mrs Flynn?'

'Shanti!' said Caine. 'You shouldn't—'

'Stigmata! I knew it! Was it the hands or the feet?'

'The hands, Mrs Flynn. But in reality it was where he was holding the guitar.'

'Ethan was chosen, Mr Caine. I always knew it. A blessing to the world. It's a sign . . . a sign . . .'

'But the trouble is, Mrs Flynn,' said Shanti, 'Vincent was just explaining that he won't be able to help with the case. He's unavailable.'

Queenie glared at him with angry bloodshot eyes. 'Unavailable?'

'Now hold on, Mrs Flynn . . .'

'Mr Caine, would you tell Ethan that? Would you tell him that you can't free him from eternal limbo and purgatory 'cos you're *unavailable*?'

'I . . . No. You're right . . . I'll do it, Mrs Flynn. I'll do it for you and for Ethan.'

'God bless you, Mr Caine. I'm counting on you to staunch the tears of a grieving mother.'

## *Chapter 7*

# Killer in the Crowd

In the small hours, as the festival finally drifted into silence, Shanti and Caine sat side by side with feet dangling from the front of the Pyramid Stage. On the hillside before them, faint smoke drifted from campfires and the tents glowed like a thousand Japanese lanterns.

'Did I say I'm glad you're on the case, Caine?'

'I think you forgot to mention that.'

'Well don't push it. You're annoying but you're useful. How did you know that stuff anyway – about guitars and amps and electromagnetism?'

'Books. Physics at school. I played in a band for a while.'

'Of course you did. Were you insufferably bad?'

'I expect so.'

'Please don't tell me what you were called.'

'Half Man Half Bull.'

'I said don't tell me.'

'Half Man Half Bull did a few gigs around the West Country. Nothing special. It was a minor tour.'

Shanti groaned. 'That was a joke, wasn't it? I thought I told you never to attempt humour.'

'It won't happen again.'

'So let's focus, Caine. What have we got? The obvious starting point is the brother, Tyrone.'

'Decades of rivalry . . .'

'. . . and a criminal record as big as his ego. OK, the next contender is your psychedelic friend Sparky Mudget.'

'He was rather taken with *you*, if I remember. It's true that Sparky has the know-how, but where's his motive?'

'Then there's Vula Plenty. You probably didn't notice . . .'

'. . . she was carrying a water bottle.'

'Damn you, Caine.'

'A lime-green designer water bottle in a leather holster. It had the word *ElkTears* on it. I think that's a Canadian company, but I can check.'

'Vula has an all-access pass. It would have been easy for her to have a little sprinkle on that stage.'

'Again, what was her motive?'

'Don't know. But we'll find out. By the way, Caine, is Vula . . .?'

'She's a trans woman, Shanti. I thought that was common knowledge.'

'To be honest, I'd never heard of her before tonight.'

'She has a very popular radio show called *Vula Has Plenty For You*. It's mainly world music. Misty is a big fan.'

'I bet she is. Anyway, one way or another, our killer is probably right here. Skulking amongst these thousands of sleeping fans.'

Caine lay back on the stage with his hands behind his head. 'Shanti, can I make a suggestion?'

'Is it to do with embracing uncertainty?'

'That's the one.'

They rose wearily, wandered past the uniforms at the back of the stage and down the steps into the VIP area, where Dawn Knightly was closing the doors of her van.

'Thanks as ever, Dawn. Don't know where we'd be without you.'

Benno, who had been briefing the night team, came over to join them.

'What's your strategy, boss?'

'Well, Mudget seemed to be throwing suspicion on Tyrone Flynn, and he's not the only person to have mentioned him. I think Tyrone will be our first port of call in the morning.'

'Already on it, boss. He's expecting you at his digs in the village at ten.'

'You're a legend, Benno.'

'You should get some sleep.'

'I agree. Let's call it a day. I noticed a Prem on the way over.'

'A Prem, boss?'

'Premier Inn. Is it too late to get me a room?'

'Ha!'

'Are you laughing at me, Sergeant Bennett?'

'With all due respect, boss, you must be joking. You won't find a room for miles during the festival.'

'So where are *you* staying?'

'The on-site team have a base above the Big Ground camping area, to the north of the site.'

'Will there be beds?'

'A few sleeping bags if we're lucky. I'm kipping in the back of the van with Dunster, and I've got lumbago.'

'So what am I supposed to do?'

'I'll sort something for you,' said Caine. 'Goodnight, Benno. Goodnight, Dawn.'

Shanti grabbed her bag and followed Caine out of the VIP area. Oh boy, her feet ached. And there was another issue too . . .

'Caine, if I tell you something very personal, will you promise not to laugh?'

'Of course I won't, Shanti. You can trust me completely.'

'I've got what you might call a phobia.'

'OK. Do you want to talk about it?'

'When I was at school, there were rumours about, you know, festival toilets. Those long-drop cubicles. The ones that make that scene from *Trainspotting* look like an advertisement for Domestos. Honestly, Caine, I'll take on a gang of bikers, but festival toilets terrify me.'

'They're not so bad nowadays.'

'People have died, Caine. Don't you know that? Drunken people have slipped through the seats into a shitty hell below.'

'Well, I've got a surprise for you, Shanti.'

'A nice surprise?'

'A wonderful surprise. Just follow me. It's not far.'

Using bat-like navigational skills, Caine steered between infinite tents, warning Shanti again and again as she almost stumbled on guy ropes and discarded items in the shadows.

When they emerged, she found a modest queue waiting patiently outside what Caine described as 'the best toilets in Glastonbury'. It was a row of luxurious miniature palaces called Toilet of Dreams, run by WaterAid to educate punters about the lack of sanitation in Third World countries. What Shanti discovered behind the firmly locked door was a gleaming ceramic throne, piping-hot water, crisp white towels, sweet-smelling soap and hand lotion, all blinged up with glitter balls, mirror tiles and the soft sound of watery music.

She came out grinning. 'OK, Caine. If you can find me a bed to match, I'll be ready for anything tomorrow. How far is it anyway? I'm more than ready to catch some z's.'

'We're nearly there; it's at the top of this hill. I don't know about you, but I sleep better in a tent than in my own bed. Something about being in contact with the earth . . .'

'What? Just stop for one damned minute . . . Where exactly are you taking me?'

'To my tent. Up above the Healing Fields.'

'Are you out of your tiny Buddhist mind? There is no way on God's earth I am sharing a tent with you.'

'Wait! Wait a minute, Shanti . . . it's a big tent. And in any case, you don't have anywhere else to go.'

'Frankly, I'd rather squeeze into a single sleeping bag with Benno and Dunster than spend a night in a tent with you and that . . . that floozy of yours. *Misty*. Isn't that her name?'

'Shanti—'

'Come and find me at seven thirty tomorrow. Don't be late. And bring me tea, Caine. Strong tea.'

## *Chapter 8*

# Intimations of Mortality

Her body ached even before she awoke. She raised an eyelid and groaned. It was insanely bright, and from outside she heard the incongruous sounds of children's laughter, warbling birdsong and the contented murmur of voices.

The police van had been parked on a slope, so that her absurdly thin nylon sleeping bag had slid downhill and she now found herself wedged painfully in a corner by the back doors. Dunster and Benno had already left, which was a blessing, but the bear-cave stench of sleeping man prevailed.

How was it possible to feel hung-over when you had drunk nothing? She pulled on her jeans, then rummaged in her bag and found a toothbrush and a packet of wet wipes. Clambering into the front seat, she located a mirror in the sun visor. When she had cleaned herself as best she could, and scraped back her hair, she crawled to the back of the van, where she tentatively opened one door.

Below her, the panorama of the festival was laid out like a

spilled toy box – circus tents, helter-skelters and a multitude of marquees. She thought of Paul and winced.

The van was parked on the edge of the police compound, overlooking a communal camping field. A few hundred metres away . . . oh my God! A middle-aged couple were enjoying their breakfast wearing . . . wearing nothing but beatific smiles.

In the distance she saw the familiar form of DI Caine making his way towards her. He was carrying a thermos flask in one hand and two mugs in the other. Christ, he'd get a shock in a second – he was headed directly for Mr and Mrs Saggybits.

But as he approached their tent, Caine simply returned their smiles. In fact, he even paused momentarily, and Shanti registered his faint voice saying something sincere about the tragedy yesterday, and something cheerful about the glorious weather, and something profound about life being a strange and wonderful journey. Then the three of them agreed to have a beautiful day and live every moment to the full.

'Caine . . . I'm up here, Caine . . .'

'Ah, there you are, Shanti. I've brought your tea.'

'Never mind the tea. Haven't you forgotten something?'

'I don't think so.'

'Yes, you have. Section Five of the Public Order Act 1986. The bit about public nudity causing alarm and distress.'

Caine merely smiled, set the mugs on the floor of the van and poured two cups of steaming chai.

The slogan on Shanti's mug said: *Don't just do something. Sit there.*

The slogan on Caine's mug said:

*What do we want?*

*Enlightenment.*

*When do we want it?*

*Sometime in the next three reincarnations would do nicely thanks for asking.*

What she craved was a cup of Yorkshire tea the colour of mahogany; but surprisingly, the insipid-looking liquid in the mug tasted delicious – milky, spicy and sweet. A faint déjà vu of long-ago holidays with her grandma in Kerala drifted upwards in the steam.

'How did you sleep, Shant?'

'I didn't.'

'I'm sorry. I did offer . . .'

'Yeah, I've been thinking about that. I suppose I'm disappointed but not altogether surprised. It must be hard to fight your primeval urges. And I guess three in a tent is every boy scout's fantasy.'

'Look, I need to explain. Misty is my sister.'

'Lying makes it worse, Caine.'

'Well, my half-sister, actually. And she has her own tent, I assure you. I've been trying to tell you that she's the reason I'm here. She's a singer, you see. Super-talented in my opinion, and guess what?'

'What?'

'She has her first proper gig this afternoon. Just a small acoustic stage at the Field of Avalon, but I'm incredibly proud. Hey! Maybe you could come. Misty would love that.'

'Are you absolutely kidding me, Caine? I can't just take the afternoon off. I'm leading a murder investigation, or maybe you didn't know that?'

'Of course. I understand.'

'Right, what I need is breakfast. Is there somewhere I can get something substantial? You know, toast, eggs, bits of animal?'

'I've arranged to meet Misty in half an hour. There's a great little place we go. They serve everything. And by the way, my sister has something she wants to share about Ethan.'

Shanti climbed down from the van and straightened her clothing and her body.

'I'm all for sharing, but don't forget we're interviewing Tyrone at ten.'

'Of course. His digs are no more than twenty minutes' walk from here.'

She followed him out of the emergency services area and past the overexposed couple, where Caine smiled and Shanti scowled.

'How do you do it, Caine? How come you're so . . . chirpy?'

'I told you, I always sleep well in my tent. It's almost light by five at this time of year, so I went up to the stone circle by the Healing Field. They say it's on a direct ley line with Glastonbury Tor.'

'The Healing Field?'

'There's a lovely sangha, and—'

'Translation.'

'Community of Buddhists. We meet at dawn for a meditation at the stone circle.'

'Of course you do.'

'It sets you up for the whole day, Shanti. Maybe tomorrow you'd like to . . .'

Misty was waiting at the Hundred Monkeys Café – an open-sided marquee already filled with bearded and braless people.

Dressed in the tiniest of skirts, and knee-length army boots, the young woman shared the same optimistic, fresh-faced smile as her older brother.

The atmosphere here, as everywhere else on the site, was numb and subdued, and Shanti heard snatches of conversations about Ethan's deadly dirge.

Caine and Misty embraced each other warmly, and Shanti knew that even if she had a brother, which she did not, they would never be that intimate.

'I hear you're a singer, Misty?'

'Yes. It's my first proper gig today. To be honest, I'm absolutely wetting myself.'

'You'll be amazing,' Caine told her. 'Just be yourself and everyone will love you.'

They queued for food, Caine and Misty selecting identical options: plain yoghurt sprinkled with seeds, fresh fruit, a single slab of dense brown bread with honey, and a glass of juice. Shanti felt almost ashamed of her choice, but she had a meaty job to do and she needed a meaty breakfast. Who knew when she might eat again?

'So is Misty your real name?' she asked, trowelling butter on her toast.

'Oh no, it's kind of a stage name. It was my nickname when I was young, wasn't it, Vince?'

'Her real name is Tina, but I think Miss T morphed into Misty, and it kind of suits her.'

'How so?'

'My sis is like mist, aren't you, sweetheart? She disappears on her travels for months on end, then turns up when she pleases.'

'You have to stop worrying about me, Vince. I'm not a kid any more.'

'I know that. But I do worry about you. I can't help it.'

'So Caine tells me you have some thoughts about the case?' Shanti said.

'I don't know how important this is . . .'

'At this stage, everything is important.'

'Well, as a performer I get a backstage pass. Yesterday afternoon I was at the back of the Pyramid and I actually had a conversation with Ethan. As I told Vince, I think I may have been the last person he talked to before he went on stage.'

It took some effort to balance her loaded forkful, but Shanti was focused. By God, these locally made sausages were good, although being watched by the saintly siblings made her feel as if tiny piglets were squealing on the prongs.

'OK, that's interesting. Tell me about it. Was that the first time you'd met? How did he seem?'

'Oh yes, we'd never met before. But to my amazement, he knew my songs – at least he said he did. Maybe he was just being kind. Anyway, he was charming. So open and interested in *me*, for goodness' sake. I mean, Ethan is . . . was just about the biggest name on the music scene. I used to run home from school to play his albums, do you remember, Vince? I can't believe he's no longer with us.'

'Let's get back to the meeting, Misty. Did *you* approach *him*?'

'Yes. I just saw him standing there, you know, barefoot and beautiful, and I thought, it's now or never, so I went over and said hi. I mean, he was about to perform in front of however many people, but he literally stopped and spoke to me almost as if we were friends.'

'What did he say?'

'It was weird. It was like time stood still . . . sorry, that's a cliché, but it really was like nothing else existed and it was just the two of us alone in the world. I couldn't believe it, but he was actually interested in my career, and he gave me advice and everything.'

'What kind of advice?'

Oh Lord, that bacon was delicious. They said it was carcinogenic, but what was a small tumour in exchange for rashers like these? Misty and Caine had barely touched their yoghurt, but Shanti was almost ready for seconds.

'Stuff about being myself – exactly what Vince tells me. He said I should create music for myself, not what I think other people might want.'

'OK, and what else?'

'He said that a good trick is to wear two hats for the two sides of the business and never get them confused.'

'What does that mean?'

'Well, he said the music world can be ruthless, so when you're doing business you need to put on your business hat and be tough and unemotional, as if you were promoting someone else's work. Sort of be your own super-agent. Then when you're writing songs or performing, you put on your emotional, creative hat. Open your heart. And he said you should never mix the two. In other words you should never be emotional about business and never be cerebral about your art. That's what I'm going to do this afternoon . . . open my heart for Ethan.'

'OK, but you said the conversation was weird?'

'Yes. I don't know how long we talked. Probably only six or seven minutes, but it felt like forever. Then Tyrone turned up with a few hard men. He seemed agitated and . . . well, frankly he was bloody rude.'

'What did he say?'

'He said, "Are we going to do this effing gig or are you going to shag her first?" It was horrible.'

'And how did Ethan respond?'

'He apologised to me, profusely. He waited until Tyrone and his boys had gone, then he held my hand – not in a bad way, quite the opposite – and he said . . . Let me try to remember this . . .'

'Take your time.'

'He said, "I'm going to die soon, Misty. I know I am. But that's OK. My work is almost done." Or something like that.'

'Jeepers! And how did you respond?'

'I was completely stunned. I kept thinking, *Did he say that? Did he actually say that?* We could hear Vula Plenty warming up the crowd, who were absolutely roaring for Ethan. I remember imagining how terrifying and utterly amazing it must be to go up there and confront that insane adoration. Then the front-of-house guys called for him, and he . . . Oh God . . .'

'What, Misty?'

'He kissed me. Right here on my forehead. So tenderly. It was beautiful. And then he ran barefoot up the steps, and I walked round to the front and joined Vincent.'

'Then we watched together,' said Caine.

'And we danced, didn't we, Vince? It was beautiful. And then, when it happened . . . when he played that fateful song . . . I felt a burning sensation exactly where he had kissed me. I can still feel it now. Is there . . . is there any kind of mark right here on my forehead?'

'I don't think so. Maybe a little redness.'

Tiny tears were streaming down her beautiful face like strings of pearls.

Shanti stood up. 'OK. I'm going to grab another coffee and make a few calls. You guys take a little time, and then Caine and I are going to meet this lovely man Tyrone Flynn. Thanks for that, Misty. You've no idea how useful it might be. I may need to ask for a formal statement at some point, if that's OK?'

'Of course.'

'And listen, do one thing for me – search your mind and see if you can remember anything else about your encounter with Ethan. Anything at all. The tiniest detail might be crucial.'

'OK, Shanti, I'll let you know. Can I just say that I'm so glad you're working with Vince. He's a very special man – I'm sure you know that. But you're lovely too.'

Shanti walked out of the marquee and found a relatively quiet spot by a huge signpost pointing towards various bizarre non-existent destinations – *HOPE, INFERNAL REGIONS, DEPT OF HEALTH, FATE* – from where she called Benno.

'I don't know what Dunster ate last night, but I never want to sleep within a mile of him again.'

'I think it was curried goat, boss.'

'What have you got for me, Benno?'

'What I've got is a bunch of jumped-up agents yelling at me about the closure of the Pyramid Stage.'

'Tell them tough shit. But say it politely.'

'I'm polite to everyone, boss.'

She made a call to Dawn Knightly, who confirmed what they already knew: that Ethan Flynn had been murdered at 21.44 on Wednesday 26 June by person or persons unknown. The cause of death had been electrocution from his guitar, Excalibur, and the amp, which had been deliberately modified. The fatal circumstances had been exacerbated by the fact that the deceased had trodden barefoot in a conductive liquid . . .

'You mean water?' asked Shanti, straining to hear above the babbling stream of people.

'As a matter of fact, I think it was water mixed with a small concentration of household detergent – washing-up liquid probably.'

'What's that about, Dawn?'

'We haven't concluded tests, but at a guess I'd say that the viscous quality of the detergent made it slightly more conductive, and it also adhered to the skin a little more effectively than water on its own. One way or another, this was cooked up by someone who knew exactly what they were doing.'

'That's all very interesting. So what are your movements, Dawn?'

'I'm in the van now. We're heading to the farmhouse in Kilton where Ethan was staying. We're going to give his bedroom the once-over.'

'Caine and I have an appointment with his brother, Tyrone. He's staying at the same place.'

'See you there, then. Oh, and there's something important I need to ask you . . .'

She hung up before Shanti could ask more.

Shanti caught her mum and Paul just heading off to school. They had been following events on the news, and she couldn't resist a little brag about the celebrities she was associating with. 'I'll probably have to interview Sista Tremble,' she said nonchalantly. After that, she wandered back to the Hundred Monkeys Café, where Caine and Misty were still finishing their breakfast. Holy moly! Did they absorb food by osmosis?

She stood out of sight and watched as they ate. Smiling gently at each other and exchanging the occasional soft word. Misty like a bright flame. Caine like smouldering charcoal.

The mindful way in which Caine consumed his food made her reflect on how the Yeovil crew ate in the canteen. Like Labradors, they were. Joking and joshing as they shovelled down their grub. Shanti suspected that if you stopped them on the way out and asked what they'd eaten, they wouldn't even remember. And maybe she was the same. Almost every night she ate in front of the TV with Mum, and to be honest, it could have been cardboard they were putting away.

As she watched Caine slip half a spoonful of yoghurt into his mouth, ninety-nine per cent of her felt the most intense irritation. And one per cent of her wanted to kiss him as he ate. To lick the last hemp seed from his smiling mouth.

'OK, Caine, you're going to have to ask for a doggy bag, 'cos we've got an interview to do and I want to check my car in the village.'

There was more cheek-kissing and eye-gazing. Jeez, it was hardly surprising she'd mistaken them for bedmates!

Misty said, 'I'll find somewhere quiet and really think about that meeting with Ethan. I know it was important.'

'I'd appreciate that, Misty. I don't want to pressurise you before your gig, but there's a good chance that you *were* the last person to speak to Ethan. Sometimes it's the tiny details that are critical.'

'I'll see what I can remember, I promise.'

'Thanks, and I hope the show goes well. Come on, Caine. Places to go. Murderers to detain.'

## *Chapter 9*

# Unworthy Farm

They set off up the concrete walkway, past Kidzfield, where grubby curly-haired tots, many with their faces painted like animals, scrambled on pirate boats.

Damn it, why couldn't she have a normal job so that she could spend more time with Paul? A tear welled in her eye, but she quickly quashed the thought. She was tired, that was all.

At last they reached the perimeter fence and showed their badges at the gate before heading up the lane into the village. Here, the scent of money wafted on the breeze. There were smart architect-designed villas with balconies overlooking the festival site, where parties of wealthy London types, dressed in shorts, Hawaiian shirts and designer sunglasses, sat and sipped Bollinger. No doubt they barbecued late into the night listening to Coldplay, and those who didn't enjoy the noise could rent out their properties for vast sums during the festival season.

Other parts of Kilton were more traditional: stone cottages where old people tended their gardens, oblivious to the heady din.

The Saab was parked exactly where she'd left it, and she was gratified to see a *POLICE AWARE* sign under the wiper.

The Somerset road names were a delight: Neat Lane and Bread Street. At the turning to Totterdown Hill, they encountered a cluster of photographers and media hounds behind a police cordon.

'Got anything for us, DI Caine?' they called.

'Is it true about the stigmata?'

'Still calling it an accident, Inspector Joyce?'

'You know the form, gents – we'll be releasing a statement in due course.'

Half a mile up the lane, they spotted the SOCO van outside a farmhouse. Dawn Knightly was loudly berating two constables.

'What's the problem, Dawn?'

'These numpties have . . . Go on, you tell her.'

'I'm sorry, ma'am, we were only carrying out orders. We were told to keep an eye on Tyrone Flynn, which we have done diligently. Then a white transit turned up with two big fellows inside. They were members of the Flynn family – Ethan's uncles, as Tyrone confirmed.'

'What did they want?'

The uniforms hung their heads.

'They'd come to take away Ethan's belongings,' one of them mumbled. 'Guitars and clothes and that. They said Queenie Flynn wanted them to bring everything home.'

'Let me get this straight,' said Shanti. 'You allowed a couple of heavies in a transit to clear out a room that was potentially crammed with evidence?'

'And it gets worse,' snapped Dawn. 'The landlady, one

Primrose Vowles, then went in and Mr Muscled the entire room. Vacuum cleaner, fresh sheets, the lot. Even disinfected the floor.'

'Sweet baby Jesus,' groaned Shanti.

'We've lifted a few prints, but if there was anything of value, it's gone.'

'So what will you do?' asked Shanti.

'I suppose we'll head off to the Flynn household and examine the stuff they moved. But I strongly suspect it's a waste of time, thanks to the Chuckle Brothers here.'

Caine had wandered across the lane, where he was surveying the property. Unworthy Farm was a classic Elizabethan farmhouse on a grand scale, with a low-slung roof like a farmer's cap. Thick oak timbers set into the stonework had been bowed and twisted by the centuries, and the windows were set at outrageous angles.

'You said there was something important you wanted to ask me, Dawn? Shall I fetch Caine?'

Eyes darting conspiratorially, Dawn took her arm. 'No. This is for your ears only.'

'Sounds intriguing.'

They stepped towards the back of the van.

'Simple question, Shanti – did you or did you not spend the night in Caine's tent?'

'What? What are you talking about? I thought you had some new evidence.'

'It's OK, I won't tell anyone. But was it an *intense* experience?'

'Jeez, Dawn. Let me make this clear once and for all. I am not interested in Caine in that way.'

'Not even a teensy snuggle?'

'Listen, I slept with Dunster and Benno.'

'Christ, you're a dark horse.'

'Right, I'll tell you what, Dawn, as you're so interested in DI Caine, you can share his tent tonight. I'm on the lookout for somewhere more comfortable anyway.'

'Oh, I'm married, Shanti, for better or worse. Mainly worse. But you . . . you're a singleton, and the two of you are so sweet together. Trust me. I have an instinct for these things.'

Shaking her head in dismay, Shanti joined Caine under the rose-strewn porch.

'What's the matter, Shant? You look flustered.'

'Nothing. I'm fine. I can't believe the amateurs I have to work with.'

With a couple of loud toots, Dawn's van made a three-point turn and set off down the lane in a cloud of dust.

'Are you going to ring that bell, Caine, or are we going to conduct the interview through four inches of oak?'

He pulled the chain by the door – a mighty brass affair with a peal like a bell tower.

No answer. He rang again, but the only sound was the distant pulsing of the festival.

'See if it's unlocked,' Shanti suggested.

'Hang on, Shant. We're a little early anyway. If it's OK with you, I'd like to take a wander around. Just to get my bearings.'

She followed him out of the porch and around the side of the building. The place had a slightly neglected air, with chickens pecking amongst sprawling cow parsley, chamomile, nettles and discarded farm machinery. An old van with one axle was propped on bricks. In a vegetable patch, to Shanti's alarm, several dead crows were suspended by their feet, as a warning to their companions.

In the large yard at the back stood a stuccoed prefab bungalow, in stark contrast to the ancient house. There were also a number of ancient sheds and outbuildings, including a ramshackle milking parlour with a hand-painted sign on the door saying *Unworthy Ices.* Peeping through a tiny window, Caine saw an industrial mixing machine, a stack of Tupperware boxes on steel-topped tables, and several ancient chest freezers on the stone floor.

In a large open-sided barn, a young man in a white boiler suit, with a cloud of blonde curls, was stacking hay bales. Caine was about to approach him when an upstairs window at the back of the main house was pushed open and an anxious voice called, 'Hello, can I help?'

They looked up at the face of a woman with complicated teeth and chaotic grey hair.

'Sorry to disturb you,' said Caine. 'We rang the bell but no one answered.'

'You're not press?'

'Police.'

'Oh dear. Not again. Well, I'd best come down. I won't keep you,' she said, closing the window.

The troubled woman who opened the door was stick thin. She stood in the gloomy interior in a floral apron, nervously peeling yellow Marigolds from skeletal hands. But it was her splayed teeth that distinguished her – each had its own navigational direction.

'Primrose Vowles? We're DIs Joyce and Caine.'

'Oh Lord. Not more trouble. It's been shocking. The whole thing is shocking.'

'Quite literally, Mrs Vowles. Anyway, I apologise for the

intrusion, but we're leading the investigation into Ethan Flynn's death.'

'My husband and I were dreadfully shaken. We had a real soft spot for Ethan. And between you and me and the gatepost, it's dreadful for business too.'

'We understand completely. We're actually here to see Ethan's brother, Tyrone.'

'As I said to your colleagues this morning, I know you're only doing your job, but we do have to consider our guests. I hope you understand.'

'We'll be as discreet as we possibly can,' said Caine.

She lowered her voice conspiratorially, stepping onto the porch and half closing the door at her back.

'The thing is, we have some very famous people staying . . . very famous indeed. And they do value their privacy. Last night my husband found two photographers with their noses pressed against the kitchen window. He had to set the dog on them. I said to him, it's only a matter of time before someone puts it all on TripAdvisor, and then where will we be? Anyway, you're welcome, I'm sure.'

She held open the door, staring at their feet. But Shanti was not about to remove her shoes. Besides, the interior was like the exterior – weather-beaten as a sailing galleon – and despite the balmy June sunshine, it felt several degrees chillier inside, with icy flagstones on the hall floor.

As they entered, Mrs Vowles adopted a loud, cheerful tone.

'Mr Flynn is in the dining room with another visitor at present. Won't you come through? You're welcome, I'm sure.'

The place had been built for a smaller generation, so that Caine had to duck beneath each arch and doorway. They entered a cavernous, low-ceilinged kitchen, which was noticeably warmer than the rest of the house. Beside a heavily chipped cream-coloured Aga was a frayed armchair with a dog-shaped hollow.

'We're still a little early, Mrs Vowles. Do you mind if we ask a few questions?'

The landlady closed the door firmly.

'With the greatest respect, we told your colleagues everything we know.'

'Once again, I do apologise, but regrettably, you and your husband may have been amongst the last to see Ethan.'

'Oh, what a thought! Chills me to the bone to think of it. I'd better put the kettle on.' She lifted the lid of the hob and swung a huge kettle into place.

'No tea for me,' said Shanti. 'You mentioned your husband . . .'

'Vowles.'

'Christian name?'

'Just Vowles.'

'Is he here?'

'I'm afraid he's out. But he'll certainly be home for his dinner.'

'We noticed someone working in one of the barns – a young man with blonde curls. Is that your son?'

'Young man? Oh my goodness, you mean Gav. Gavin Blackmore. Farmhand. He don't say much, but he gets on with the job. We do have a son, as a matter of fact, but you know what they're like at that age. Seth only drags himself out of bed for two things – that festival and his football.'

'So it's a working farm?' said Shanti.

'Working? We don't never stop working. But between you and me and the Aga, it's a thankless task these days. If it weren't for the B and B I don't know what we'd do. The only people who prosper in these parts are our neighbours at Worthy Farm, what with the prize-winning herd and the festival and the like. Don't s'pose they know what to do with all the money.'

'But the festival has been good for your business too?'

'It would be wrong to deny it. We've taken them all in over the years. Tom Jones was sat right where you are eating an egg . . . soft-boiled, if I remember rightly. I walked in on that Alice Cooper in the bath once, and don't talk to me about Amy Winehouse. This week I've got Sista Tremble in the Old Dairy . . . in fact the house is overflowing with international megastars.'

'And what about Ethan Flynn?'

'Proper gentleman. Lovely. Even cleaned round the toilet when he'd been. We looked forward to him staying and that's no word of a lie. It's shocking to think what happened to him. Vowles was saying only last night it's a shame it were him and not the brother, but I told him straight out, "That's inappropriate, Vowles. Even in jest."'

'Has Tyrone been problematic?'

Mrs Vowles glanced about furtively, her fanned teeth glowing in the ochre light.

'All manner of comings and goings. Uncle this and cousin that. In and out, out and in. Some of his minders smoke in the house, and we can't have that, can we? An old place like this would go up like a haystack. And the state he leaves his room . . . You'd think I had nothing better to do than pick up his underpants. No one dares say anything, though, 'cos he's a little . . .'

'A little . . .?'

'A little confrontational.'

'But generally people in the village are happy with the festival? It must be a big intrusion with the music going all day.'

'I don't know about happy. We certainly didn't have no crime in Kilton before the festival. Not so much as a stolen apple. And now look at it . . .'

'I understand. Fortunately these kinds of events are incredibly rare.'

'I should hope so. Now, if that's everything, you really must excuse me. I've a lot to do.'

She opened the door and ushered them into the cold corridor. Once more her voice became amplified and artificially jolly.

'There we are then! Now, you'll find Mr Flynn in the dining room at the end of the passage. Mind your head as you go. You're welcome, I'm sure.'

She reached out a thin hand, and when Shanti took it, she found the flesh as cold as clay.

In the long, low corridor, two hulking men were guarding the dining room door like mighty oaks bent over a lane.

'Looking for someone?'

'We have an appointment with Tyrone Flynn.'

'Feds, is it?'

'We're police, yes.'

'See your badge.'

'Would I say I was with the police if I wasn't?'

'People say all kinds of things. Our job is to mind Tyrone. You know what happened to Ethan; we can't be too careful.'

Shanti and Caine showed their IDs and one of the giants knocked and poked his head briefly into the dining room. There was a mumbled conversation.

'Tyrone's got someone with him, but he says you can go in and watch.'

He held the door ajar as the two DIs ducked beneath the bridge of his over-inflated arm. The dining room was vast and low, with a wide fireless hearth and an oak table the size of a landing strip. On the walls were the mounted heads of many mammals. In glass domes and cases on highly polished surfaces their smaller cousins had been lovingly taxidermed. The air was thick with the sinus-aching smells of soot and polish and age . . . and a strange buzzing like an agitated hornet.

In obvious pain at the head of the table sat Tyrone Flynn, his shaven head bent awkwardly beneath the gloved hands of a young Asian woman, who appeared to be drilling into his skull.

'Tyrone Flynn?'

'Guilty.'

'My colleague and I are from Yeovil Police HQ. We're investigating the unfortunate death of your brother Ethan, so we'd appreciate a little of your time.'

'She won't be long— Aah, fook!'

As they pulled out two dining chairs, Shanti realised that the woman was a tattoo artist, who was adding to the extensive gallery on Tyrone's skin. This one was being sited on the top part of his neck, just below the right ear.

'That fookin' hurts!'

'You want me to stop, Tyrone?'

'No. I like it. Finish the job.'

'Mr Flynn, we can't really talk while—'

'She's almost there. Just sit and watch, will you? FOOK!'

They sat in silence as Tyrone's heavily pierced face creased in ecstatic agony. He was wearing a white T-shirt that at first glance appeared to have been made for a child. After a moment, Shanti realised with a shudder that it was not the shirt that was undersized; rather the body inside it was oversized, the heavily veined muscles of his arms, neck and chest bulging like party balloons.

'Right, that's enough. Leave me now. I'm bleeding, look.'

The tattooist applied a swab to his neck, but Tyrone brushed her aside. She swept her belongings into a case and exited the room.

'Christ, did you know you've more nerves in the base of your skull than anywhere else in your fookin' body?'

'I'm not sure if that's true . . .'

'Well it's true for me, and I'm the one who's suffering.'

His inky face was intensely hostile.

'PRIMROSE!' he yelled. 'PRIMROSE! I'm gasping for another beer!'

An instant later, Primrose Vowles scuttled into the room, anxiously levering the lid off a bottle. 'There we are, Mr Flynn,' she chirruped. 'You're welcome, I'm sure.'

When she had gone, Tyrone necked the beer in long, greedy slugs, then slammed the empty bottle on the table and glared at Shanti.

'I'll start by saying that I don't like the police and they don't like me. So how can I help you, Cuntstable?'

'I'm a detective inspector, Mr Flynn. And if you don't mind me saying, you don't seem especially pained by the death of your brother, or have I got that wrong?'

'Pained? What would you know about pain? Look at that . . . go on, look!'

He contorted his gleaming pate so that they could see the bleeding blue tattoo – a single word in Gothic letters . . .

'You've had Ethan's name tattooed on your head.'

'On my head. On my heart. On my fookin' balls.'

'But when he died, you simply walked away . . .'

'Right. Listen. I'll say this once only. When it happened, I thought he was fookin' about. More big-drama-queen games. Another piece of arty-farty theatre. I didn't know he was dead, did I? And neither did a single one of the hundred thousand Stigs in front of the stage.'

He rose from his seat, hauled a hefty set of dumb-bells from the floor and began to work out. With every pull, the veins on his tree-trunk neck rose like throbbing slugs.

'I'm interested in the name . . .' said Caine.

'Ooh, you're interested in the name, are you? What fookin' name? Ethan? You're interested in the name Ethan Flynn?'

'No, the name Stigma.'

'Get a dictionary.'

'I know what it means, Mr Flynn. I just wonder who chose that particular name for the band, and why.'

'Well as a matter of fact, that's one thing I can claim credit for. Stigma was my idea. The Flynns are a travelling family and for generations we suffered prejudice and racism the like of which you can't imagine. In the end, most of us were driven off the roads and forced to settle. But the discrimination never stops. It's always "gyppos" and "pikeys" and "them lot". And plenty of the stigma comes from the boys in blue.'

'I noticed you have a bit of a police record . . .' said Shanti cautiously.

He dropped the dumb-bells, which clattered, bounced and rolled on the flagstone floor.

'See, there it is again.'

'I'm just stating a fact.'

'Listen, I was raised to sort things out for myself. Within the community, and outside too, we settle things with our fists. We have to. You lot aren't there for the likes of my family.'

'We're here for your family now, Tyrone,' said Caine gently. 'I made a promise to your mother that I'd do the right thing for Ethan.'

'So the first person you accuse is me . . .'

'No one is accusing you of anything,' said Shanti. 'But it's well known that you had a certain amount of contempt for Ethan.'

'Ah, most of that was show. And Ethan was no angel either. He pretended to be all holy, but he could be a right bastard.'

'Can you give an example?'

'Well, take yesterday. Did you see that thing where he stopped the whole fookin' world and pointed at the sunset? Everyone thought it was magic. But I'll tell you something, you couldn't even see the Tor from where we were standing. It's directly behind the stage.'

'So how . . .?'

'He got one of the lads to give him the nod when the sun was in exactly the right place. Then he did the whole pointy thing and the big dramatic silence. And by coincidence, that happened to be the very moment when I was about to do my bass solo, which I'd only been rehearsing for about two years. See, that's the kind of brother he was.'

'I'm a little confused,' said Caine. 'You said that most of the rivalry was for effect; what were your true feelings for your brother?'

'I hated him. I've always hated him. I hated him when we were kids, 'cos he was Mammy's favourite, you know. He could do no wrong in her eyes. She actually believed he was some kind of saint or something. And another thing I hated was the way he patronised me.'

'Can you explain?'

'Ah, you know, people thought he was the big talent and I had none of my own. But like I say, there was another side to Ethan, which no one saw, not even Mam – a subtle thing, the way he worked on me. He was a bully.'

'Then perhaps you shouldn't be surprised if people start putting two and two together and—'

'And what? It's not a crime to hate someone, is it? There's nothing in the law that says you have to love your brother.'

'To be honest, you appear conflicted,' said Shanti. 'I mean, you've just had his name tattooed on your scalp . . .'

Tyrone returned to his chair, massaging his illustrated fists.

'Listen, Ethan was blood. We shared a womb, for fook's sake.'

'All noted. So who do you think wanted to harm him? Someone else in the family?'

'Oh yes, it's bound to be a Flynn.'

'Did Ethan know he was going to die?' asked Caine.

'What?'

'Did he have a premonition of his own death? Did he ever mention that to you?'

'Sounds like the sort of thing he would say. But guess what? *I'm* gonna die. And so are you, Policeman Plod . . . Creepy, eh?'

'Let's try something else,' said Shanti. 'Can you tell me about Ethan's movements before the show?'

'Like I say, we weren't exactly bosom buddies. In any case, my missus is expecting, so I've had plenty to attend to. But I do know that he spent most of the morning in Glastonbury.'

'OK, that's helpful. Why was that?'

'He was a great one for all the hippie-dippy spiritual bullshit. He liked to visit some Mystic Meg in the town to have his cards read.'

'That's interesting. You wouldn't have a name for this lady?'

'As a matter of fact, I do – it's not a name you'd forget. She's called Medusa Cole.'

'And the name of her shop?'

'Fairy Farts. Troll's Tits. How the fook would I know?'

'Was she a close friend?' Shanti asked.

'You mean was he shagging her? I've no idea, but he thought she had some kind of wisdom, meaning he handed over stupid sums of money. Oh, and she was the one who made those ludicrous costumes.'

'Costumes?'

'The costumes the dancers were wearing. Tarot characters.'

'You didn't approve?'

'Listen, I'm old-school rock 'n' roll. I used to think that was what the fans wanted too. The whole mystical thing was Ethan's doing.'

'You say you used to think that? Have you changed your mind?'

'It's no secret that seven years ago, when we went our separate ways, I made two rock albums, which . . . put it this way, they didn't do as well as I'd hoped. Ethan made about five of them dreamy spiritual albums including *Heartstrings*, which . . . well, you know . . .'

'*Heartstrings* went multi-platinum, didn't it?' said Caine.

'I don't know. I expect so . . . Look, my fookin' head is splitting. I need to lie down.'

'Of course. Final question . . . Was your brother in a relationship at the time of his death?' said Shanti.

'He was always fookin' someone.'

'But who was his most recent partner?'

'I'm not his personal assistant, you know. There were girls, and there were boys, and there was everything in between.'

'Sorry, you've lost me.'

'Pansexual, he called himself. Right . . . interview over. You'll see yourselves out.'

'Yes, that'll be all for the time being, but there may be more questions later. I understand you and your wife live with your mother, Queenie, near Frome. But we'd prefer it if you stayed here for a few days, if it's all the same to you.'

He jabbed a stumpy finger at her with amused menace.

'Now let's get a couple of things straight: I'll go where I fookin' please, when I fookin' please. Is that absolutely clear?'

'It's your call, Mr Flynn, but you'll find everything a lot easier if you cooperate. OK, we'll leave you in peace now.'

'Peace? There'll never be peace for the Flynns . . . BOYS! These fookin' amateurs are leaving.'

## *Chapter 10*

# A Shadowy Huddle

They found Primrose Vowles expertly rolling pastry in the kitchen, all darting eyes and forked teeth. She appeared more than a little reluctant to let them see Ethan's room.

'I don't mean to be unhelpful,' she said, 'but it's all nice and clean and ready for the next guest now. Besides, I've steak and kidney pie to make for sixteen.'

'We appreciate that, Mrs Vowles. But we also have a job to do.'

She muttered something, and wiped her spindly hands on her apron. Then she selected a large key from a rack behind the door.

'Oh dear, yes, that's another problem . . . I gave poor Ethan his own set of keys – bedroom and front door, like I do for all the guests. But with all the shocking events, his keys have disappeared. You see, these keys are very old – antique, I suppose – and I only have one spare. If I lose this, I don't know what I'll do. I'd be most grateful if you could keep an eye out for that set while you go about your business.'

Promising her that they would, Shanti and Caine followed her bamboo body along a maze of corridors, up two flights of stairs, and along seasick landings with threadbare carpets, more animals in glass cases, and melancholy oil paintings of prize-winning livestock.

'The Lilac Suite is the best room in the house,' she said as she unlocked a Hobbit-sized door. 'It's where lovely Ethan always stayed.'

It was indeed a fine bedroom, with slanting oak floors and lilac wallpaper. A large window looked across the valley, although little of the warm sunshine permeated the thick walls.

'And this bed has been in the Vowles family for centuries . . .'

Around a corner stood a colossal four-poster, with intricately carved pillars and frayed curtains.

'There's an en suite too,' said Primrose proudly, pushing open an inner door to reveal a low-ceilinged bathroom with an iron tub the size of a fishing boat.

As she and Dawn had said, the bedroom had been scrubbed clean, with crisp sheets and neatly folded towels on the bed. A strong smell of disinfectant lingered in the air. On one wall, a heavily framed oil painting of a Vowles ancestor stared gloomily at Shanti. He was a tiny, red-nosed man with mutton-chop side-burns beneath a wide hat. He wore a burgundy tailcoat and bloated white breeches, and he was posing in front of the very house in which they were now standing.

Nothing remained of the dead superstar's possessions.

'There's the Tor in the distance,' said Caine, leaning over the window seat. 'And I expect you can see the lights of the festival at night.'

'Course, I'll have the greatest trouble renting it now,' fretted Primrose. 'Everyone who wants a room has found one.'

'Well, wait a minute,' said Shanti. 'I need somewhere myself. I'd be prepared to move in until the end of the festival.'

Primrose seemed a little taken aback. 'You're most kind, I'm sure. But I'd have to speak to Vowles.'

'Sorry . . . you said you would have trouble finding someone, and I'm offering to move in straight away.'

Primrose shifted awkwardly from one skeletal leg to the other.

'With all due respect, it's just that some of the guests might not be happy having, you know, police on the premises.'

'On the other hand, they might be glad to have someone watching out for them, in light of what happened yesterday.'

'Yes, I s'pose . . . Oh dear, what a dilemma!'

'I'll tell you what, Mrs Vowles, there would be no need for anyone to know I'm a police officer, except you and Tyrone Flynn. How about that?'

'I'd have to tell Vowles.'

'Fine. You tell your husband, but I won't mention it if you don't.'

'Would that be both of you?'

'No, Mrs Vowles. Just me.'

'I apologise. You never quite know these days.'

'That's fine. DI Caine has his own accommodation. So are we agreed?'

'It's peak season, mind, so I'm afraid the room won't be cheap. And with respect, we ask for a deposit against damages.'

'I won't do any damages.'

'You see, Miss . . . Mrs . . .'

'Joyce. Shanti Joyce.'

'With respect, Mrs Joyce, that's what they all say till damages are done. Also you'll need to pay for breakfast and an evening meal, whether you take it or not.'

'That's all fine, Mrs Vowles.'

'And the room gets rather chilly at night. No central heating, see.'

'You've sold it to me. Shall I take the key?'

'Oh dear! The trouble is. . .'

'I know. It's the last one. I'll take the greatest care, I promise.'

Mrs Vowles handed over the old, cold key, took the money that Shanti offered and stepped onto the landing.

'I hope you have a pleasant stay at Unworthy Farm,' she broadcast. 'Dinner is served at eight p.m. prompt. Please inform the kitchen of any special dietary requirements. You're welcome, I'm sure.'

'Thank you, Mrs Vowles.'

When the landlady had gone, Shanti threw herself onto the fat mattress.

'Jeez, that was hard work. She's not exactly hotel receptionist of the year.'

'I'm amazed you want to stay, Shanti. In any case, won't you be stretching the budget? What will the super say?'

'Think it through, Caine. That VIP area at the back of the Pyramid is heavily guarded, right?'

'It seems to be.'

'Well doesn't that suggest that the perp had a VIP pass?'

'You're saying it might have been one of the guests here at Unworthy?'

'Yes, it's possible. It certainly won't do any harm to talk to them. What we know for sure is that this is where Ethan spent his final nights. Besides, it's an opportunity to keep an eye on that pumped-up Popeye Tyrone Flynn.'

'Take care with him, Shanti.'

'But top of my list of priorities is a long, hot soak. And this monster bed is nice and soft. Ooh, I ache in every joint of my body!'

'Whatever makes you happy. Just make sure you obey the house rules . . .' Caine was studying a handwritten notice on the back of the door:

*No music smoking pets or drugs except prescription.*

*We use a septic tank pee poo and paper only in toilet.*

'Crumbs! I'll do my best. So what did you make of Tyrone's statement? Talk about Mr Angry. If I heard him right, he was suggesting that Ethan was in multiple relationships. Pansexual, was that the word?'

'Yes, that's what he said. And I agree, it could be significant.'

'I think we need to compare notes. But maybe not here. There's a pub at the bottom of the lane. I don't know about you, but I could use a shandy and a packet of cheese and onion.'

In a former life, the Five Heads had been a fine building, but the interior had been systematically stripped of character, and now it was an unlovely potpourri of swirly carpets, fake horse brasses on nicotine-stained walls, and faded velvet curtains.

Drinking alone in a shadowy corner was the curly-haired farmhand, Gavin Blackmore, while a small group of locals in overalls and working clothes were huddled around a table, at the head of which sat a tiny weather-beaten man with bushy white eyebrows and a red nose. At his feet lay a ratty white and tan terrier, which bared its brown teeth at the two DIs.

'You mind your manners, Boner,' laughed the tiny man.

The barmaid wore a red leather jacket and an armoury of studs and piercings. She eyed Caine approvingly through heavily mascaraed lashes.

'Hello. What d'you fancy?' she said.

'What would you recommend? Something local, perhaps?'

'I'm local . . . Oh, I see what you mean. The cider's not bad. Strong, mind.'

The red-nosed man drained his pint and stood up. He reached down to tell the dog to stay put, and to Shanti's surprise, the critter appeared to nip at its master's hand. The man made his way slowly across the carpet, swinging one leg rigidly as he walked. When he arrived at the bar, he appeared no more than child-sized at Caine's side.

'Folk round here call it Suicider,' he said with a tinkly laugh.

'Ha! Perhaps I'll give it a try. What about you, Shanti?'

She chose half a shandy, a packet of crisps and a bar of fruit and nut chocolate, and the two of them found a seat across the room from the group.

'Enjoy your drink,' said the snowy-eyebrowed one.

'I bet the fun-sized animal lover is Primrose's husband,' whispered Shanti.

'That's what I thought,' said Caine. 'He looks exactly like the chap in the painting in your bedroom.'

They clinked glasses.

The cider was indeed murderously strong. Caine caught notes of wasps' nests in ancient apple groves.

'So, what are your thoughts?' he asked.

'Spoiler alert. Tyrone did it.'

'Hold on, Shanti.'

'Fratricide, isn't that what they call it?'

'Tyrone is aggressive, that's true. But Ethan's death was carefully staged. Don't you think spontaneous assault is more Tyrone's style?'

'Ah, you may be right,' she sighed. 'It's as if the killer was trying to send out a message in a very public way.'

'Personally I'd like to track down some of Ethan's lovers. I'd also like another chat with Vula Plenty – I think she knows more about him than she was letting on. She seems abnormally affected by his death.'

'I've also been thinking about your sister's encounter with Ethan. Was he scared that someone was out to get him?'

'Or was that just his Byronic temperament?'

'And now we have a new lead,' said Shanti. 'The Mystic Meg he visited yesterday. What was her name?'

'Medusa Cole.'

'The clock is ticking, Caine. Tick tock. We need a plan. Benno thinks we'll be able to interview Queenie Flynn tomorrow. The family home is near Frome, which is twenty minutes away. I suggest we head over there first thing in the morning.'

'I agree. And if you don't mind, I'll ask Benno to arrange another meeting with Vula in the afternoon. I think it would be better to visit her in her own domain. Apparently she has a yurt.'

'Is that a pet? Or a disease?'

'A round tent used by nomads.'

'And this afternoon we can interview some of the Tarot dancers. Only please don't make me talk to Sparky Mudget.'

'But he worships you.'

Caine returned the glasses to the bar. His was still half full.

'Couldn't manage your cider, then? A big chap like you?' The pierced barmaid stared deep into his eyes.

'It was delicious, just rather . . .'

'Strong body.'

'Yes . . .'

'Warm and sweet on the tongue.'

'I . . .'

'Nice head, too . . .'

As he left the bar, Caine strained his ears for conversation, but a contented silence had fallen over the drinkers in the Five Heads, broken only by the sawing snarl of the dog.

When he emerged into the balmy morning, he felt a pleasant swirl in his head. He saw Shanti affectionately checking her Saab, and his heart warmed towards her.

They walked down the leafy lanes in the direction of the ever-pounding festival. Below them rose the surprisingly grand spires and towers of Kilton parish church.

'Sorry, Shanti. Just give me five minutes, will you?' said Caine, pushing open a gate at the side of the cemetery.

'For God's sake, Caine. Where the hell are you going?' she said, hurrying to catch him.

'It's just a thing I have. I can't resist a graveyard. I think of them as the autobiography of a community. The monks in Thailand used to meditate in the charnel grounds.'

'Caine, it's nearly midday. We barely have the beginnings of a lead on this case, and you're wandering about looking at gravestones. There's only one body I'm interested in, and that's the fried half of Stigma.'

'Take this, for example. Fresh flowers. Placed there today, by the look of it.'

'Why the hell should that concern me?'

'Look at the inscription on the stone – *MYRTLE VOWLES, BELOVED MOTHER AND GRANDMOTHER. TAKEN TOO SOON.*'

'Caine, you are so far off the beaten track it's untrue. In a place like Kilton, everyone is related. I imagine half the village is called Vowles.'

'See the date? It's almost exactly ten years since she died.'

'Ah, now I get it – Myrtle Vowles, aged eighty-three, rose from the grave and rewired Ethan's amp. Can't believe I didn't crack it sooner.'

'You're right. It's probably nothing. Just the funny way my mind works.'

'Don't take this personally, Caine, but the funny way your mind works is the reason you live alone in a cabin on the Undercliff.'

## *Chapter 11*

# The Truant Tarot

Any thoughts Shanti might have had about the festival quietening down at lunchtime were dismissed as they re-entered the site.

If anything, the crowds had increased as the weekend approached. The two DIs fought their way past deafening arenas, and Caine pointed out that several bands were performing Stigma tributes in various musical styles. A mime act known as the Tiresome Butchers had put together a surrealist homage to 'While My Guitar Gently Kills', and an identikit family of sisters from Tennessee were working their way through a country version of 'Tiger in the Subway'.

When they reached the Pyramid Stage, they found that it was now fully screened and the cordoned-off mosh pit in front had been transformed into a sea of bouquets, which obliging coppers carried to and fro on behalf of grieving Stigs. Against the screen at the front of the stage stood a shrine to Ethan – a spotlit mandolin on a stand, draped in garlands of flowers.

They found Benno in the backstage area, looking more than a little flustered.

'I've never known a case like it, boss. We've got the world's media demanding answers, and there are dozens of conspiracy theories circulating.'

'OK, well Caine and I are around all afternoon. We'd like to talk to the Tarot dancers if we can.'

'I told them to stay on site. You'll find them by their bus over there.'

There were eight of them – four men and four women – sitting forlornly in canvas chairs or doing half-hearted stretches beside the tour bus. Shanti and Caine introduced themselves, and it became apparent that the troupe was still traumatised by the events of the previous day.

'Could you tell us a little about your act?' asked Caine. 'And anything odd or unusual you might have noticed.'

'We'd rehearsed everything,' said a slender woman with eyes like a porcelain doll. 'But Ethan always pulled out a surprise. That was his way.'

'What kind of surprise?'

'Well, none of us knew about the costumes until an hour before the show. Ethan loved spontaneity, you see. He'd ordered eight Tarot outfits – they were amazing, weren't they? Then he gave us a little talk about adopting the identity of our characters. For example, I was the Priestess, and Ethan talked about stepping into her persona as I stepped into the clothes.'

'Let me get this straight, you had no idea you were going to be Tarot card characters until just before the show?'

'That's right. We had rehearsed the basic choreography, of course, but it was such a thrill to tailor our moves accordingly.

Those fabulous costumes were his gift to us. Ethan's little surprise.'

'You were magical, Kirsty. You truly shone,' said one of her companions.

'Thank you, darling. We were all magical. You see, Inspector, Ethan inspired us. Most of us had worked with him many times, and we adored him. He was so sure everything would work that . . . it just did.'

'Does everyone agree with what's been said?' asked Caine.

'Not me,' said a young man raising his arm lazily at the back.

'Oh yes, sorry, Fabrizio. It was rather disappointing for you,' said Kirsty.

Shanti and Caine turned towards the athletic young man, who rose from his chair and sashayed towards them. Everything about his posture suggested decades of *pliés* and practice at the barre – the elegantly turned-out toes, the upright carriage, the extended neck and open chest.

'Fabrizio, is it? You had a different experience?'

He spoke in a thick Italian accent. 'It was a nightmare. Ethan handed out these glorious costumes, and we were so excited to find out who we'd be. But me? I was last in line, as usual, and there were only seven costumes.'

'There wasn't one for you?'

'No. Just my luck. This kind of thing always happens to me.'

'Darling, you seem to be forgetting that poor Ethan actually died,' said another young woman.

'It wasn't personal, Fabrizio,' said Kirsty. 'You know that. Ethan was just as disappointed as you. Do you remember, he even talked about sending someone back to the shop to see if it had been left behind?'

'But it was too late.' Fabrizio was a picture of sorrow. 'And now I'll never have this opportunity again.'

'So to be clear,' said Shanti, 'seven of you went on stage dressed as Tarot characters, while you waited here, Fabrizio?'

'I lay in the bus and cried.'

'And the rest of you, do you still have your costumes?'

'Your forensic people took them for examination,' said an impossibly perfect young man.

'But you noticed nothing unusual before or during the show? No one tampering with the amplifiers or guitars?'

There was much sighing and shaking of heads.

'We've been through it a thousand times,' said Kirsty. 'It was just another show. Ethan was his same lovely self.

'No one spilt water on the stage?'

'Water? Why?'

'I'm sorry, I can't go into detail, but I need you all to consider whether you might have accidentally spilt anything on stage. Or whether you saw any liquid near where Ethan was standing.'

They stared at each other blankly.

'All right, let's try something else,' said Caine. 'Could you confirm which of you ran over to attend to Ethan when he fell?'

Several of the dancers raised their hands.

'He was clearly dead.'

'I wanted to give him mouth-to-mouth, but his face was . . .'

'And the smell! Oh God, the stench of burning flesh . . .'

'But you decided to carry him off stage?'

'What else could we do?'

'We couldn't leave him there for all the world to see.'

'I had to . . . prise his hands off the guitar,' said the perfect man mournfully.

'It must have been deeply traumatic,' said Caine. 'If you need to speak to someone, please ask one of our team and they can put you in touch with a counsellor.'

'I want to ask about Tyrone,' said Shanti. 'Did any of you speak with him before the show?'

There was an uncomfortable pause.

'We tended to keep away from Tyrone,' said a shaven-headed woman. 'Especially right before a gig. He could be a bit . . .'

'More than a bit.'

'. . . a bit moody. And he had a thing against dancers in general, so we avoided him if we could.'

'Right, thank you, everyone. You've been most helpful. If you plan to leave the festival site between now and Sunday, we would be most grateful if you could let one of our colleagues know. In the meantime, if you think of any other details, no matter how trivial they might seem, don't hesitate to speak to one of our officers.'

By the time Shanti had written up her notes and debriefed Benno, she felt utterly exhausted. Who knew that a festival would involve so much footwork?

She spotted Caine signing the magazine for the young constable who had driven her the day before.

'Looks like you've got a fan there, Caine. Did you tell her about Half Man Half Bullshit?'

'Oh Shanti . . .'

'Anyway, I've got a ton of paperwork and a press release to attend to before dinner, so I'll catch you later. What's your plan? Tantric massage? Colonic irrigation?'

'You know what I'm going to do – I'm going to hear Misty sing.'

'Of course. I'm glad you've got your priorities in order. Let me know when you're ready to resume work.'

'I've just messaged her to say that I'm on my way. And she says . . . oh, hang on, Shanti, you may want to hear this . . . she says she's remembered another detail from her meeting with Ethan.'

'What detail?'

'She doesn't say. But she thinks it might be highly significant. She says she'll tell us when she comes off stage.'

'Damn it, Caine. Is this a ruse to get me to hear your sister sing? I don't think you realise how little time we have to solve this case. Four days – three and a half now.'

'According to Sparky Mudget, time is liquid.'

'There's only one thing time does, Caine, and that's run out. Your sister had better have some useful information, because my patience is running out too.'

## Chapter 12

# A Remembrance of Death

The young singer was set to perform in a glade surrounded by swaying silver birches in the Field of Avalon. The two cops picked their way through the modest crowd and found a space on the grass in front of the small acoustic stage.

As they waited, Shanti realised that her normally serene partner was writhing with apprehension at her side.

'For God's sake settle down, Caine. You're worse than Paul at school assembly.'

'I'm so grateful you came, Shanti. You've no idea how big this is for Misty. My kid sister on stage at Glastonbury. I can hardly believe it.'

A familiar figure stepped onto the stage. Vula was dressed in her usual Afghan hippie style – colourful headscarf, harem pants and a beautifully embroidered waistcoat. Her heavily lacquered fingers clutched the microphone, her molten Canadian tones drawing the audience's attention.

'My friends, we have a very special treat for you on this

magical afternoon. Two days ago, my dear friend Ethan Flynn ... yes, yes, Ethan ... asked me to listen to a couple of songs he had come across. They'd been written and performed by a young artist I had never heard of. But that was Ethan all over. It was his favourite thing to spot emerging talent, because for him there was nothing more precious than authenticity, before it becomes sullied by fame and money.' Vula's pale face was wet with tears. 'You know, I'm certain that Ethan would have been here in person if he wasn't ... if he wasn't double-booked at another celestial gig. I don't know about you, but I feel his presence very strongly amongst us. Please take a moment to hug your neighbour ...'

Shanti winced and pretended to be fascinated by her phone.

'I've been trying to recall the phrase that Ethan used to describe the songs you are about to hear – "pure auditory gold", that's what he said, ladies and gentlemen. My friends, please give all the love you have to ... MISTY!'

To Shanti's surprise, Misty was alone. No band. No backing singers. She wandered on stage carrying an acoustic guitar, like a child walking in a meadow. If she was afraid, she didn't show it. Instead, she appeared baffled and dreamy, as if she had woken from sleep.

Half of Shanti's mind was doing what it always did – churning and turning on the case in hand. There were so many elements and so many persons of interest. Caine was right – even now, Vula seemed inordinately sad at the loss of Ethan Flynn. Of course they had known each other professionally for many years, but she appeared hollowed out with grief.

And then Misty began to sing – a self-penned ballad of childlike simplicity, rendered in such unique and authentic tones that Shanti's brain stopped in its tracks. Her ears and her entire being opened towards this woman-child, whom she had dismissed as a silly thing – the lighter half of Caine's annoying New Age persona – and she realised that the whole audience was silenced, all of them enraptured by Misty's auditory gold. From amongst the trees and tents, dozens of mourners drifted wide-eyed towards the haunting sound, seeking solace like the thirsty to a freshly flowing waterfall.

The song was about hurt and healing. The way in which humans were condemned to cause pain, because of their own pain. And the promise of solace in love.

When Shanti turned to look at Caine, he appeared blurry, and to her annoyance she found that tears had filled her eyes. Caine was weeping too – proper, unrestrained man-tears. And when she looked about, she saw that people of every age and gender and race had tears coursing down their faces. For Ethan. For everything good and pure that humans had destroyed.

How long the concert lasted, she could not say. The afternoon was measureless, but by the time the applause had faded and she found herself queuing to have CDs signed for Paul and Mum, the light was already beginning to fade.

Misty rose to her feet and hugged them, as if Shanti as well as Caine was a beloved sibling.

'Did you like it?' she breathed.

'No words,' said Caine. 'Just beautiful, sweetheart.'

'And you, Shanti? Thank you for coming.'

'It was . . . it was . . . Jeez, Misty, I have a limited emotional vocabulary. But you touched parts I didn't know I had. That's all I can say.'

At last they were walking together through the trees, and

Misty was telling them in excited tones about offers and introductions from producers and journalists; an invitation to perform on Vula's radio show, and the many glowing things that people had said.

'But I won't let it go to my head,' she said. 'I don't want to get tied down at this stage in my life. Everything will happen in time.'

Time? Jeez, Caine had been right, damn him. And Sparky Mudget too. Time was indeed liquid, and the afternoon had evaporated like water sprinkled on a stage. Shanti had almost forgotten the reason she came.

'Misty, I know you have a lot on your mind, but Caine told me you had remembered something new about your conversation with Ethan . . .'

'Of course. Yes, it came to me while I was rehearsing before the gig. I was halfway through a song when suddenly a picture came into my head – a memory. It may be nothing at all, but it made my blood run cold, so that I forgot the lyrics and had to begin the song all over again.'

'Go on.'

'When Ethan was talking to me . . . you remember I told you that he took my hand . . .'

'After Tyrone insulted him.'

'Yes, it was just before Vula went on stage to warm up the crowd. You see, most artists have a rule about having the stage completely clear before a gig. But I noticed someone coming down the steps at the back of the Pyramid.'

'Can you describe them?'

'Oh yes. I won't forget that person.'

'Go on. This could be important.'

'It was only a fleeting glimpse, but there was something about their behaviour that caught my eye. Sort of furtive.'

'Would you recognise them if you saw them again?'

'It was one of the Tarot dancers.'

'Jeez. You realise this could be our killer? Think hard now. Which of the dancers was it?'

'It was Death,' she replied.

# Chapter 13

# The Hollow Eyes of Doom

Inside the mobile unit, Benno and Shanti sat in the half-light peering at a screen, while Caine stood behind them.

'OK, Benno. We're looking for something very specific. We've obviously got thousands of images of the Stigma gig and Ethan's death . . .'

'More like millions, boss.'

'. . . but what I'm interested in are the minutes immediately before the concert. To be precise, the ten-minute time slot between Sparky Mudget and his technicians exiting the stage, and Vula Plenty coming out to introduce the band.'

'OK, boss. The problem is the stage was dark and empty, so it wasn't very photogenic, if you see what I mean.'

'There must be something,' said Shanti.

'There is. There's a fixed webcam, which runs 24/7. Mind you, it's a bit grainy.'

'Let's take a look. OK, this is good . . . I can just about make out the amp that was connected to Excalibur. See, there in the shadows. That's what I'm interested in.'

'I'll start running it here at 20.43, while things are still relatively busy. Here's Sparky Mudget with a head torch, making his final checks.'

'I'd recognise that podgy white arse anywhere,' said Shanti.

'It's a bit murky, but you can make out a few of the Spark1Up team inspecting bits of kit. Now Sparky gets up and looks around. Double-checking everything. Finally he gives the thumbs-up. He rounds up his techies and they exit the stage together.'

'This is where it gets interesting,' said Shanti. 'We're entering the key time. Go carefully, Benno, we don't want to miss anything.'

'The stage is unoccupied for nearly ten minutes . . .'

Caine leaned forward. 'But at 20.50 . . . Look!'

'Holy crap,' said Shanti. 'There's someone creeping about in the shadows!'

'It must be one of the dancers,' said Caine. 'They're wearing a long red cloak with a big hood and what appears to be a skeleton costume underneath.'

'That is one weird costume! What's he got in his hand?'

'A carrier bag. Tools, probably.'

'Right. Run it as slow as you can, Benno. Look, he's bending down by the amp.'

'The nerve of it!' said Benno. 'Tampering with the equipment in front of that huge crowd!'

'Not one of them would have noticed,' replied Shanti. 'It's what you call hiding in plain sight.'

'He's working swiftly,' said Caine. 'I reckon that's a screwdriver in his hand. It's impossible to see exactly what he's doing . . . but it looks there like he's replacing the casing on the amp . . . What's he up to now?'

'My God!' said Benno. 'He's taking out a bottle and . . . Look! He's deliberately pouring it around the guitar stand!'

'Now he stands and turns,' said Shanti. 'As if he's double-checking that he's done everything he should. Freeze it right there, Benno! Unless I'm mistaken, this is our man.'

'Or woman, Shanti.'

'Right, Caine. Take a good look at that figure of Death. Does it have chest bumps?'

'It's difficult to say.'

'Well I don't think so. Granted, the body is concealed beneath the cloak, and the light is poor. But in my eyes, that's a fella.'

'You can't even gauge their height.'

'Give me strength. Right, Benno, tell the team to search the festival site for a man – or a woman – who could be tall . . . or short. Is that helpful?'

'Not very, boss.'

'You heard him, Caine. You're not very helpful.'

'Should I make printouts?' asked Benno.

'Good idea. One for each of the crew. Let's send a couple of teams amongst the crowds. Double Brownie points if anyone spots him.'

'Maybe they'd be better in civvies, boss. Then they can mingle.'

'Good thinking. Uniforms tend to scare people away. But hang on – maybe we're making things more complicated than we need. We interviewed those dancers this morning, right? So, which of them was Death?'

'None of them,' said Caine.

'What do you mean?' asked Shanti.

'I'll show you. Let's find the dance sequence on YouTube . . .' He turned to a laptop and began searching. Moments later, he opened a link. 'OK, this is about twenty minutes in to the Stigma gig. Here are the dancers moving frenetically around Ethan – he's playing a mandolin at this point.'

'That choreography is well OTT.'

'There are seven dancers – there should be eight, remember, but Fabrizio didn't appear. You can see the Priestess, the Fool, the Hermit, the Devil, the Magician, the Sun and the Moon. But Death isn't amongst them.'

'I suppose you're right as usual. OK, Benno, please can you wind back that webcam footage? I want another look at the quiet period before Stigma come on stage. This is it. Now then, is it possible to zoom in on the suspect? I want a good look at his face.'

'It's fuzzy, but . . . Bloody hell, this gives me the willies, boss.'

Benno fiddled with the computer, so that the outlandish character knelt and rose, rose and knelt repeatedly. In one gloved hand he carried the bag, and in the other an electrical lead and a glinting screwdriver. At last Benno found the moment he was searching for – where the robed figure turned and stared directly into the lens. The footage was grainy, but the effect was startling.

'Do you mind if I swear, boss?' said Benno.

'I think that would be perfectly appropriate.'

'Fuck me, boss. Fuck me forwards. Fuck me sideways. Fuck me upside down.'

For a brief moment the three cops found themselves staring into the hollow eye sockets of Death.

'There we have it,' whispered Shanti. 'This is who we're after . . . Find Death and we've found our killer.'

## *Chapter 14*

# Starry Starry Night

Pausing to collect a few essentials from the festival's pop-up shops, Shanti commandeered a ride through the tides of people into Kilton village.

She was pleased to find that the Saab started first time. As she drove up Totterdown Hill, she realised that the two uniforms were still stationed on the lane outside the farmhouse.

'You can knock off now,' she called through the open window. 'Everything been quiet here?'

'Yes, guv. Tyrone's moved out now.'

'You what?'

'Gone home to his mum's.'

'Jesus! That man . . .'

'He said you'd already questioned him, and in any case, he wasn't under arrest, so he'd go where he fookin' likes, when he fookin' likes.'

Shanti always enjoyed a hot bath at the end of a long day, but this was something special. The small plastic tub at home, which she shared with a bundle of scratchy toys, was fine. But the huge lion-footed affair in the Lilac Suite was a different experience altogether. She lounged for nearly an hour, up to her ears in the fragrant water, which was as hot as her body could bear.

On the opposite wall, a large and ancient map had been mounted in an oak frame. It took Shanti a while to realise that it was a beautifully rendered illustration of Unworthy Farm from the 1800s. Back then, the land extended over hundreds of acres, with numerous workers' cottages. In the lower left-hand corner, a red-jacketed hunt was setting out on fine horses, with a pack of hounds and hunting horns, as a poor fox scurried beneath the roots of a tree.

Vincent Caine showered and shaved at the WaterAid facilities and changed into a clean shirt. Then he enjoyed a modest, mindful meal at the Hundred Monkeys Café, before joining Misty and some of her friends at the trance tent.

'Vince, I want you to meet my best friends in the world – Tempest, Zara and LukeyLuke. This is my big brother, everyone. Isn't he lovely!'

At first, Caine's dancing was a little awkward. He couldn't help feeling slightly self-conscious alongside these cool young things. But as the insistent rhythms swept over him, he found that conversation, and even thought, became impossible. Soon there was nothing to do but smile and give himself up to the ever-increasing tempo as the rest of these twisting, sweaty bodies were doing.

As she dried herself on Primrose Vowles' freshly laundered towels, Shanti barely noticed the throb of the festival.

She only meant to rest in bed for ten minutes, but it was almost dark when a brief but deeply disturbing nightmare woke her. It had been so vivid. Someone had been kneeling on the mattress beside her, whispering in her ear. When she sat up, she was freezing cold and there was no one there, but her head churned with disturbing thoughts and sensations. This ancient four-poster had been where Ethan Flynn had spent the last night of his life. For the first time, she noticed a row of skilfully carved oak faces staring down at her from the upper panels of the bed, each baring its teeth or crying out in dumb anguish. Or so it seemed.

She would need to hurry if she was going to sample Primrose's cuisine. She pulled on the red and gold patterned dress she had selected in an instant from a festival boutique, realising now that it was an Indian design, like the saris her mother wore on special occasions. Then she tidied her hair and applied a little make-up. The woman who stared back from the full-length mirror was almost unrecognisable from the tough and somewhat cynical cop she had been a couple of hours ago – *Cinderella, you shall go to the ball!* If only Caine could see her now, she thought, instantly banning the notion.

On the dance floor, in front of the raised booth where DJ MixxyBlasta was spinning his magic, DI Vincent Caine had peeled off his shirt and allowed Misty, Tempest, Zara and LukeyLuke to daub his torso with glow-in-the-dark UV body paint. Beneath the strobe lights and walloping beat, he disappeared into a fluid ecstasy of movement. Hands twisting in wavering oscillations like the classical dancers he had seen in Thailand. Eyes closed in rapture, body whirling, twisting, gyrating, until the dance became a meditation in which there was no dancer; only the pulsing heartbeat of sound, and the euphoric warmth of friendship and love that washed over him.

The starry tenants of Unworthy were already assembled in the great dining room where Shanti and Caine had interviewed Tyrone. Now the fire roared and the place was like the green room at a glittering award ceremony – filled with so many famous faces that Shanti's heart skipped many beats, as if she were suffering from stage fright.

Wine flowed. Voices were raised in animated conversation, accompanied by the guffaws of a dozen entitled stars of the music industry, who felt as relaxed in an ancient English farmhouse as they did in their own mansions and holiday villas around the world.

Some she identified immediately: Manchester grime artist Lil Bisto; lounge-bar crooner Zulu Waters; an impossibly pretty K-pop trio called Safe Squad. On the very chair where Tyrone had received his tattoo sat the lead singer from 6th Sense. In earnest conversation by the fire stood three silver veterans of the music world: Royal Bronson, Gilish, and Marcel Snapper. Already drunk or high, tabloid bad girl Ulalla Strump tottered precariously on towering heels.

They all took their seats at the huge table beneath the steady gaze of the mounted animal heads. Shanti found herself beside Lil Bisto on her left, and an unusually large carved chair to her right.

'I seen you, ain't I?' said Bisto.

'I'm sorry?'

'I seen you on stage, innit?'

'No . . . no. I'm not in a band.'

'Right. You *look* like you was a music star.'

'Thanks. No, I'm—'

Before she could finish, a huge presence entered the room, swearing as she ducked beneath the beams. It was Sista Tremble.

'Got goddam motherfuckin' spiderwebs in my hair!' she exclaimed.

'Oh babe! Let me help you with that,' said a petite man-child known as Glamdos. He leapt to his feet and began plucking invisible strands of cobweb from Sista's towering Afro.

At last, Sista Tremble fell with a sigh into the throne beside Shanti, a huge smile on her immaculately made-up face.

'And you are . . .?' she said.

'Shanti Joyce,' said Shanti Joyce. 'I have to say, I grew up on your music, Ms Tremble. Really, I have every one of your songs, you know, on vinyl. I can't believe—'

'You are precious!' roared Sista Tremble. 'But I assure you, when I'm not on stage I'm just a regular girl.'

'A regular girl who likes a regular glass of wine,' said Marcel Snapper, massaging her powerful shoulders. He poured a full glass of red for Sista and another for Shanti, and waited with bottle poised as Sista downed the glass, refilled, downed and refilled again.

'Thank you, Marcel. Now I'm human again,' she sighed.

At that moment, an overloaded hostess trolley entered the room, followed closely by the anxiously obsequious figure of Primrose Vowles.

'This is why we return again and again,' announced Marcel Snapper, as Primrose unloaded steaming platters onto the table. 'Never mind the Opium Club or Nowadays, what we want is

Primrose's steak and kidney pie, and you *wait* till you try her home-made ice cream. More wine, ladies? Nonsense, you've barely had a drop!'

'A toast, ladies and gentlemen!' boomed Sista Tremble, and her powerful voice silenced the rattling and chattering in the room. 'A toast to our dear companion, gone before us. Gone before his time.' Every glass was raised. 'To Ethan, divine messenger of love.'

'TO ETHAN!' yelled the megastars.

'But not that ass fuck of a brother!' whispered Sista in Shanti's ear.

In a nameless abyss of sound, the entity formerly known as Caine was at one with the music of the spheres. He was absent. In his place was an animalistic body, grinding and grinning in orgiastic contortions.

As Shanti lay on her back, staring queasily at the shifting gargoyles on the bed frame, she struggled to recall some of the conversations she had shared during the long evening. Her normal practice would be to dictate notes into her iPhone, but that would necessitate a series of manoeuvres her swollen belly and fragile head would not allow. If she fell asleep now, though, she might forget everything. No. What she needed to do was replay the evening in her mind, so that she could discuss various salient points with Caine in the morning.

The night had been a swirling cascade of wine and food and hilarity, reflected in the taxidermy domes on every sideboard. But amongst the hurly-burly, there had been valuable intel. For example, she recalled a fascinating conversation with Lil Bisto about Sista Tremble. Despite her gushing tribute to Ethan, it transpired that the soul legend shared a long and acrimonious history with the Flynns. According to Bisto, it had all started ten years previously, right here at Glastonbury, when the youthful Stigma had ousted the great diva from the Sunday-night headline slot that had been her rightful place. It was, according to Bisto, a moment from which her career had never fully recovered.

'I mean, she's still big, ain't she?' he had confided furtively. 'But Sista is more of a retro thing, you feel me? More for the oldies.'

And this year Sista Tremble had returned like an avenging queen to reclaim that Sunday-night slot, only to discover that Stigma had once again stolen the limelight by opening the festival in such dramatic fashion. It seemed that no one could compete with Stigma. Could it be, Shanti wondered in a fuzzy kind of way ... could it possibly be that Sista Tremble had returned to Glastonbury to exact a soulful revenge?

What else had transpired in the great dining room of Unworthy? She recalled the poignant moment when a melodious cappella rendition of 'Legend of You' had broken out, as artists of every age and genre united in a spontaneous commemoration of Ethan Flynn, accompanied by an astonishing percussion solo by Gilish, using cutlery on pots, pans and glasses. The only witness to that seminal musical moment had been Shanti Joyce, a working-class cop from Camden Town. And not one of those luminaries had questioned her place amongst them.

The truth was that Shanti had been privy to so many scandals and rumours that night, she found it impossible to separate fact from fiction. Had she imagined it, or had there been an uproarious conversation about a mysterious intruder laughingly known as 'the Unworthy Wanker'? Someone who wandered the silent bedrooms during the day, rifling through the intimate belongings of the female guests.

'All I can say is you'd better double-triple-quadruple lock your door, girl,' Sista had warned.

'You know how I hate gossip . . .' interjected Royal Bronson.

'He loves it,' said Sista.

'. . . but did you hear the rumour about poor Polly?'

'Polly?' said Shanti.

'He means Polly Darton,' interpreted Sista. 'Country and western tribute act.'

'Apparently the poor woman had more than a dozen 40DD brassieres removed from her portmanteau.'

'No way!' gasped Shanti.

'Way!' said Sista. 'I mean, where would you conceal contraband of that magnitude?'

And then Shanti and Sista Tremble, both outrageously drunk, had settled into a hilarious guessing game about the identity of the mysterious Unworthy Wanker.

'Just look around the room,' whispered Sista. 'It could be *him* . . . or *him* . . . or *her*! Or any one of them . . .'

'Maybe *all* of them!' squealed Shanti.

'OK, the next person to speak is him,' snorted Sista.

'What are you two laughing at?' asked Marcel Snapper.

'Oh, nothing, honey,' Sista had replied, practically bursting her ample sides. 'Just a little guessing game . . . Oh my! I do believe I have wet myself!'

'Well, my vote goes to old man Vowles,' Shanti had said.

'After all, he has the room keys and a leaky red nose. He even has a dog named Boner.'

'I don't believe that is the first time that suggestion has been made. All I know is that I place a loaded mousetrap in my underwear drawer. So keep your eyes open for swollen fingers . . . or other parts!'

'But then why do you choose to stay here?' Shanti had demanded. 'I mean, is it just me, or is it damned *cold* everywhere?'

'England *is* cold,' replied Sista. 'And that's why my people always provide electric blankets and heaters. Lots of them. You should go into my room – I call it Sista's Sauna.'

'Yes, but don't you find Unworthy a tad . . . rustic? And the family are a little odd, aren't they? And now you're telling me about—'

'About the Unworthy Wanker. Listen, honey, I've stayed here more than a dozen times, and I shall continue to stay as long as the Glastonbury gods allow. It all comes down to three words: *authentic English charm*.'

Towards the end of the monolithic meal, Primrose had scuttled in to clear the table and serve her home-made ice cream, which was indeed divine. This time she had brought her son, Seth, to help. Everything about the skinny teenager with the drooping red Mohican suggested that he was reluctant to be there.

When Sista Tremble had grabbed the boy's arm and teasingly invited him to sit on her abundant lap and share her mulberry scoop, Seth's acned face had blushed a deeper shade of purple than the ice cream.

'Can't I go now, Mum?' he had wailed.

'S'pose so,' Primrose replied. 'But you make sure you're back before midnight.'

'Midnight! You're 'aving a laugh. It doesn't even kick off till then.'

Once Seth had left the room, Primrose had complained bitterly that he was off to join his mates down at the Cider Bus. It seemed that every resident of Kilton received a free pass to the festival – a kind of compensation for the disruption it caused. And that consequently Seth and his friends spent 'far too much time in that den of iniquity'.

'Lord knows what they get up to . . .' she muttered as she reversed the trolley into the passageway. 'You're welcome, I'm sure.'

At that point in her recollections, Shanti must have slept, because when she awoke, the ancient farmhouse was bathed in moonlit silence. Faintly bilious and chilled to the bone, she stumbled from the bed, stubbing her toe painfully on a medieval chair. Tipping out her bag, she located a pack of aspirin and swallowed three, with a glass of lukewarm water.

But how could she sleep now? The huge bed was a cold as a tomb.

At the trance tent, Caine embraced his sister and her friends. What a night it had been. The young ones would be here until dawn, but he had work to do, and his warm sleeping bag awaited. Somewhere along the way, he had lost his shirt. But that was OK. The night was still warm. He slipped outside and made his way up the hillside towards his tent, pausing to do a few t'ai chi moves and inhale the fresh night air. His body felt delightfully stretched by the frenetic yogic dancing. His head was clear and rested. He extended metta – loving kindness – to all at the festival; in particular, his heart went out to the grieving mother, Queenie Flynn. Just before he fell deeply into peaceful sleep, he sent gratitude and tenderness to his colleague Shanti Joyce. And hoped that she too was at peace.

## *Chapter 15*

# A Hot Brick

Shanti Joyce was not at peace. In fact she was at war. At war with the strangulating blankets. At war with her throbbing head and churning belly. At war with the arctic conditions of the bedroom.

She fumbled for her phone. The time was 1.15 a.m. Draping a blanket around her shoulders, she meandered barefoot through the labyrinth of corridors and landings, down the oak staircase and along the icy flagstone corridors to where a light was burning in the kitchen. Pushing open the door, she saw that every plate and item of cutlery had been washed and dried and stacked tidily, and a solitary figure sat bent over a plate of leftovers at the table.

When the terrier raised its rodent head and snarled at her from the armchair, Shanti realised that the person at the table was not Primrose, but her husband – Farmer Vowles, the tiny red-nosed man from the Five Heads.

'You be quiet now, Boner,' he chuckled. 'That's no way to greet a lady.'

'That's all right,' said Shanti unhappily. 'I'm sure his bark's worse than his bite.'

'That's what they say, isn't it?' twinkled Vowles. ''Cept in Boner's case it's the other way round. His bite's far worse than his bark, ain't it, you little rascal?' He reached affectionately towards the dog, and once again he was greeted with a snarling air-nip. 'He's a hunter, see. Put 'im down an 'ole and he'll pull 'em out with those sharp little teeth, no matter what they are. Weasels, rats, rabbits, badgers, it's all the same to Boner.' He chuckled appreciatively at the thought.

'Well I'm sorry to disturb you,' Shanti said. 'I was looking for a hot-water bottle. I don't want to complain, but it's bloody freezing upstairs.'

'Oh dear, we can't 'ave that,' he replied, raising one snowy white eyebrow. 'See, that's the trouble with an old place like this. Folks these days are used to central heating an' all that. We don't have none of that 'ere. But you come and sit yourself down, my dear, and get warm. Now, let me see . . . no, we don't have no hot-water bottle, far as I know.'

'Well, an extra blanket . . .'

'Trouble is, that's Primrose's department, an' she's getting her beauty sleep in the bungalow. I'll wake her if you want me to . . .'

'Oh no! Please don't do that. I assumed you slept in the house.'

'Not since we started the B and B. No room, see. We're cosy enough in the bungalow, me an' Primrose. But I like to slip over here and sit by the Aga from time to time. Reminds me of the old days.'

Shanti noticed a large drip on the tip of his hooked nose. It wavered but did not fall.

'I'll tell you what I'll do,' he said. 'I'll teach you the old Somerset way to heat a body. Mother used to do it for me when I were a boy, God rest her soul. Now you stay 'ere. I won't be long.'

He rose to his feet, grinning mysteriously, and swung his leg stiffly towards the back door. There he pulled on wellingtons, fumbled with antique locks and stepped into the night.

Shanti sat alone with the rumbling, musky dog quivering in the chair. Christ, what was the old man up to? She had a busy day tomorrow and she really didn't feel too bright.

The door opened again and Vowles stepped inside and removed his boots. In his leathery hands was a brick, which he displayed proudly. The cop part of Shanti prepared to defend herself, but the small man oscillated past her towards the Aga. Opening one of the oven doors, he slipped the brick inside.

'I do this for Primrose sometimes,' he said, beaming sentimentally. 'She's like you – always cold. Like sleeping with a fish, it is. Now, we'll give it ten minutes, and it'll keep those pretty toes warm till morning.'

The rich gravy from the steak and kidney pie threatened a second coming.

'None of my business, but Primrose says you're police,' said Vowles, continuing with his meal.

'That's correct.'

'I don't mean to pry, but you don't look like police. More like one of them singers.'

Oh Lord! She was still wearing the sari. She must have fallen asleep fully clothed.

'Well I assure you, I'm a detective inspector from Yeovil. And you wouldn't want to hear me sing.'

'I'm sure you have a lovely voice,' he chuckled. 'And 'less I'm wrong, you're looking into the death of poor young Ethan. Shocking business. We had a soft spot for him, me an' Primrose.'

The last thing Shanti fancied was a late-night chat, but in sickness or in health she was a cop, and you never knew what you might glean from an accidental encounter.

'You knew him well?'

'Not well. That's more Primrose's department. But we were fond of him in our way. He were always respectful. On the other hand, there's no gettin' away from it – they live hard and they die hard. That's their way, ain't it? Me an' Primrose have seen it all over the years. Young Ethan wasn't the first and he won't be the last, I'm sorry to say it.'

She was mesmerised by the quivering nose drop.

'Do you have any thoughts about his death, Mr Vowles?'

'You see, I'm just a man of the soil. What would I know? In my opinion they bring it on themselves. Some it's drugs. Others it's drink . . .'

'And Ethan?'

'Him? It were sex.'

'How do you know that, Mr Vowles?'

'There now, I've said too much already. He were a fine young gentleman, I'm sure, an' some poor mother will be grievin'.'

'No, I'm genuinely interested.'

'Let's just say, me an' Primrose noticed more'n a few visitors popping up to the Lilac Suite. The night before he was taken we heard all manner of histrionics up there.'

'You heard an altercation?'

'Heard it. Saw it. I were sittin' here mindin' my own business – it was late, mind – an' one of them came runnin' in, all weepin' an' wailin' an' discombobulated. I tried to help, but she ran out the back and disappeared into the night.'

'That's interesting. Could you describe her?'

'Pretty thing. All dressed up like she were in a pantomime. Oh, an' she were American.'

'Could she have been Canadian?'

'With respect, my dear, they're all different nationalities these days, aren't they? I don't mean to seem prejudiced . . .'

'Of course not.'

'. . . I've got nothing against no one of any race, so long as they pays their rent. But what I fail to understand, and maybe you can answer this for me, is why there are suddenly so many of them. I mean, where was you all before? You didn't suddenly pop up from nowhere . . .'

Up close, Shanti observed the craggy landscape of his face. Below the pebble eyes, and eyebrows like snow-capped hedgerows, his cheeks were laced with intricate blue and purple veins, from decades of labour on the Levels. The dome of his head was bald as a planet, but white hair was swept backwards on either side. And still the trembling bead on his beaky nose defied the laws of gravity.

'. . . All I know is there's been Vowleses in Kilton since records began and a good deal longer. Interestin' fact: Kilton were a quarantined village during the plague.'

'That's wonderful. Congratulations.'

'Thing is, me an' Primrose is the first generation who've met folk from . . . you know, other parts. An' I don't mean no offence to no one.'

'Of course not. And it's always hard when we're forced to confront our little prejudices.'

He beamed benignly. 'You're a very understanding young lady. But you won't hear me complain. I count my blessings every day. I have a pretty wife with a clever business mind; she saved Unworthy, did Primrose. Makes me choke up to say it.'

'You mean the bed and breakfast?'

'Bed and breakfast, Unworthy Ices, she never stops, that girl. She's a phenomenon.'

'Ah yes, the famous Unworthy Ices.'

'Ain't you tried 'em? Trust me, you will. Primrose has a shed full of the stuff.'

'Come to think of it, I did have some ice cream with my dinner. Mulberry, I think it was. Anyway, it was delicious.' Her stomach lurched at the thought.

'Hee hee . . . Here, I'll tell you somethin' that'll make you laugh! If Primrose had her way, I'd be drivin' an ice-cream van round that festival. That was another of her little schemes. But I draw the line at that.'

'I don't blame you.'

'See, miss, it's difficult for you to understand, but I'm a farmer through an' through. Just like my father, and his father before him, going all the way back through time.'

'Primrose told me that farming is tough these days.'

'Tough ain't the 'alf of it. Them supermarkets shaft you every direction you turn. "You need to diversify" is what the Farmers' Union tells us. Diversify? What? Start a pop festival on my land?' He laughed aloud. 'All I know is the soil. I can't think what my forefathers would say if they saw the place now – Unworthy Ices in the milkin' shed, bedrooms full of pop stars.'

'I think there's a portrait of one of your ancestors in my bedroom.'

'I were born in that bed.'

'It must be nice to have that heritage. And I suppose your son will take over one day. Seth, isn't it?'

He pushed his plate away, and in an astonishingly unguarded moment, a long tongue flickered upwards and snatched the drip from his nose.

'Brick's ready,' he said.

Swinging his leg across the room, he opened the oven. He reached inside, swaddled the hot brick in an oven glove and handed it to her with an unnerving smile.

'Me an' Primrose spent our wedding night in that bed, and many a night since. So I feel qualified to say you'll not find a more comfortable restin' place in a hundred mile.'

Shanti felt his small eyes on her back as she shuffled along the dark passage and up the stairs of his ancestral home.

'Sleep well, my dear,' he called.

Barely had she settled on the pillows than the festival began to stir and throb, like a colossus awakening in the hills.

## Chapter 16

# Villa del Flynn

Sipping tea outside his tent, Vincent Caine watched the dawn rise over the sleeping festival. It was one of those precious moments in which an embryonic sun and a pregnant moon shared the same sky.

The slogan on his mug said: *The cup is already broken.*

Laying a few sticks on the small fire and pulling a blanket around his shoulders, he fell into meditation. A memory came to him of his first teacher, old man Tu, cross-legged on a bamboo platform in the forest. A copper bowl of glowing coals illuminated his parchment face.

The young Caine was entranced by the skinny man. Beneath the saffron robe, Tu's ancient wiry chest rose and fell, his protruding ribs like the abandoned rowing boat on the beach. For the benefit of his student, he was making a strange gesture – grasping with one hand and pushing away with the other. He was trying to illustrate the way in which humans tried to select that which was desirable, and push away that which was not.

'But all of this is folly,' he said. 'We cannot cling to youth, to beauty, to health, to our children, to our status. The more we cling, the more we suffer. All things change. All things are impermanent.'

To the novice, the concept seemed frightening. Caine thought of Dylan's song 'Everything Is Broken'. Did we really lose it all?

The old man drained the last drop of tea. 'You see this cup. I have had it for many years. I love to hold it and feel the warmth in my hands. But look carefully. It is covered with fine cracks, like the wrinkles on my hands. "The cup is already broken," says the Buddha.'

Caine gently removed the cup from the master's hands and turned it in the light. He saw a glaze laced with innumerable fine cracks, like the leafless branches of a winter tree. In that moment he comprehended that the cup was beautiful *because* of the cracks.

'Be with the change,' said old man Tu. 'When we accept change, we embrace freedom. In meditation we sit with arms at ease, neither grasping nor pushing away. Be in the moment. Accept imperfection. Be with what *is*.'

The moment Shanti awoke, she knew that everything was wrong. It was way too early, the room was obscenely bright, and her head was as rough as the fox's head in the dining room. As she turned over and buried her face in the pillow, she stubbed her toe on the cold brick.

By chance, the shrill alarm on her iPhone was a Sista Tremble jingle.

A lukewarm wash didn't begin to shift her headache, and she

couldn't open the window because of the demonic drumming outside. *It's time to go home now*, she pleaded silently. *Why don't you all go home?*

Looking in the mirror was a catastrophic error – sari-clad Cinderella had morphed into the Ugly Sister.

What she needed was tea. A cup of tea as strong as creosote with enough sugar to strip the enamel from her teeth.

In less than an hour, Caine would be waiting for her, and the anticipation of his dewy face infuriated her.

Half falling down the stairs, she re-entered the kitchen to find Primrose in a faded floral apron at the stove. There was someone else there too – the taciturn farmhand Gavin Blackmore, silently munching toast in his white boiler suit. With his cumulus of blonde curls, his pink face and even teeth, he seemed far too wholesome for Unworthy Farm.

Primrose turned her toothy face and began to chirrup a greeting in nervous little sentences.

'You're bright and early. Vowles said you had a nice chat last night. Most of the others won't be down for hours. Me and Gav's been at it since five. Already done the milking, haven't you, Gav?'

'I have,' he muttered.

'We were just saying it's going to be another scorcher, weren't we, Gav?'

'We were.'

'Perfect washing day, anyway. Now, you sit and chat with Gav and I'll do you a fry-up.'

'Just tea,' pleaded Shanti. 'Strong one, please.'

'Well you may as well have the full works as you've paid for it. Eggs is laid. Pigs is butchered. Tell you what – I'll serve something up and I'm sure you'll change your mind when you see it. Won't she, Gav?'

'She will.'

Raucous chair legs scraped the floor as Shanti took a seat beside the melancholic man, who gathered a few items from the tabletop and built a protective wall around himself.

She heard the sizzle of the pan; the dull tick of the kitchen clock; the munching of Blackmore's white teeth on toast; the bass beat of the distant festival; and the heavy thumping of her own head.

After a while Primrose levitated a mug of tea and a towering plate of food towards her – 'You're welcome, I'm sure.'

Shanti stared at the haemorrhaging black pudding, the seeping fried bread, the blubbery bacon, the staring egg yolks, the testicular beans – sights that would normally have made her taste buds boogie. But today, her stomach reeled.

'Right,' said Primrose. 'If you'll excuse me, I'll sort out the washing. Anything you need, you ask Gav. That's right, isn't it, Gav?'

'It is.'

Shanti piled sugar into her tea and the two of them settled into welcome silence.

Her companion was young – late twenties, thirty at the most, although it looked like he was barely shaving. Beneath the blonde halo, his ruddy face was square-chinned and almost handsome, and yet there was something desolate about the man. As Shanti nibbled bravely at a corner of toast and sipped her tea, he glanced cautiously towards her and retreated as far as the table allowed. What was it that scared him so much? That she was a woman? That she was Asian? That she was a cop? Or was he nervous of everyone who was not Primrose?

'Had a few too many last night,' she explained.

'Oh.'

'To be honest, I'm still a little woozy.'

'I see.'

'Don't want to offend Primrose, but this is more than I can manage.'

'Righto.'

'You don't fancy helping me with some of it?'

'No, ta.'

'Well, I can't sit here chatting all day. Busy, busy, busy. You know how it is.'

She dumped her full plate by the sink, swallowed the sugary dregs of her tea and stepped into the yard, where the acrid smell of slurry suffused the morning air.

She found Primrose pegging washing on the line. But these were not Vowles vestments. Dancing strangely in the warm breeze was a peculiar array of multicoloured garments – suede miniskirts, conical bras and sequinned corsets, belonging evidently to the glitzy guests at Unworthy Farm. A half-remembered phrase echoed from the night before . . . *the Unworthy Wanker.*

'Thanks for the breakfast, Primrose. I'm off now.'

'You're welcome, I'm sure. Will you require supper? It's rack of lamb with roast potatoes.'

Before Shanti could answer, the morning was split by the echoing report of gunfire. Her cop instincts exploded. Spinning on her heel, she grabbed Primrose by the apron and hauled her to the ground.

'Jesus Christ Almighty!' she gasped.

Sprawled on her back, Primrose stared at her in toothy amazement. 'Goodness me!' she said. 'It's only Vowles. He's out crowing.'

'Crowing?'

Shanti helped Primrose to her feet, noticing again the coldness of her hands.

'Well he might have got a badger. Though that's more of a night-time thing.'

'Oh, I see,' said Shanti. 'Where I was stationed in north London, if you heard a gunshot, someone was dead.'

As they spoke, Gavin Blackmore came outside, pulled on his boots and walked forlornly towards a quad bike, which he sparked into life. A moment later he was speeding across the fields, staring despondently towards the horizon, his curly top like a fast-moving cloud.

With the empty basket propped on her thin hip, Primrose watched until the quad bike was a distant gleam.

'He's a man of few words,' observed Shanti.

'Poor Gav. Bit of a loner since the tragedy. Such a shame. He's clever, you know. Went to college. Could have done great things with his life, could Gav. Me an' Vowles always said he might have been rich and famous in another life, like Ethan Flynn. But then, like a crow caught on the wing, it all tumbled down.'

'What tragedy, Primrose?'

'Oh, we don't really talk about it, if it's all the same to you,' she said, popping a peg on a tiger-skin thong. 'Everyone just gets upset all over again.'

Shanti drove jerkily down Totterdown Hill towards the Five Heads, where Caine stood waiting, precisely where he should be, at precisely the agreed time, looking precisely as annoying as she had anticipated.

'Morning, Shanti. Sleep well?'

'Why are you so loud?'

'I'm sorry. Was I raising my voice?'

'You were sort of squeaking, Caine, which is even worse.'

She climbed out of the car and walked around to the passenger side, tossing him the keys.

'You're driving,' she said.

'Come on, Shanti. We've talked about this before. You know I don't drive.'

'Caine, I am not in the mood. I have actually seen you drive.'

'But why?'

'Because I have just driven four hundred metres from Unworthy Farm, and trust me, it didn't go well. So either you let go of your pathetic eco-scruples, or many people will die and your karma will be stained for several lifetimes.'

Caine climbed reluctantly inside, fastened his seat belt and started the engine.

'Well done, Caine. Just like a big boy.'

'If you don't mind me saying, you seem a little delicate, Shanti.'

'Just remind me what we're doing today. And do it quietly, in short words.'

'We have an appointment with Queenie Flynn at ten a.m. She lives with son Tyrone, his wife, Ophelia, and from what I gather, several generations of the Flynn dynasty. Their house is modestly named Villa del Flynn, and it's about a mile outside Frome. Could you put it in the satnav?'

'You do it, Caine. Nice and quietly.'

Caine entered the location, indicated left at the Five Heads and accelerated gently onto the A361 towards Frome.

'So what's it like at Unworthy?' he asked.

'Christ, I don't know. The Vowles clan are a Somerset version of the Addams Family.'

'Well you could have—'

'It was like Siberia in that bedroom. I barely slept at all.'

'Well, I did offer—'

'On the other hand, I established some significant facts while you were relaxing. Fact One: Vula spent the entire evening in Ethan's bedroom before he died. Apparently there was some kind of altercation and she ran outside . . .'

'You're saying they were in a relationship?'

'. . . Fact Two: Sista Tremble has a long-standing grudge against Stigma.'

'You interviewed Sista Tremble?'

'Caine, I sat late into the night with just about every music legend on the planet. Sista and I are like old mates.'

'Good work, Shanti.'

'It seemed meaningful last night, but I suppose it's too far-fetched that someone in her position would act on a petty grudge.'

'I've always thought that murder is the great democratiser. No one is above their base instincts.'

'Do shut up, Caine.'

'It's not like you to overdo things, Shanti.'

'Do you know who Marcel Snapper is?'

'Seventies crooner. Newly cool in a retro-ironic way.'

'Right, well a few years ago, Marcel Snapper's doctors told him that if he didn't stop drinking, he would die instantly. He hasn't touched a drop since, but in revenge, he's on a mission to turn everyone he meets into an alcoholic. I was one of his victims.'

'I see. But don't you think that ultimately we are all responsible for our own actions?'

'Caine, would you look in the pocket by your side and see if there's anything I can hit you with?'

'I've been thinking, Shanti – normally we'd be narrowing our list of suspects by this stage, but it seems to be growing all the time. There's Tyrone, of course. Also Vula, who omitted to mention a possible relationship. Then there's Sparky Mudget, or one of his crew, who would have had the technical skills to meddle with the wiring. We also have the Tarot dancers. And now you're suggesting it could have been a rival artist like Sista Tremble. So what do we actually know? That Ethan was murdered by Death. But even that doesn't help very much. I must admit this puzzle is getting more intriguing by the minute. What are *you* thinking, Shanti?'

'I'm thinking of crawling into the back and having a short kip before we arrive.'

As Caine steered through winding green tunnels, Shanti had a déjà vu of long, vomity car rides with her dad at the wheel. And Caine appeared to be in a particularly loquacious mood . . .

'I'd like to understand more about Ethan. He's such an enigmatic figure, isn't he? Like quicksilver. It's almost as if he was a different person to everyone he met. Misty was charmed by him. His fans were mesmerised. To Queenie he was a kind of seer. Vula and the dancers saw him as someone with an unlimited capacity for love. Yet Tyrone said he could be devious and spiteful.'

'Too many words, Caine.'

'I'm sorry, Shant. What can I do?'

'There's a box of paracetamol and a can of Red Bull at your side. Pass them over and drive quietly, there's a good boy.'

The immense gates of Villa del Flynn were tightly closed. Around the perimeter of the grounds stood thick laurel hedges and black railings with gold tips. Each of the towering gateposts was crowned with a roaring concrete lion.

Caine leaned out and pressed a buzzer on the brushed-steel intercom. A remote voice said, 'If you're from the press, you can fuck off.'

'DIs Caine and Joyce. We have an appointment with Queenie Flynn.'

'Wait.'

'Jeez,' said Shanti. 'I hope these people aren't going to be trying. I'm really not in the mood.'

'I hadn't noticed, Shanti.'

They waited a full five minutes. Then the gates parted.

Caine steered up a long paved driveway, passing an impressive stable block with a clock tower, where teens in jodhpurs groomed gleaming stallions. Wherever they looked, people were busy – mowing pristine lawns or weeding flamboyant flower beds. From a fenced stockade, a baffled herd of llamas and a single ostrich watched them go by. In a children's area, noisy kids bounced on an inflatable castle, drove about in a small-scale Bentley or booted a football at a half-sized goal. It dawned on Shanti that there was a strong family resemblance here. Every one of these people had those distinctive Flynn looks – symmetrical features, dimpled chins and startling emerald eyes.

The house itself was an immense, sprawling single-storey affair, which had been endlessly extended with no real sense of cohesion. Caine parked alongside a series of costly cars, each polished to a glittering sheen.

Glancing briefly in the mirror of the sun visor, Shanti saw puffy eyes staring back at her. She grabbed her bag and followed Caine, who was making his way up the wide steps to an elaborate Greco-Roman doorway – all pillars and polished marble.

As they reached the huge lacquered door, it swung open, revealing Queenie Flynn, dressed from head to foot in black, like an Italian widow.

'Ah, Mr Caine. I see you answered Ethan's call. I hear him night and day. Day and night.'

'Thanks for seeing us, Mrs Flynn. You remember my colleague, DI Shanti Joyce?'

'You're both most welcome. The house was built by my late husband, Frankie Flynn. Would you please follow me?'

The handsome widow led them along a marble hallway, past gaudy paintings of Queenie and her late husband; the boys, Ethan and Tyrone; prize-winning racehorses and landscapes of rural Ireland. At one point they emerged into a huge circular room with a glass-domed roof, which seemed to be the epicentre of the house, like the body of a spider from which numerous legs emanated.

In the centre of the hemisphere stood a bow-topped gypsy caravan on a plinth. Every surface had been intricately hand-painted and thickly lacquered. On either side were elaborate water features, in which koi carp gawped and gentle fountains played.

'This is the very caravan in which Ethan's grandmother was

born,' Queenie explained. 'Her ashes lie in a casket within. I think of this as the soul of the house, and Ethan did too. In fact the dome was his own design. He had a marvellous relationship with his nan as a boy, and when she passed, he was inconsolable. Whenever things got too much for him, he would come and sit in the caravan. It was a sacred space for him. Many's the time I heard his voice from inside, pouring out his troubles to her. I hope he wouldn't mind me telling you, that.'

'That's very touching,' said Caine.

'The caravan represents something different to me. It's about overcoming adversity and . . . yes, stigma. You see, the council hated us when we arrived, but we prevailed. No one can beat a Flynn. Over the years we bought little pockets of land and, just like Ethan's musical career, expanded in every direction to create what you see today. All on one level, Mr Caine. The Flynns don't do stairs.'

She led them along more corridors until they emerged into an immense uPVC conservatory filled with elephantine plants and colossal white leather sofas.

Beyond the glass, a gaggle of Flynn children splashed and bombed in an immense swimming pool. A pair of opulent peacocks strutted their stuff without a care in the world.

'You sit yourself over there, Ms Joyce, and you beside me, Inspector Caine. If you'd be so kind.'

'Please call me Vincent.'

'Like the saint.'

'Or the artist.'

'And you must call me Queenie. Ah, it's too hot in here with all the glass. Ms Joyce, would you nip next door and ask one of the lads to open the doors for us?'

As she left the room, Shanti was amazed to see that Queenie had taken a firm hold of Caine's hand. Jesus, they were actually sitting side by side in that minging conservatory, holding hands.

She wandered down a corridor until she found a couple of oversized Flynn menfolk working out in a gym.

'Queenie says would you mind opening the doors in the conservatory. It's too warm.'

At the mention of the matriarch's name, the boys threw down their equipment, gave themselves a swift wipe with towels, and bounded along to the conservatory.

'Thanks, lads,' said the black-laced widow, as the young men unfolded a dozen doors onto the pool area. She clapped her hands at the children. 'Off you go now,' she bellowed. 'The grown-ups have business to attend to, and besides, it's not appropriate. Leave us now!'

Without a murmur, they gathered their belongings and left.

'I love to see them really,' said Queenie. 'The pool is mainly for the kids. Ethan and Tyrone never learned to swim, and I'm not one for the water.'

'Would you like anything, Queenie?' asked one of the muscle-bound lads.

'I'll take a fruit melange, thanks, Damon. It's all I can manage. And something for our guests?'

'Sounds lovely,' said Caine.

'Whatever they said,' said Shanti.

The pool area was surrounded by more single-storey extensions, like a Californian motel. Now the ripples settled and the water fell silent.

After a while, the drinks arrived – cocktail glasses crammed with slices of fruit and paper umbrellas, the liquid inside sickly sweet.

'May we ask you some questions, Queenie?' said Caine.

'You may. But first let me ask you one.'

'Of course.'

'Do you have faith, Vincent?'

'I do, Queenie.'

'And what about you? Ms Joyce, wasn't it? You'll be a Muslim, or a Hindu, no doubt. It's all right, I don't mind. It was Ethan who opened my eyes to the fact that there's more than one stairway to the Holy Throne.'

'None of the above.'

'A woman of no faith then . . . a cynic, perhaps?'

'Mrs Flynn, with the greatest respect, my faith is the rule of law. It may not be a divine belief, but in my humble opinion it's the system that is most likely to bring your son's killer to justice.'

'There it is. Like vinegar on the wound.'

'I'm sorry, I didn't mean to—'

'No, you're doing your job. Ask me what you will.'

'Well, could you give us a little background? Ethan and Tyrone were twins, were they not? Did they have other siblings?'

'Oh, there were others. Six I lost in childbirth. So when the twins were born it was a miracle. A few years later, my Frankie was taken from me too. And now . . . now my beautiful Ethan. That's why I lie awake and ask the Lord, why do you send me these trials?'

As tears flowed down her face, Caine clutched her hand

tightly and Shanti heard him whisper, 'It's hard to see it now, Queenie. But each of these tragedies has made you stronger. They've made you the woman you are today. You will get through this.'

'Bless you, Vincent. But you see, there's nothing left of my heart now. I have no more tears to shed. The only thing that keeps me going is the certain knowledge that we will all meet again. A Flynn reunion in paradise.'

'You were telling us about Ethan's childhood . . .' said Shanti.

'He was the seventh son of the seventh son. Ah, I can see the sceptical look on your face, Ms Joyce, but according to legend, that makes him a person of unusual qualities. There's no question about it: Ethan was born with a gift, and – look around – he transformed the lives of all he met.'

She waved at the walls, which were hung with photographs of Ethan and Tyrone in the company of royalty and celebs. On another wall was an arrangement of gold, silver and platinum records in frames.

'When did his talent become evident?'

'From the very start. He was a prodigy. I'll tell you something – Ethan could read music before he could read words.'

'Like a little Mozart,' said Caine.

'Precisely, Vincent. You've got it in one.'

'Was it you who taught him, Queenie?'

'Bless you, no. The musical gene passed me by, though I've a fine ear. His father, Frankie Flynn, was handy on a guitar, but Ethan's real inspiration came from my mother – rest her soul – whose ashes lie in the caravan beneath the dome. Even as an old lady she had the voice of an angel, and she adored Ethan. The two of them were inseparable.'

'That's a precious thing for a child,' said Caine. 'So how old were the twins when they began to perform?'

'Ah, it was a marvel! At five or six years old we took them into pubs and hostelries, and he played ... little Ethan played. He charmed people. Whatever instrument they gave him – a fiddle, a flute, a penny whistle – he jumped up on the table and the whole place fell silent. And when he finished, they begged for more, until the poor mite was exhausted and I implored them to let him rest. Then the money rained upon him. At fourteen, the Flynn brothers gave their first big performance, at Puck Fair in Kerry, and they were the sensation of the year. After that, it was television and radio and festivals, and there was no stopping them. When Frankie passed, I became both father and mammy to them. I guided them and fought off those who wished to exploit them – the men in suits, as I call them. And there were many.'

'You talk about Ethan's gift, Queenie,' said Caine. 'But what about Tyrone?'

'Ah.'

'Could you tell us about him?'

'Well now, Tyrone found life a little harder. Ethan had only to pick up an instrument and the strings would fly. For Tyrone, it wasn't so easy. But I have a picture in my head of little Ethan patiently helping his brother to learn. Hour after hour. Tyrone did all right, but he was always a little ... how should I put it?'

'In Ethan's shadow?' said Caine.

'Perhaps. I need to mind what I say, because Tyrone is here with his wife, Ophelia. They're expecting their first child at any time.'

'We heard she was expecting. That must make you very happy.'

'I shall be happy when Ethan and I are reunited, and not a moment before.'

'Tell us more about Ethan, Queenie.'

'You remind me of him a little, Vincent. He had a gentle heart.'

'That's kind of you.'

'He was not like Tyrone and the other boys. You've seen them – the cousins and uncles and nephews. Built like prize-fighters. Frankie was the same. But Ethan was a sensitive child. Fragile. Prone to fatigue. He needed his rest, did Ethan.'

'Now, Queenie,' said Caine. 'This may sound strange, but did Ethan ever talk about his own death?'

'Oh, many times. He was a seer.'

'You think he had some kind of spiritual quality?'

'I don't think it. I know it.'

'Look, this is all very interesting,' said Shanti. 'But could we stick to the actual facts?'

'She's a non-believer, Vincent, so I'll say no more about it. All I can tell you is that our Lord and Saviour rose again on the third day. Ethan was taken from us on Wednesday night, so watch out tomorrow, that's all I'm saying . . . I'll leave it there.'

A silence fell. Caine held Queenie's hand; Shanti sipped her drink. Suddenly a murderous shrieking tore the air.

'Jesus Christ!' said Shanti. 'What the hell was that?'

'Only the peacocks,' said Queenie. 'And I'd ask you not to blaspheme in this house.'

'I'm sorry. It gave me a fright. I've never heard that sound before. It chills the blood.'

As they spoke, a majestic young woman with a cascade of golden hair emerged from one of the many poolside doors. She slipped off her robe and Shanti saw that between the two halves of her bikini, her belly was swollen like an overripe fruit. Gripping tightly to the handrail, she lowered herself slowly into the turquoise water.

'There she is,' hissed Queenie. 'Miss Hoity-Toity-Lah-Di-Dah.'

'That must be Tyrone's wife, Ophelia?' said Caine.

'I'll say it quietly: I can't abide the woman.'

'And why is that?'

'She's not one of us. But that's all right. I could live with that. No, it's just that Ophelia is what you might call stuck up. A ballet dancer. All nose in the air. We're plain folk, Vincent. We say things as they are. She's not right for Tyrone and it will all end in tears.'

'I'm so sorry you feel that way.'

Caine seemed transfixed. After a couple of elegant lengths, the young woman turned and floated on her back, her long tresses rippling around her and her distended belly projecting towards the sky.

'We're nearly finished now, Queenie,' said Shanti. 'If it's not too personal, I need to ask you about Ethan's love life. Did he have someone special?'

'He had his mammy.'

'Of course. But a girlfriend? Or, you know . . .?'

'I think there was someone.'

'Go on.'

'One night, a week or two ago, I was in the corridor just out there, on my way to bed. I heard Ethan sitting in here by the pool with his guitar. I never liked to disturb him when he was with the Muse, so I said nothing. But I must admit that I waited out of sight and listened. He was playing a song I had never heard before, and it moved me to tears. Next morning, I said to him, "What was that lovely song I heard last night, son?" He said, "Ah, that was a new one, Mammy. A love song. Look, I wrote it down." He waved a piece of paper. I said, "Son, it's the finest thing you've ever written." And he said, "Well, I've never felt like this before."'

'That's interesting,' said Shanti. 'But you never met this special person?'

'He never brought anyone back here is all I can tell you.'

'Why would that be, Mrs Flynn?'

'This may surprise you, Ms Joyce, but I'm from a different age. I raised my boys with a sense of morals. If you want to sleep with a person, you marry them first.'

'I gather Tyrone and . . . and Ophelia over there are married.'

'I'm afraid so.'

'You've been enormously helpful, Queenie,' said Caine. 'And we are acutely aware of how painful this is for you. I think that's all I want to ask for now, unless you have anything, Shanti?'

'Can you think of anyone who might have wished Ethan harm, Mrs Flynn?'

'Ah now, that's the sixty-four-thousand-dollar question. Who would harm a divine man like Ethan? Well, I'll tell you . . .' she dissolved into shuddering tears, 'a bloody Judas, that's who!'

Caine put his arm around her quivering shoulder and promised they would do everything in their power to track down the perpetrator. And all the time, the golden daughter-in-law glided up and down the pool like a bloated goddess.

Shanti rose to her feet.

'Thank you for your time. And for the drink. Before we leave, would you mind very much if DI Caine and I had a look at Ethan's rooms?'

'What? Don't you know that your lot have already crawled all over it?'

'If you would indulge us, Mrs Flynn.'

'Well. All right then. I'll take you there and leave you. It's too painful for me to enter. Would you follow me, please?'

They trailed along more dog-leg marble corridors. Past a door to a lavish recording studio. Past more garish paintings, more Flynns at work and play. At last they reached an annexe that seemed somewhat separate from the main property.

'This is Ethan's apartment in here. It's not locked. I beg you not to touch more than you have to. It's like a shrine to me. When you've finished, someone will show you out. I'll bid you farewell. Vincent, it's been a pleasure . . . Ms Joyce, may you find the one true consolation in this life.'

Caine and Queenie squeezed hands, then the black widow lowered her veil and retreated down the long white corridor, stopping once to call, 'Don't forget what I said now. About the third day. Even Doubting Thomas believed when he saw with his own eyes.'

Once she was gone, Shanti and Caine snapped on latex gloves and entered the tranquil refinement of Ethan's quarters.

'*Ooh, yes, I am a man of faith . . .*' mocked Shanti. '*Call me Vincent, Queenie. Like the saint . . .* Damn it, Caine, if you could hear yourself.'

'How's your head, Shant?'

'Sore, Caine. But I expect it's divine punishment.'

'Take a look at this apartment. It's so different from the rest of the house.'

There were three rooms in all – an elegant bedroom, a large living space and an understated bathroom. As they wandered about, Shanti took dozens of photos.

'Bloody hell, he liked his instruments. What a collection!'

They were everywhere, on stands and racks and shelves. Hand-made lutes and mandolins, flutes, oboes and many more that Shanti could not name.

'Check out these books,' said Caine. 'Celtic mythology, poetry . . . and all the classics. He truly was an exceptional man.'

'*Like a little Mozart, Queenie!* Well, he had shit taste in art.'

'Shanti, I don't know how to break it to you, but these are original oil paintings by Jack B. Yeats, brother of the poet. They are actually signed.'

'Expensive shit, then.'

'They're beautiful.'

'I'll take your word for it. OK, so what did we learn from the tragic widow?'

'I think she's extraordinary.'

'Well she certainly liked you, Caine. I expect you could move in any time you wanted. What on earth was all that garbage about Ethan rising again?'

'She thinks it'll happen tomorrow night.'

'OK, well I had a good look at Ethan on Wednesday, and if he rises again he'll be walking about like a chargrilled kebab.'

'But did you see the girl, Shanti?'

'The girl?'

'The girl in the pool.'

'I saw a woman, yes. And I saw you gawping at her. There was actual drool hanging off your chin.'

'She was like a Rossetti painting . . . floating on her back with all that golden hair.'

'She was pregnant, Caine. Heavily pregnant. In fact she was about to drop at any moment – I was looking for a net. Is that really your thing? Pregnant women?'

'Why are you always trying to gauge my sexual preferences?'

'Because you are an enigma.'

'Well, in answer to your question, I didn't say I was attracted to her; I said she was like a figure from a Rossetti painting. I wish you'd realise there's only one woman—'

'Hang on, Caine. What's this?'

Shanti had lifted a book from the shelf. An expensively bound complete works of Shelley. From between the pages she plucked an opened envelope.

The letter inside bore a Harley Street address.

Dear Mr Flynn,

Following your echocardiogram of 12 June, Dr Mamtora has repeatedly attempted to contact you. She requests that you make an appointment at your earliest convenience to discuss the results. I would therefore be grateful if you would phone me as soon as you receive this letter.

With kind regards,
Hazel P. Duncan
pp Dr Nilima Mamtora

As they stepped into the corridor outside the apartment, Shanti noticed a figure at the far end wrapped in a bulging dressing gown and a turban of towels.

'You're in luck, Caine. It's Ophelia. Try not to dribble.'

As they drew closer, the DIs realised that the woman's face was wet. Either she hadn't dried herself after her swim, or the delicate features of the mother-to-be were coursing with tears.

'Hello, can we help you?' asked Caine.

'Oh. No, I'm fine. Everything is so sad.' Her voice was refined – aristocratic, almost.

'Yes, a terrible time for all of you. Were you and Ethan very close?'

'I'm sorry. I have to go.'

She buried her face in her hands and rushed past them. Shanti felt the warmth of her body and the brush of the robe as Ophelia let herself through a door and disappeared from view.

The two DIs looked at each other in wonderment. From inside the room they heard muffled tones – Ophelia wailing in anguish, and another, deeper voice swearing and shouting in the most aggressive manner.

'You fookin' bitch! Mammy was right! I should never have married you. You ruined my life!'

'Right,' said Shanti, seizing the door handle.

Caine touched her arm. 'Hold on, Shant. We can't just storm in.'

'So what do we do? Walk away? I'll tell you what, if there's one thing I can't stand, it's a bully.'

She rapped firmly on the door. Inside, the shouting ceased. A moment passed, then the door opened and the raging tattooed face of Tyrone Flynn confronted her.

'What the fook are you doing here?'

'We came to speak to Queenie. Then we heard shouting . . .'

'I'LL SHOUT AS MUCH AS I FOOKIN' LIKE IN MY OWN FOOKIN' HOME!'

'Could we speak with your wife? Ophelia, isn't it?'

'You can fook off out of my house.'

Then she was there. Towel in hand. Wet locks hanging like molten gold. Her exquisite face streaming with tears.

'I'm quite all right, thank you. Absolutely fine. Thank you so much for your concern. Goodbye.'

## *Chapter 17*

# When the Earth Trembles

'Let me ask you something,' said Shanti as she followed Caine through the turnstiles into the festival site. 'I've been wondering about it all morning.'

'Of course, Shanti. What is it?'

'Why do you have yellow and pink paint on the side of your neck? Is it a Buddhist thing?'

'Oh, that. It's body paint. You know, glow-in-the-dark. It's from the trance tent.'

'There's a whole side of you I don't know, isn't there, Caine?'

'And how about you? Have you recovered?'

'I'm fine, thank you. Never better. All I need is a few carbs.'

'You're in luck. Look, two rows of food stalls. Caribbean . . . Moroccan . . . Sicilian . . . Hmm, I like the look of that whole-food van.'

'Yeah, I fancy wholefood too – whole pigs, whole sheep, whole cows . . .'

They found a place to sit where an ancient Rastafarian crooned melodies to a steel guitar.

'That letter was a lucky find, Shanti. It could be important.'

She tore a sachet of ketchup with her teeth and squeezed it onto her burger.

'No luck involved; basic rookie training. People use letters, receipts, all kinds of stuff as bookmarks.'

'Silly me. And clever of you to notice the connection with Shelley.'

'Shelley?'

'The poet Percy Bysshe Shelley and Ethan Flynn. Both had premonitions of death. Both died at the age of twenty-nine.'

'I find it's best to avoid being too clever. Tends to lead to false trails. Anyway, I zapped a photo of the letter to Benno and he'll follow up with the Harley Street quack.'

Caine had salad. Lots of it. In a biodegradable cardboard box. Shanti felt almost sorry for him. By the end of the day he'd be faint with hunger. As a gesture of goodwill, she offered her chips.

'You know what would make me happy, Caine ... I mean orgasmically happy? If I could nail that bastard Tyrone. It would be the climax of my career. I know I shouldn't say it, but he pushes my buttons. Reminds me of someone ...'

'I agree. To be that aggressive to the mother of your child is beyond comprehension. Mind you, Queenie didn't like Ophelia either. The mystery deepens, Shant.'

Near an oversized Range Rover, Benno was pacifying an over-sized person with an oversized voice.

'No, you listen to me, Officer! Now I appreciate you have a job to do. But I also have a job. And maybe my job is more important 'cos I have thousands . . . many thousands of fans waiting on me. Do you realise that I have flown halfway across the world to perform on Sunday night? Ain't no one gonna take that moment from me.'

'I'll handle this,' said Shanti. 'Ms Tremble, we are sympathetic to your situation. I want to assure you that my team are working flat out to make the Pyramid available for your set on Sunday night. If that proves impossible, then the festival organisers have promised the very next best venue . . .'

'I don't want the very next— Hey! Don't I know you?'

'We sat together last night.'

'Yes, we did. And you informed me that you were an artist.'

'I never actually said that, Ms Tremble. My name is Detective Inspector Shanti Joyce. This is my partner, DI Caine. We're leading the investigation into Ethan Flynn's death.'

'But you tricked me. If I'd known you were a police officer, I would never have said half the things I said.'

'About the Unworthy Wanker?'

'Not that . . . I . . . To tell the truth, I can't recall exactly what I did say. Marcel kept the wine flowing and . . . I find I have the most intolerable headache.'

'I understand. I had the same problem. So let's start again, shall we? I want to ask you some specific questions about an altercation you had with Stigma ten years ago.'

'Just one motherfuckin' moment . . .'

'I simply want to eliminate you from my inquiries.'

'And if I say no?'

'That would raise a red flag for me, and I would be forced to request a formal interview. Now, would you prefer to talk somewhere more private?'

'I'd prefer not to talk at all.'

'I'm afraid that isn't an option.'

'Then I shall require my lawyer.'

'No problem, shall I call them for you?'

'He lives in Birmingham.'

'OK, that's around a hundred miles . . .'

'I mean Birmingham, Alabama. That's around four thousand miles. He is *very* expensive, Officer, and I will forward the bill to the British constabulary.'

'As I said, I am not requesting a formal interview at this stage, Ms Tremble. Only a little chat, if you'd be so kind.'

'Look, maybe you don't realise who I am . . .'

'I know exactly who you are. As I told you last night, I have followed your entire career. But this is a police matter, and the more you resist, the more questions it raises in my mind.'

'You know, I don't need to put up with this bullshit any longer. Just make sure that stage is ready on Sunday night, or *you* . . .' she prodded Shanti hard on the shoulder, 'will be held accountable.'

Turning on her heel, Sista Tremble marched towards the Range Rover, where a uniformed chauffeur was holding the door.

'Oh, and by the way,' she boomed, 'I will make it known to my friends – my true friends – at Unworthy Farm that we have a two-faced, double-dealing turncoat *spy* in our midst! As from this moment you are . . . What's the phrase I'm searching for? *Persona non grata*. I wish you a pleasant afternoon.'

As a half-sized assistant held down her monumental hair, the mighty diva ducked into the vehicle, which sped away, sending clods of earth raining on the exasperated cops.

## *Chapter 18*

# Within the Sacred Dome

The inside of Vula's yurt was like the warm belly of a beast. A yak, maybe.

Vula reclined on a fat cushion, while Caine sat cross-legged and Shanti perched awkwardly on some kind of rustic milking stool.

The floor of the dome was layered with exotic rugs. Near a wood-burning stove, a huge mattress had been spread with richly coloured blankets and cushions.

Vula looked like she hadn't slept. Within the dimly lit interior, her Moorish clothing seemed apposite. Like a Matisse odalisque, thought Caine.

But as Shanti started her questions, the serene atmosphere dissolved.

'Thanks for seeing us again, Vula. Forgive me for being direct, but time is running out. We have reason to believe that you and Ethan were in a relationship immediately before his death.'

'My God! The gossip in this place.'

'So it's not true?'

'Look, I . . .' She dissolved into tears.

'Take your time, Ms Plenty.'

She reached for her ever-present water bottle and swallowed audibly. Her soft voice was frail.

'This is almost impossible to describe, but Ethan was different from other men.'

'You said that before.'

'Yes, but different from anyone you could ever meet. He was a fragile artistic soul, searching for answers to life's big questions.'

'That's not what I asked.'

'No, but you need to understand that he was unique. He was in love with everyone.'

'You still haven't answered—'

'Yes, he loved me. Yes, I loved him. There, now you know. And yes, we had many precious moments. Ethan suffered from terrible fatigue, so we would lie here together for hour after hour. He loved this yurt. He called it my sacred dome. He would stroke my hair and whisper that I was his sleepy creature. I truly believed we had a future together . . . but it wasn't to be.'

'He broke it off?'

'Not exactly. I discovered there was someone else. Is this relevant?'

'It's very relevant. But a moment ago you said he loved everyone. You knew there were other people.'

'All right, you might as well know . . . The night before the festival opened, I discovered that Ethan had found someone special.'

'Why didn't you tell us this before?'

'Because . . . don't you see, it's like reopening a wound? Ethan's death was tragic enough, but the fact that we parted in that vile way . . . It's just too much to bear.'

'Tell us what happened, Vula.'

'We ate together at a little restaurant in the countryside. It was perfect. Then we spent time alone. We kissed. And in spite of the big gig the following day, Ethan seemed calmer and happier than I had ever known him. He discussed his plans for the concert – the costumes he'd commissioned for the dancers. He was so happy because they'd turned out even better than he imagined. He was like Peter Pan. It was all a wonderful game.'

'Was this in his bedroom at Unworthy Farm? The Lilac Suite?'

'It was.'

'And how did he break it to you – that he had fallen for someone else?'

'With a song.'

'A song?'

'Yes. I . . . I told him I loved him. But instead of responding, he got up from the bed . . .'

'You were both on the bed?'

'Yes. It was cold in there so we cuddled up on that great beast of a four-poster. Ethan was in a funny, dreamy mood. I wondered if he had been smoking something.'

'Had he?'

'I don't think so. He picked up his guitar – a beaten-up acoustic that had belonged to his father – and began to play and sing. A love song I'd never heard before. It was astonishing! So mysterious! So perfect! I've been involved with music all my life and I have antennae. I *know* when something is unique. And this song touched my heart. I just knew that it will . . . that it *would* have been the greatest hit of all time.'

'But how did this lead to an argument?'

'This is the thing. I was deluded. So blind. You know what Ethan's lyrics are like . . . He was a poet. The words were a mysterious riddle. Like an idiot, I thought he was singing about me. I can't recall every word, but he seemed to be describing me in such a tender way – as a sleepy creature here in my yurt . . . my sacred dome. I was in ecstasy. Every verse seemed to be about me. He said he loved me *like darkness loves the light . . .*'

'And then?'

'Then he started singing that our love could never be. I felt it like a stab in my heart. And finally, in the very last verse, which was a kind of chorus, he mentioned her name, over and over again.'

'Whose name?'

'The one he loved more than any other. The one the song was dedicated to. And in one cruel word, my life was finished. I knew that Ethan didn't really love me at all.' A stream of tears flowed onto her silken jacket.

'Vula, what was the name Ethan mentioned?'

'I don't know. I can't recall. A stupid name.'

'A long name? A short name? A girl's name?'

'Short. Eve. Or Eva. Something along those lines. Yes, come to think of it, that was the title of the damned song – "Song for Eve", or something like that.'

'Do you know an Eve?'

'No. I'd never heard the name mentioned.'

'So he carried on playing . . .'

'He had this faraway look on his face, as if he was in rapture.

He'd forgotten I was there. I jumped up and stormed about the room, but he carried on playing – experimenting with harmonies. He had a piece of paper with the chords and words written on it and he kept crossing out, and adding new ones. Trying to make it even more perfect – as if that were possible.'

'OK. And then . . .?'

'I was shouting. Yelling at the injustice of it all. I told him that he had never really cared about anyone. I said that I – along with all the loves of his life – was only ever an accessory. A distraction. A momentary muse. But he barely heard me. So I stormed out the room. Almost blinded by tears, I ran down the stairs of that horrid old farmhouse. I didn't know where I was going. I stumbled into the kitchen and a beastly little man was sitting there with a beastly little dog. I ran to the back door and outside into that filthy, shitty yard. And all the time, through the whole nightmare, I imagined that Ethan would come after me and tell me that everything was all right. But he never did. And do you know what made it even worse?'

'Go on.'

'People recognised me at the festival. You get used to that, of course, but I was in such a state, and a crowd of drunken lads surrounded me, taunting and taking photos. By the time I got back, I was demolished. Completely and utterly devastated.'

'Devastated enough to kill Ethan?'

'What? No! God, no!'

'You didn't steal a costume from the dancers?'

'No. I swear it.'

'You didn't enter the stage and tamper with the electrics?'

'Good God!'

'You see, Vula, when we interviewed you on the night of

Ethan's death, we were very impressed by your knowledge of all things technical.'

'I'm a DJ. I've worked at music gigs for years. Of course I know something about it.'

'Then you will know that if you sprinkle water where someone is about to stand barefoot with an instrument that has been made live, it will surely kill them.'

'Oh God! When will this nightmare end? I've lost my dearest, dearest friend. And now you're accusing me of his murder.'

'Just questions, Ms Plenty. Just questions.'

# Chapter 19

# No Ruder Intruder

'So what am I going to do, Caine?'

'About what, Shanti?'

'Well I'm not exactly gagging to have dinner at Unworthy. You heard what Sista said – I'm *persona non grata*. Oh Caine, it's such a shame . . .'

'Because you were such a fan?'

'No, because Primrose is cooking lamb. With roast potatoes and everything.'

'Well you've paid for your room and you're adamant that you don't want to stay with me. But listen – there's nothing to stop us spending the evening together. I'll cook for you and no animal will die.'

'You're a mate, Caine. I know I'm a bit scratchy sometimes.'

'It's what I like about you.'

'Do you really? I seem to have a way of upsetting everybody – Sista Tremble, Vula, Queenie Flynn, they all hate me and they all love you.'

'That's how we work. Good cop. Bad cop . . .'

'Yeah, but maybe it's time we swapped roles.'

'. . . and I do like you, Shanti, more than you know.'

'All right, don't push it. Where's the tent? Or is it a tepee? I bet it's a tepee. With loads of dreamcatchers. Do you have dreamcatchers, Caine?'

'Just a tent. It's not far now, but look! What a night! It's like *A Midsummer Night's Dream*. Everyone out enjoying themselves in spite of what happened. Or maybe it's drawn everyone together. Did you know that the Dalai Lama appeared on the Pyramid Stage in 2015?'

'What did he sing? "The Sound of Silence"? "Karma Chameleon"?'

'He just talked. It was his eightieth birthday. He said that the concept of war is outdated. That countries need to think less competitively and more globally, because the environment is a global issue. It was beautiful. He even visited the stone circle at dawn.'

'What do you think about Vula, Caine? Was she really traumatised or is she a great actor?'

'I think the tears were genuine. But as a matter of fact, you're right – she trained at the Canadian College of Performing Arts.'

'See, I knew it. I had a husband who could fake anything. I was looking around in her yurt to see if I could spot that Death costume. It would fit her very snugly.'

Caine's tent was easily identifiable – a large white canvas affair, with laces instead of zips. The giveaway was the row of colourful prayer flags suspended between a hawthorn bush and one of the wooden tent poles. Somehow he had secured the best camping spot on the entire site – a tranquil corner of a field with sweeping views across the whole valley, sheltered by a hedge where a late-night blackbird sang to its mate. Everything was orderly, and Caine had even prepared sticks and charcoal within a circle of stones.

He unfastened the tent and pulled out mats and blankets. Then he lit the fire and began to prepare a meal.

'Let me look in there, Caine. Do you mind if I look?'

It was absurdly homely inside – a large sleeping bag on a nest of soft blankets, neatly folded clothes and even a small pile of books. The man had set up a miniature shrine with a stick of incense, a tiny vase of wild flowers and a weeny Buddha, all softly illuminated by a sweet-smelling candle.

As she tried out the bed, a sentimental memory came to her of Caine helping Paul to sling a hammock between two trees near the cabin on the Undercliff. The boy had been going through a difficult phase, but he had responded so naturally to Caine's easy-going ways. They had chatted happily together while Caine taught Paul to sharpen a stick with a knife. Those simple tasks had brought him so much joy. There was no getting away from it – Caine was good for the lad. How often had Paul asked when they would meet again?

And he could cook, too. The food he served up was astonishingly good. Some kind of spicy vegetable curry with naan bread and cold beer. Although Shanti didn't like to admit it, it felt good to sit there with this most unlikely of cops, beside the gently burning coals.

As they ate, they gazed at the Pyramid Stage far below, where the strange events of the week had unfolded. From up here, there was a different perspective on everything.

'I keep thinking about poor Queenie,' said Caine. 'What she

must be feeling now. The loss of a child must be the hardest thing to bear. It's unimaginable.'

'She told you what she wanted from you.'

'I know. I will do it, Shanti. We'll do it together. We'll bring Ethan's killer to justice.'

'In the meantime, I'm exhausted,' she said. 'I've barely slept all week. And that bed has a whole history of its own. But it's too early to head back.'

'Stay as long as you want. Come a little closer. Have a sleep by the fire. I wonder, Shant, do you ever . . .'

'Ever what, Caine?'

'Do you ever think about that night?' he whispered.

'What night?'

'By the bay near my cabin.'

'Right, listen, Caine. We're on a case. There was no night. There was no bay.'

'Of course. I understand. But I just thought that maybe if we . . . you know, solve this case . . . it would be nice to think—'

'Maybe you should embrace uncertainty, as you're always saying.'

'Yes. I'm sorry, Shanti. My feelings got the better of me.'

'See this?'

'I'm sorry, I don't see anything.'

'I'll give you a clue – it's thin and blue.'

'I'm not with you . . .'

'There's a line between us, Caine. Call it the line of duty.'

They settled on their backs, gazing at a huge moon encircled by a ghostly aura. A full moon? No, it was one nail-clipping short. It would be full tomorrow.

There was something hovering high in front of that gentle astral eye. Shanti saw the spiralling silhouette of a magnificent buzzard. It was almost as if the creature had followed Caine from his woodland home.

'Tell me a story, Caine. You know, one of your Buddhist tales.'

'A story, eh? Well, back in Thailand I knew an old, old man named Tu.'

'You told me. He was your teacher.'

'And Tu used to tell stories, which were funny or moving or wise.'

'Such as . . .'

'Such as the story of a grieving mother called Kisa Gotami.'

'Sounds cheerful.'

'She had a beautiful young child, who she loved more than anything in the world . . .'

'And the child died . . .'

'. . . and Kisa was inconsolable. Wherever she went, she carried the cold body . . .'

'This is deeply unpleasant, Caine.'

'Everyone pleaded with her to lay the child to rest, but she sat all day in the marketplace holding the body and begging people to bring her a cure for death . . .'

'I've changed my mind. Forget about the story.'

'Day after day she sat there, until at last someone told her to walk out into the countryside until she found a Bodhi tree near a stream, and here she would see a holy man. So Kisa Gotami carried her lifeless child and walked, weeping, into the countryside until she found the stream and the holy man in meditation beneath the tree. Straight away she knew it was the Awakened One.

'As she approached, the Buddha reached out and very gently drew the cloth from the dead child's face. Then he asked what he could do for her.

'"Lord Buddha, give me a cure for death and bring the light back to my little one's eyes."

'The Buddha said, "Little sister, the world weeps with you. I would give my own blood if I could take away your pain. Now go and bury your child."

'But Kisa Gotami kept asking, "Give me a cure for death."

'At last the Buddha said, "Go and knock on every door you can find and ask for a handful of mustard seeds. Then bring them to me."

'Kisa said she would go straight away, but the Buddha caught her hand and said, "There is one more thing, little sister. The mustard seeds must come from a household where no one has died."

'So Kisa carried her child back to the town and began to knock on every door, and although every house was happy to give her mustard seeds, there was not a single family who had never lost a loved one.

'For days she carried the little body from door to door, and at last she returned to the Buddha, still in meditation beneath his tree.

'"Dear Kisa," he said gently. "Did you find the seeds?"

'"I found the seeds, Lord, but not a single house untouched by death."

'And as she said this, it dawned on her that there are infinitely more people dead than alive. That all things must pass, and that suffering comes from holding on to that which is impermanent.

'"This was the bitter seed I had to give you," said the Buddha.

'So Kisa buried her child, and with it a mustard seed, which flowered and grew. And she became enlightened.

'You see, Shanti, what I love about old Tu's tale is that it shows the Buddha as a human being. He doesn't perform a miracle. Buddhism is about fully accepting the dappled quality of reality – grief and joy, life and death. That is wisdom. When Kisa understood, she became enlightened.'

Caine sat for a while marvelling at the respectful silence with which Shanti was meditating on his profound story.

But when he looked closer, he realised that she had fallen asleep, lulled by the steady rhythm of drums and the distant grieving of Ethan's followers.

It was well after midnight when Shanti left the festival site and climbed the steep lanes of Kilton. Something had changed in her perception. When she had arrived at the festival, she had hated it. The place had seemed chaotic, overwhelming and threatening. But now she thought of it with something like affection. It was a safe place, filled with kindly, if somewhat naïve, people.

As she passed the moonlit cemetery, she realised that it was this strange little village that made her uneasy. The festival was a potpourri of diversity – not unlike Camden Town, where she had begun her career. But in places like Kilton, she would always be an outsider.

On either side of Totterdown Hill, the swaying shadows of the hedgerows took the form of primitive dancing figures. Within the foliage, nameless animals rustled and cried.

Exhausted and uneasy, she entered the luminous porch and

slipped the iron key into the door. The lock turned, but the door would not open. Damn it! Someone had thrown the bolts inside.

Aching with fatigue, she walked around the side of the hulking building. A few lights burned inside, but she was reluctant to tap on a window. She passed the vegetable patch, where the silhouettes of dead crows swung uneasily, and entered the yard, which the silvery moonlight had transformed into a snowscape. She noticed the weirdly shaped clothing on the line, the ugly prefab bungalow where the Vowles family lived, and hanging over everything, the sweet and sour stench of slurry.

Approaching the horizontally divided stable door of the kitchen, she tapped lightly and waited. Soft voices emanated from inside.

'Someone's out late, Vowles.'

'Best see who it is, Primrose.'

The top part of the door opened like a puppet booth, revealing the Punch-like face of Farmer Vowles.

'It's our young guest,' he said, opening the door and letting her in.

'You're welcome, I'm sure,' said Primrose. 'I set a place for you, but I'm afraid Vowles has finished the scraps.'

It was the first time Shanti had seen them together – wild-haired, wild-toothed Primrose, a head and a half taller than her elfin husband.

As she stepped inside, a turbulent commotion erupted at her feet – a snarling, devilish whirling. Before she could register what was happening, a set of incisors buried themselves into her lower leg, and she let out a whoop of pain.

'Boner! Boner! You rascal! That's no way to treat a lady.'

Vowles grabbed the beast by the scruff of the neck and managed to prise its powerful jaws apart.

'Jumping Jesus!' yelled Shanti. 'Your bloody dog has bitten me!'

'Don't take it personal,' agonised Primrose. 'He does that to everyone.'

Ten minutes later, following abject apologies from Primrose and Vowles, Shanti hobbled along the chilly landing towards her bedroom, clutching a conciliatory mug of cocoa. In her bag was a bottle of antiseptic and a wad of cotton wool, which she had finally managed to persuade Vowles she would apply herself, rather than succumb to his nursing skills.

Rummaging for the key, she was puzzled to find that the door was already unlocked.

Every cell in her body sprang to attention. Her breathing quickened. Her heart rate increased. At the front of her mind was the fact that a killer was still at large.

She turned the handle silently and slipped inside, placing the hot mug on a table whilst vainly fumbling for the pepper spray in her cluttered bag.

Someone had turned on a light – Primrose, perhaps – but there was a strange sound in the room: the creaking and groaning of springs. As Shanti turned the corner, she saw to her absolute horror the legs and body of a man standing upright within the canopy of the four-poster. His head was concealed inside the awning, and he seemed to be probing the nooks and crannies of the bed.

'Who goes there?' she yelled. It was an unexpected phrase, one she had never used before. It came, perhaps, from the war films her mother used to watch. But it seemed to fit the occasion.

With muscular arms, the man seized the beam at the top of the bed and swung himself down. Now she saw the bulging physique and heavily inked cranium of Tyrone Flynn.

'What the fook are you doing?' he snarled.

'I . . . How dare you? This is my room. I'm staying here.'

'The fook you are. You're lucky I didn't lay you out – creeping in like that.'

'Don't threaten me, Mr Flynn. You might not find me such an easy adversary. So I'll ask politely: what are you doing in my room in the middle of the night? And why are you standing on my bed?'

He stepped towards her, pulling himself up to his full height. Not tall, but unbelievably wide. Those small eyes bored into hers. His muscles twitched and flexed like a buffalo on crack. He jabbed a stumpy finger at her face.

'You're the bitch who questioned me downstairs. And came sticking her nose between me and my wife.'

'You may bully Ophelia, Flynn, but you won't bully me.'

He took a step nearer, dimpled chin jutting, until their faces were almost touching. She smelt his odour – beer and something toxic, like acrid sweat squeezed from punished muscles.

'Right. This here is the room my brother was staying in. That's why I've got a key, see?' He dangled it in her face. 'Stigma management booked and paid for rooms for me and Ethan, and seeing as we've had no refund, we're still renting both rooms.'

'OK, well in that case, there's been a misunderstanding. Either that, or Primrose is taking double rent. But I rented this room in good faith, and now . . . I'm going to bed.'

Flynn returned to the four-poster and threw himself onto his back in an elaborately casual pose, bulging arms tucked behind his neck and a smirk across his jaw.

'Go on then. Don't mind me.'

'Get out, Flynn. One call is all it would take and I'd have half the Avon and Somerset force here in five minutes.'

'Ooh, you're scaring me! I'll go when I'm ready, bitch.'

'You don't frighten me, Flynn. So are you going to tell me what you were looking for?'

'Looking for? What makes you think I was looking for anything?'

'Because I saw you rummaging about.'

He sneered at her with the amused menace of a pit bull at a playground. 'I was looking for your knickers.'

'Oh my God! You're the Unworthy Wanker!'

'What? What the hell did you call me?'

'I . . . Never mind. I suppose that was some kind of sick joke. So what *were* you looking for?'

'Just seeing if my brother left anything behind.'

'Like what?'

'Like none of your fookin' business. Right. It's late. I'm not in the mood for games either. I'll be on my way . . .' He rose and jabbed his finger again. 'But a little warning for you, Cuntstable – you keep the fook out of my affairs. And the affairs of my wife. And the affairs of my mam. You hear me?'

'Oh, I hear you, Mr Flynn, but I'll carry out my duties in whatever way I see fit. Now, would you close the door on the way out? And I think Primrose would like her key back.'

In spite of her brave words, Shanti slept with the pepper spray beneath her pillow and a chair jammed under the door handle.

Slept? There were better ways to describe how she passed the night.

*Chapter 20*

# The Magic Mountain

If you've never visited Glastonbury, you might picture a charming English market town, redecorated in psychedelic poster paints by a posse of neopagans on LSD.

The kaleidoscopic shops are crammed with paraphernalia from a hotchpotch of New Age belief systems. You might wander the cobbled streets alongside druids, goddesses, hippies, tree sprites, a green man in a mistletoe crown and, of course, tourists from every corner of the world.

All are drawn by the myriad legends of this mystical place. Did the child Jesus walk here with his uncle, Joseph of Arimathea? Or, as William Blake put it, *did those feet in ancient time walk upon England's mountain green*? Is Glastonbury the final resting place of King Arthur and Guinevere? Or the sacred home of the Holy Grail?

In the cemetery gardens of St John's Church, which dates back to around AD 950, you might spot the local goth vicar offering tea and words of comfort to sunbathing winos and druggies, who represent the queasy underbelly of this intriguing town.

What is certain is that in Glastonbury it is easier to find an astrologer than an accountant, easier to balance your chakras than check your bank balance.

It didn't take the detectives long to find The Third Eye, Medusa Cole's purple emporium, in a shadowy side street. Shanti stared vainly though the dark glass, but all she saw were cats sleeping amongst the dangling crystals.

'What time is it, Caine?'

'A little after nine.'

'It says here: *We open around eleven a.m. during festival season.* Around eleven? Holy Moses! Yet another waste of time.'

'Relax, Shanti. We'll come back. Let's use the time to clear our heads and reflect. Do you fancy a walk?'

'Caine, I've done nothing but walk since we arrived, and in case you hadn't realised, today is Saturday. We now have two days to catch the killer before the festival closes tomorrow night. I don't want to reflect. I want to arrest someone.'

'I know all of that, Shanti. But it's essential that we interview Medusa. Besides, you can't visit Glastonbury without climbing the Tor.'

As Shanti puffed and sweated at his side, Caine ambled up the steep slope of the Tor towards the tower. Infuriatingly, he was not out of breath. And to make things worse, he had pulled a tattered book from his bag and was now reciting rambling passages about the spiritual associations of the place.

'The Tor is one of the most sacred places in the world. It's sometimes called the Magic Mountain, the Glass Hill of the Faeries, the Spiral Castle or the Land of the Dead.'

'It's great that you know this stuff,' gasped Shanti. 'Because when this case collapses and we both lose our jobs, you can get a job as a tour guide.'

'It's also known as a Druid initiation centre, an Arthurian hill fort, a crossroads of ley lines, a place of fertility rites, and a converging point for UFOs.'

'UFOs? What have you been smoking, Caine?'

'I'm simply telling you what it says here. It was actually a police officer who witnessed eight egg-shaped objects in formation over the Tor.'

'It wasn't you, was it?'

'Apparently there have been many reports of strange psychic experiences.'

'I think I'm having one now.'

'Some people feel suddenly disorientated, or they tumble into subterranean passages. Feelings of weightlessness are common too. Other people want to leap in the air.'

'Not that one.'

'On May the first, they hold a druidic ceremony on the summit. Wouldn't you love to see that?'

'I have to wash my hair that night.'

'Local people sometimes feel an overwhelming impulse to climb the slopes of the Tor . . .'

'. . . while others feel an overwhelming impulse to stay home and eat cake.'

'Some say this is Avalon, Shanti, where Arthur's sword Excalibur was forged. Ethan must have known about all of this. Legend has it that it's the resting place of the Holy Grail, which

Joseph of Arimathea brought from the Holy Land.' He turned and pointed to the foot of the hill. 'Water from the grail is said to emerge in a blood-red spring from the Chalice Well down there. Say what you like, Glastonbury Tor is a place where the veil between the worlds grows thin.'

'I feel that. I feel a thinning of my veils.'

As they neared the summit, Shanti saw the tower rising like a proud nipple on the breast of the hill.

'Ah,' said Caine as he settled on the grass. 'It's good to see the horizon.'

He pulled two mugs and a thermos from his bag. 'Look, there's the festival way down below . . .'

She followed his pointing figure; there indeed were the multicoloured canvas spires, the vast car parks and the dense termite nests of people, crammed into a fold of the boundless eiderdown plains.

The slogan on Shanti's mug said: *OMG without God is just OM.*

The slogan on Caine's mug said: *Breathe in. Breathe out. Repeat.*

'It's amazing to think that for centuries the Tor was an island sticking out of the sea. Everything below us would have been underwater. Imagine that, Shanti. You and me on a tiny island.'

'One of us would need to drown.'

'The whole area is very low-lying, you see, and that's why the Somerset Levels are so prone to flooding. The name Somerset is actually a shortened form of "summer settlement", because it was uninhabitable in the winter. And of course there have been many times when the festival has been a washout . . . I hate to say it, but there are dark clouds over the horizon. I hope this beautiful weather doesn't break.'

'All I know is that somewhere down there our murderer is walking free. While we're sitting here drinking tea.'

'Don't worry, Shanti, the truth will emerge. Like the land from the sea.'

'You know something, Caine? I can't even be bothered to think of a sarcastic reply. That's how tired I am.'

'Do you want to talk about it?'

'Talk about what, annoying man?'

'Something happened last night. You seem out of sorts.'

'Look at this . . .' She rolled up her trouser leg.

'A bandage. You hurt yourself.'

'No, I didn't hurt myself. A little rat of a dog hurt me.'

'Vowles' dog? I'm so sorry.'

'That creature has actual fangs, Caine.'

'Maybe you should get that looked at.'

'Forget it. The dog was the least of it. There was a far more aggressive animal waiting in my bedroom – Tyrone still had Ethan's key and he was rummaging around in there. Gave me the fright of my life.'

'That's terrible, Shanti. If only I'd been there . . .'

'I can look after myself, thanks very much. I won't let a bully like Flynn intimidate me.'

'You are amazingly brave.'

'You know what they say: it's possible to be scared and brave at the same time. Someone should put that on a mug.'

'That's incredibly true. But Flynn is a powerful man and not entirely stable. I wonder if he's on steroids. You know, for the bodybuilding.'

'And guess what I was thinking, the whole time he was standing there? Could this man fit in that Death costume?'

'Although Tyrone probably wouldn't do that himself. Don't forget he has a whole entourage working for him.'

'Anyway, he scared the crap out of me. At first I thought he was the Unworthy Wanker . . .'

'Hang on, Shant. Have I missed something here? I heard you using that phrase when you were interviewing Sista Tremble.'

'Ah, it's nothing. Just idle dinner-table chat. There's a rumour that people . . . women, I suppose, have had personal items stolen from their rooms over the years.'

'I'm struggling to find the appeal of that place.'

'Well, there's no need to fret. Shanti's scanties remain unscathed.'

'So what was Tyrone after? He must realise that the room had been turned over by forensics. And that was after his own boys had removed every last musical instrument.'

'Yeah, the Flynns got away with the lute.'

'That's really very good, Shanti.'

'Anyway, whatever he was after, it must have been tiny, or very well concealed.'

'More tea? There's another drop in here . . .'

'Let me ask you something, Caine. You're a Stigma fan, aren't you?'

'Well I wouldn't—'

'What exactly *did* Tyrone bring to the proceedings? From what I gather, he has no talent whatsoever.'

'Hmm. I don't think that's quite true. He did bring something. The albums Ethan made on his own are a bit, you know, saccharine.'

'Hang on, Caine – *Heartstrings* went multi-platinum. Everyone knows that.'

'Of course. People bought it because they were in love with Ethan. But he was better with his brother. Tyrone brought that funky rock 'n' roll element. A hefty thumping bass. It was the contrast between their personalities that made the music so unique. It was like—'

'You're going to say yin and yang, aren't you?'

'That's exactly what it was. And it's perfectly encapsulated in songs like "Legend of You" and "Heathen Child" – tender love songs, but with that heavy bass groove.'

She handed him the empty mug and climbed to her feet.

'Right. Well thanks for the tea, Caine, and the TED talks – you know, folklore and music and everything. I don't know how I managed before we met.'

'Oh Shanti . . .'

'So, how about that meeting with Medusa Cole?'

'Yes, hopefully The Third Eye will have opened.'

'And by the way, you may be right about the rain. I think I just heard a rumble of thunder . . . you know, a heavy bass groove.'

## *Chapter 21*

# The Third Eye

The door of The Third Eye had been wired to a large wind chime, which tinkled and jangled as they stepped inside.

In spite of the melodious din, no one appeared, and the detectives were left alone with the cats to browse the wands, didgeridoos, incense sticks, crystals, cauldrons, glass figurines of faeries, wizards and witches, Celtic bracelets, and a fibreglass Buddha in vivid pink.

'Look, Caine. Here's your mate.'

'He rather loses his significance amongst all the . . .'

'Tat? Is that the word you're looking for? Bling?'

'To each their own, Shanti.'

'I mean, look at this. A whole rack of essential oils. I ask you – is there anything less essential than essential oils?'

'I don't quite agree. The lavender might help you sleep.'

At the back of the shop, a bead curtain parted and the elusive proprietor emerged – all pale face, black and purple tresses, and purple shawls and skirts.

'Can I help with anything?' she asked, scooping up a passing cat. 'Or are you just browsing?'

'You must be Medusa Cole.'

'Hello. Yes. Do I know you?'

'Detective Inspector Shanti Joyce, and my colleague, DI Vincent Caine. We're investigating Ethan Flynn's death.'

She turned a whiter shade of pale, and clutched the cat to her purple bosom.

'I gave a very full statement to one of your officers. I explained that I made some costumes for Stigma.'

'Yes, we'd like to ask about that. We understand Ethan was a frequent visitor.'

'Well I wouldn't say frequent. He travelled abroad a lot, you know.'

'But he visited several times in the weeks before his final performance.'

'He did, yes.'

'So his death came as a complete surprise?'

'I'll have to choose my words carefully – no, it wasn't a surprise. Although the manner of his death was horribly unexpected.'

'I think you're going to have to explain that.'

'Ethan had a kind of premonition. A couple of days before his final gig, he asked for a reading. I remember that I wasn't keen because I was so busy with last-minute touches to the Tarot costumes. But he told me he needed some insight, and . . . well if you'd ever met Ethan, you would understand that he was impossible to refuse.'

'OK, so can you tell us what the cards revealed?'

'You're joking, of course.'

'I'm sorry?'

'What happens in a reading is between the client and the spirit world. I wouldn't have any customers at all if I went around blabbing their intimate secrets.'

'But Ethan is dead.'

'I know that. I'm as devastated as everyone else. But even so . . .'

Caine's eyes had been drifting around the shop. High in a corner he noticed a blinking CCTV camera with a sign saying: *THE THIRD EYE IS WATCHING.*

'Medusa, I wonder if you could let us see the footage of Ethan's visit?' he said.

'Footage? Oh, I see what you mean. This may sound stupid, but that camera is a dummy. In fact I completely forgot it was there. You wouldn't believe how much stock gets nicked, and I suppose it's some kind of deterrent.'

'Can we come back to the costumes?' said Shanti. 'You made a set of Tarot outfits for the dancers. Is that correct?'

'Yes. Designing and creating clothes is my passion. There's no better place than Glastonbury to do it. You've seen what people wear around here. And it's not just the pagans, travellers and hippies; I also make period clothing for military re-enactments, as well as costumes for plays and performances of all kinds. But what Ethan asked me to do was in a different league. A dream come true. It's like he really respected my creativity. He wanted me to take it to another level.'

'What do you mean?'

'Well, he got the idea from the cards, but he wanted those costumes to be extraordinary – really disturbing.'

'You certainly achieved that. So how many costumes did you create?'

'Eight in all. Only . . .'

'Only what?'

'Only some bugger nicked one. And in my opinion it was the best of the lot. A figure of Death with a burgundy velvet cape and a papier-mâché skull. Wait a minute – I can show you.'

She pulled out her phone and scrolled through various images of the Tarot costumes, laid out on a cutting table or fitted onto mannequins. She stopped at the figure of Death, and Shanti immediately recognised the hooded face that Benno had shown them on the webcam footage.

'I was particularly proud of this one. Ethan was very clear that he didn't want anything jokey or cartoonish, so I searched online and came up with a Mexican deity named Santa Muerte. You can see the way I stained the skull brown and added decayed teeth. See the maggots wriggling from the eye sockets? The ribs are padded with foam and stitched onto black velvet.'

'It's truly grotesque.'

'Thank you. It was a hell of a lot of work. So you can understand why I was pretty pissed off when it disappeared. If I find out who did it, I'll kill them. Thank God it was only one costume that went walkabout, but that was bad enough. I didn't have time to make a replacement, so one dancer couldn't perform at all.'

'So you're saying that someone walked into the shop in broad daylight and lifted this costume before the performance?'

'No. It happened when the shop was empty. In the dead of night. Look, I'll show you . . .'

She poured the cat out of her elaborately ringed hands and led them through the beaded curtains into a cluttered back room, where sewing equipment was arranged – trestle tables with rolls of cloth, sewing machines and long-handled scissors, all overlooked by a silent family of antique tailors' mannequins. Around the walls were bizarre masks and rails of finished or half-finished costumes. At the far end of the room was a small booth faced with black felt.

'That's where I do my readings,' said Medusa. 'To be honest, I don't make much from the shop, but the readings and the sewing just about make it work. Look, that's where the bastards came in . . .'

She indicated a large double window at the other end of the room, which opened onto a dank yard. One pane had been roughly repaired with polythene and tape.

Caine examined the thin glass and the latch. Even for an amateur, forced entry would be a doddle.

'Please leave the window as it is,' said Shanti. 'We may need to check for prints.'

'Christ, do you really think there's a connection between the break-in in my little shop and Ethan's death?'

'It's quite possible. Now I need you to think really hard, Medusa. Could you have mentioned Ethan's commission to anyone? I mean, could anyone have known that the costumes were waiting here?'

'God, yes.'

'What do you mean?'

'Listen, the Stigma contract was the biggest thing that ever happened to me. It's not every day you get a personal invitation to work for Ethan Flynn. Of course I talked about it. To be honest, I think my family and friends in the village were sick of me bragging about it. Everyone knew the costumes were hanging here, and I suppose I showed them those photos too. The only people who weren't supposed to know were the dancers.'

'But you told me your clients expect discretion.'

'Well hang on, that's slightly different, isn't it? I mean, your inner world is one thing; showing costumes to your mates is a bit different, isn't it? Would you like one, by the way?'

'One what?'

'A reading. I'll do a discount, seeing as you're helping Ethan.'

'Not for me, thanks,' replied Shanti.

'It sounds fascinating,' said Caine.

'No problem,' said Medusa. 'Just give me a mo.'

She stepped inside the booth and closed the black-felted door.

'We're on duty,' hissed Shanti. 'What the actual hell do you think you're doing?'

'Bear with me,' he said. 'There might be more to glean.'

After a moment, Medusa emerged with a mysterious smile on her pale face and another cat in her hands.

'All ready,' she said. 'I'll have to ask your friend to step outside, if you don't mind. Oh, and Shanti . . .'

'That's DI Joyce.'

'. . . could I ask a tiny favour? Would you mind watching the shop? I doubt we'll get many customers as everyone's at the festival, but you never know. All the lanterns and candles are half-price, except the skull lamps. We won't be more than twenty minutes.'

Outside it had begun to rain steadily, and Shanti sat behind the counter feeling sad. Her mum was taking Paul to Saturday Soccer School and it would be a miracle if the boy knew who Shanti was by the time she returned. Even worse was the sinking feeling that she would go home defeated. Most people had jobs that involved some kind of resolution or progress, but a large proportion of crimes were never solved. Come to think of it, most cops worked with colleagues who didn't waste valuable time gazing at their astrological auras. And the harsh reality was that most women her age had loving partners waiting for them at home.

She peeped in a drawer beneath the till and flipped half-heartedly through an order book. Jeez, there was the account for the Tarot costumes. Well, at least Ethan had paid a decent fee for Medusa's handiwork. It was certainly more than a DI earned in a month.

One of the cats leapt onto her lap, impaling her thighs with its talons. Just as she was struggling to unhook the feline, the wind chimes pealed and the shop door opened. To her absolute dismay, a coachload of Chinese tourists spilled into the shop, talking loudly and shaking umbrellas as they began to enthusiastically examine the artefacts. The leader of the group asked if it would be OK if some of them took photographs of Shanti, with the crystals and dreamcatchers above her head.

It seemed like a frantic age before they departed and Caine emerged from the back room. He appeared pale and visibly shaken.

'All quiet, Shanti?'

'You wouldn't believe . . . Oh, never mind. Look how much I just made for Medusa. I'm telling you, I'm in the wrong trade. What's the matter with you? You seem more abnormal than usual.'

'Shanti, I know we're pressed for time . . .'

'Pressed isn't the word, Caine. Strangulated comes a little closer.'

'. . . but I think you should go through.'

'Go through where?'

'I told Medusa to wait for you.'

'Are you pulling my boobies? Grab your man bag. We're leaving.'

Caine was holding the savage cat, which seemed close to climax beneath his caressing fingers.

'Shanti, listen. I know you're a sceptic, and it's not exactly my thing either. But trust me, Medusa has some kind of inner vision. Besides, I've already paid for you.'

'You haven't!'

'My little present. I bought you some essential oils too. Go on. She's waiting.'

The inside of the booth was lit by flickering candles, which reflected in the eyes of Medusa's cats, the many beads around her neck, and the glistening orbs on the table.

Medusa laid down the deck of cards she had been shuffling, and stepped around the small table to Shanti's side. Within the dark space, she spoke more softly.

'Shanti, I can tell you're a little less physical than Vincent, but I hope you won't mind if I hug you?'

'Hug me?'

Instead of replying, Medusa Cole put her purple arms around Shanti's body and embraced her tightly. She stayed there for a long, long time. Far longer than was comfortable or appropriate. And all the while she whispered in her ear, 'I need to touch people before I work. What I'm doing is reading you. I'm feeling your energy. Ooh, you're so-o-o tense . . .'

'Jeez, I—'

'What you really need is a deep massage, but that's not my practice. I'm journeying deeper than the physical, Shanti. Much deeper . . .'

At last she was released. 'That's fine,' said Medusa. 'Why don't you take a seat?'

Medusa stepped around the table, which was covered with a lacy black cloth. On the surface sat a multitude of cards, cats, and crystal spheres on ornate brass stands.

'I can feel your resistance, Shanti. But that's fine. I can work with that. Look on the table – you'll see various items, but none of them have any inherent value.'

'Good. I agree. I'll get along—'

'They're only tools. What you have to understand is that the spirit world lies so close, and these devices help to penetrate. Have you seen one of these before?' She lifted a cloudy sphere from its stand and rotated it in her hands.

'I think so. My mum's got a thing for trash movies.'

'An antique ball like this is very valuable. The guys who raided the shop missed a trick. This ball is worth thousands, probably. I inherited it from my grandmother and I love it. Now look, I hold it in front of the candle . . . and perhaps a question arises in your mind . . .'

'Do you have a fire certificate?'

'Gaze deep, Shanti. There are infinite shapes and shifting visions. Did you ever stare at the clouds?'

'Maybe. When I was a kid.'

'And you thought you could see figures and images. I see them now. It's called scrying.'

'Don't be a scry-baby.'

'The funny thing is that beneath the stress and the bluster

and the tough facade, I'm sensing something huge ... something immense.'

'That's my overdraft.'

'Ha! Oh, this is lovely, Shanti! It's so vivid. So close to the surface. What I'm getting is ... *love.* Pure unadulterated love. Are you in a relationship right now?'

'Nice try, Medusa. In fact I'm recuperating from a fairly shitty divorce. My current companion is pizza.'

'No. You're wrong.'

'I assure you it's true. Have you tried mac and cheese with those little pineapple pieces? Oh Lord, that's real love!'

'I'm saying that the love of your life is closer than you realise.'

'You mean there's a pizza shop next door?'

'Shanti ... Shanti! Stop fighting. Yes, love is very near for you. All you have to do is stop resisting and reach out ...'

Shanti felt a strange sensation. A blush that started on her throat and bloomed around her chest.

'Wait, there's something else!' gasped Medusa. 'Hush, you lot! Ooh, they're being so noisy! How can I hear if you all talk at the same time?'

'I'm sorry,' said Shanti. 'Was it the cats?'

Medusa's eyes were strangely glazed as she stared deeply into the smoky orb, which did indeed seem to fill with swirling, drifting clouds.

'It's Ethan, Shanti. He has a message for you.'

'That's nice. You'd think he'd be ex-directory.'

'It's all about love. Ethan is telling you to find the one he loved above all others and then you will understand.'

'You mean like Date-a-Corpse? That's very niche.'

'He says to take good care of her. Remember, Shanti. It's all about love. Love is everything.'

'Right. I need to get along now, Medusa. Thanks for showing me your balls.'

# Chapter 22

# A Skeletal Scuffle

'Get many customers, Caine?' asked Shanti as they ran along the wet pavements towards the car.

'Not one,' said Caine. 'But I'm dying to know what happened to you in there. You look a little flushed, if you don't mind me saying.'

'I do mind, Caine. What happens in a reading is between the client and the spirit world. Hang on! What are you doing now? I'm getting soaked.'

He had stopped in his tracks, as if struck by an idea.

'Shant, could you hold on for just one minute? I want to check on something Medusa said.'

Any complaints she had tumbled into the streaming puddles that spewed down the Glastonbury drains. As Caine turned on his heel and doubled back towards The Third Eye, she ducked under the awning of a shop offering *Everything for the Discerning Witch.*

What was Caine up to now? And what the hell had Medusa

been talking about? *The love of your life is closer than you realise.*

Three minutes later, he returned, wet hair straggling to his shoulders, and they sprinted towards the car.

'What was that all about?' Shanti said as she whacked on the air con to de-mist the screens.

'Interesting, Shant. You remember Medusa admitted that she had talked publicly about the contract with Ethan? "Bragging about it" was the phrase she used.'

'Yes, I did register that. Meaning it's possible that someone in Glastonbury knew about the costumes.'

'Well, yes. Only it suddenly struck me that she didn't mention Glastonbury at all. What she said was "I think my family and friends in the village were sick of me bragging about it. Everyone knew the costumes were hanging here."'

'So what are you saying?'

'Glastonbury is a town, right? I went back to ask her why she had used the word "village". It turns out that she doesn't live here at all. That's why she's usually late to open during festival season. She lives in a little village a few miles away, and the lanes are solid at this time of year.'

'And the village is . . .?'

'The village is Kilton.'

'Cripes!'

'And that's not all . . .'

'I'm listening.'

'Medusa's best mate is the barmaid at the Five Heads.'

'You mean that biker girl who couldn't keep her eyes off you? OK, I'll admit that may be of some significance. But I'm buggered if I can figure it out. In return, I'll tell you something

Medusa said to me, which is almost certainly a pile of horseshit. Apparently Ethan spoke to her from the other side. He said it's all about love. If we can discover who Ethan loved above all others, then we will understand.'

'Yes,' said Caine 'We need to find Eve.'

The hot raindrops pounded the tarmac with such force that they rebounded towards the dark heavens. Behind the thundering wipers, Shanti slowed the car to walking pace.

'OK, Caine, I've risked the wrath of the spirit world by telling you what Medusa said. So how about you? You looked like death when you came out of there.'

'It was Death I saw.'

'Oh my God. You know what? I am sick of people blathering on in pseudo-mystical riddles. Just tell me in plain English what happened.'

'She used the cards and a glass ball. It was so vivid . . . like a lucid dream . . .'

'Like high-definition bullshit?'

'I was in a race with Death. I could feel my lungs bursting as I tried to catch him. His cape was billowing as he ran. Then we were wrestling on the ground. His face was horrible – all brown and decayed.'

'You wrestled with Death?'

'That's right. But he eluded me.'

'OK, Caine. You know that extended period of sick leave you took a while back? I'm going to have a word with the super. Let's see if we can get you a little more time out. Just resting and taking things steady. You'll be fine. In fact . . . in fact . . .'

'In fact what?'

'In fact it's me that's losing it. We have literally got one and a half days left and all we have is a pile – a steaming dung heap – of festering half-baked ideas about skeletal electricians and avenging divas and murderous twins and love-ins in yurts and . . . Damn it, Caine, I think my head will burst. And if you DARE to suggest meditation, massage, mindfulness, or anything beginning with M, then your premonition about wrestling with Death may be closer than you thought.'

'Murder begins with M.'

'Shut it, Caine. Just shut it.'

They drove in silence to Unworthy Farm, where Shanti parked up and Primrose lent them an umbrella – 'You're welcome, I'm sure.'

Side by side, the two DIs walked through the deluge; down the waterfall of Totterdown Hill, past the Five Heads, alongside the glistening gravestones of Kilton cemetery. The air around them was filled with a sweet, dank aroma as the dusty earth drank its fill.

'I'm going to track down Sista Tremble,' said Shanti loudly beneath the drumming umbrella. 'Maybe she'll be a bit calmer now and answer some questions about her history with Stigma.'

'You don't really think she was involved?'

'Look, I have no idea. But I have to do something. I think we need some time apart anyway. We're not joined at the hip, are we? What are you going to do? Work, rest or play?'

'I suppose the Buddha would recommend doing all three simultaneously.'

'That makes so little sense, it almost makes sense again.'

'I'm going to look into the doctor's letter you found in Ethan's room. I'll have a catch-up with Benno and some of his uniforms.'

'Only they aren't uniforms, remember. I told Benno to get them to change into civvies.'

'Anyway, let's hope this rain passes before long – there are some great bands performing tonight and tomorrow.'

'Do you know how much I care out of ten? That's a one, Caine. Possibly zero. Why do you have to stand so close?'

'I'm sorry. The umbrella isn't very big. Here – you take it.'

'I'm happy to share, but let's not get physical.'

The rain at the festival site was biblical. The mood had changed from sun-baked relaxation to frenetic scurrying and gloomy sheltering. Stallholders desperately covered their wares. Groups of teens who had pitched their tents sloppily in low-lying areas were busily rescuing drenched possessions. A few drunken fools were mud-sliding in black puddles.

'Afternoon, miss,' said a voice at Shanti's side.

She turned to see a long-haired man with a Zapata moustache and blue sunglasses sheltering at the dripping edge of an open marquee.

'Give me strength, Spalding. I said civvies, not pantomime dress.'

'Trying to blend in, miss. Like you told me. You wait till you see Dunster . . . Hang on. This is him now.' From beneath his poncho, he furtively pulled a radio, from which a stream of animated communication erupted.

'What's he saying, Spalding?'

'You're not going to believe this – Dunster's spotted him down at the Other Stage.'

'Spotted who?' asked Shanti.

'Death,' said Spalding. 'He says he's made a comparison with the image from the video and he's ninety per cent certain this is our man. Seems that Death is a Lil Bisto fan.'

'Right,' said Shanti. 'I want this properly handled. Tell Dunster to keep a sharp eye on the suspect. If he moves, he should follow at a distance. Tell him we're on our way.'

'It may be quicker if I run ahead,' said Caine. 'I'll see you there.'

Before she could respond, he had darted off, weaving nimbly through the surge of sodden people, leaving Shanti and Spalding to follow in his trail.

In spite of the ever-increasing downpour and the ominously rumbling skies, a large crowd dressed in polythene capes and sou'westers were nodding and jigging enthusiastically as Lil Bisto pranced and yelled on the stage. Caine drew himself to his full height and scanned the throng. No sign of Dunster, and no sign of the suspect.

As he eased towards a slightly elevated area, where people were huddled beneath an oak tree, an irregular movement caught his eye. Less than five hundred metres away, an extraordinary exchange was taking place. Only at Glastonbury could a confrontation between such strangely clad adversaries be thought of as nothing more than an irritating distraction from the performance. As Caine pushed and squeezed and apologised, he saw Dunster, dressed in an outrageous costume-shop police uniform – a blue onesie with huge silver buttons, a tiny helmet and oversized boots – doing his best to apprehend the hideous red-cloaked figure of Death. Struggling through a tangle of umbrellas, he heard Dunster say, 'Could I have a word, please, Mr Death?'

From within the maggoty sockets of his decayed face, Death

glanced at the comedy policeman, then shook himself free and legged it, with Caine in rapid pursuit.

It was hard to run on the sodden grass, but Caine chased the skeletal figure through the irritable crowds, who swore and shoved as they passed. As he reached the perimeter of the arena, Death disappeared down a narrow alleyway between dripping tents and marquees; hurdling ropes, cables and wooden stakes as he ran.

With an overwhelming sense of alarm, Caine thought he had lost him. The skies had darkened to such an extent that he had to stop and peer about in the deluge, soaked to the skin and vaguely aware of muffled thunder and sheets of lightning overhead.

He searched vainly for Shanti, Dunster, Spalding or anyone else who would understand the urgency of the situation. But he was alone.

In his peripheral vision he caught a fleeting flash of red beneath an awning where a children's art workshop was taking place. He heard screams and yells as terrified children evacuated into the rain, and entered in time to see the fantastical fugitive darting out of the other side. To the horror of her parents, Caine leapt over a small child asleep on a blanket as he pursued the fleeing figure.

Death had sprinted across a clearing towards a marquee where a heated political rally was taking place. The politician onstage was arguing his case ferociously, but the crowd clearly disagreed. The hooded figure shoved his way through the audience, overturning cameras and tripping on cables, Caine pushing through after him, apologising furiously as he ran. Now the caped cadaver made a sliding sprint across an open field where a forlorn queue waited their turn at a toilet block. Here the ground had dissolved into a suspicious ooze, which bubbled through the brown grass. As Caine arrived on the scene, gasping for breath, he saw Death skid, tumble and fall headlong into the mire. In an instant, he was on him.

'Utterly pathetic,' said a woman in disgust, as the pair brawled and tussled in the mud. 'Glasto used to be a celebration of love and kindness. There are children here, you know. If you idiots want to fight, why don't you do it in the pub at home?'

Caine wanted to explain. He wanted to say that he was on her side. He truly was a man of peace, and the last thing on earth he wanted to be doing was wrestling a hideous corpse in this fetid quagmire. But he could not find the words. The task in hand was so utterly exhausting that it took every ounce of his energy. He managed to force one skinny arm behind the man's back, but his adversary was as slippery as an eel. Every time Caine attempted to raise himself to his knees, he slithered further into the mud.

Now a muscular man in a wheelchair rolled forward and hauled Death to his feet.

'No,' pleaded Caine. 'You've got the wrong man.'

But Death had struggled upright, his cloak as waterlogged as a whaler's oilskins. Caine caught one last glimpse of that ghastly grinning skull before the cloaked figure staggered away and was lost amongst the crowds.

Not far away, in the area known as Shangri-La, dedicated to outsider art and underground culture, Shanti had become separated from Spalding.

Shaking her umbrella, she walked into what could have been

a set from a dystopian movie – oppressive graffiti-lined alleyways and the two-storey facade of a neon-lit hotel. Passing through a huge doorway constructed from recycled plastic bottles, she found herself in a demented hospital ward, with rows of iron beds on which bearded nurses in skimpy uniforms, carrying enormous syringes, were caring for hung-over festival goers.

At last she stumbled into a gloomy cabaret bar called PugUgly, where punters were sipping cocktails and sheltering from the rain. On the podium in front of her, tonight's performers were rehearsing. Dressed in macabre S&M gear, they ground and gyrated beneath green strobe lights. Shanti bought herself a large Diet Coke and found a chair at a table near the back.

As she vainly tried to reach Caine on his phone, a peculiar thing happened. At first she barely reacted; almost everyone here was wearing some kind of strange garb, so when the dripping, mud-coated figure of Death entered the pulsating green space, it took a moment for her adrenaline to kick in.

He was standing directly in front of the small stage, clearly exhausted from his efforts. She rose to her feet, walked briskly towards him – and dived.

As the fetish dancers tumbled backwards, Shanti pinned Death to the stage. In a series of swift movements, she rolled him face downwards, clipped handcuffs around his wrists and hauled him onto his back.

Then, inserting a finger into each maggoty socket, she removed the papier-mâché mask.

## *Chapter 23*

# The Man Behind the Mask

'I ain't done nothing,' said the thin-faced man behind the skull.

'Like hell you haven't,' said Shanti. 'I'm arresting you on suspicion of murder. You don't have to say anything . . .'

'Sick,' said one of the latex cabaret dancers. 'Nice act.'

With one knee pressed firmly on the man's chest, Shanti pulled out her phone. 'Benno, I'm in the . . . Excuse me . . . where the hell am I?'

'Shangri-La,' shouted a woman in the audience.

'Used to be called Lost Vagueness,' said another.

'Shangri-La, Benno. In a bar called . . .?'

'PugUgly,' called the audience in unison.

'In a bar called PugUgly. Get over here, soon as you can. I've got our man. Oh, and bring Caine if you can find him. There's a hospital here in case he needs a lie-down.'

By the time Benno, Caine and a small team had pulled up in the 4x4, Shanti had hauled the man against a corrugated-iron wall on the grass area outside, where the rain was beginning to ease.

Caine climbed out, looking exhausted and utterly sodden. His face and hair were plastered with sludge.

'I'm sorry, Shanti. He got away from me. How did you . . .?'

'It's about being in the right place at the right time, Caine. Right, sir. Would you like to tell my colleagues what you told me?'

She pushed the fugitive across to Benno, who seized his arm firmly. The man beneath the mask was dark, unshaven, late twenties, with a gold-tipped front tooth.

'Like I said, I ain't done nothing.'

'You broke into a shop and stole this costume.'

'No. I never did.'

'Let's start from the beginning,' said Benno. 'What's your name, sir?'

'Ben.'

'Full name.'

'Ben Dunnit.'

'So where did you acquire the death costume, Mr Dunnit?'

'Like I've been trying to tell her – I've got a festival ticket and everything. I'm totally legit. I hitched down from Newcastle, but it took longer than I thought, so I only got here this morning.'

'The costume?'

'It was just a laugh . . . I didn't even know I'd got it.'

'What do you mean, you didn't know you'd got it?'

'I . . . All right, I'll put my hands up – I nicked a bike.'

'You nicked a bike?'

'Look, it took me nearly two days to get here. I spent last night sleeping in a service station. I was bloody knackered when

I arrived and the place was swarming with cops. I went into a pub and had a few drinks. Everyone in there was talking about . . . you know, Ethan Flynn. I must have been the last person in the country to hear about it. When I came out, I suppose I was a bit the worse for wear. I walked down a lane towards the festival. I was dying for a leak, but there were cops everywhere, so I nipped into some bushes. I saw the bike just lying there in some undergrowth, so I liberated it. I only used it for the last bit, to get to the festival. It was downhill all the way.'

'Let's get this straight – you hitched to the festival from Newcastle . . .'

'It took nearly two days.'

'You stopped at a pub for a few drinks. When you came out, you went into some undergrowth and found an abandoned bicycle?'

'It wasn't even locked.'

'So you decided to help yourself. You cycled to the main gates.'

'Showed my ticket, but they wouldn't let me take the bike inside. They said I had to leave it with the other bikes and motorcycles in the car park.'

'But what about the costume?'

'It was in a bag inside the pannier. I thought it would be stupid not to check the pannier, but there was nothing in there except a few random tools and this lot – the robe, the mask and the skeleton. I could see it was quality kit.'

'So you put it on and came onto the site.'

'It was just a laugh.'

'Where are the tools?'

'Still in the pannier, as far as I know.'

'Then what?'

'Then nothing. I was minding my own business watching Lil Bisto when this joker tried to grab me . . .' He pointed an accusatory finger at Dunster. 'I managed to escape. But then *he* came after me . . .' He turned the finger to Caine. 'Chased me for bloody miles. I ended up in a pool of muck. Look at the state of me.'

'Why did you run if you'd done nothing wrong?'

'I just admitted it. I took a bike.'

'So, we'll find this bike in the car park, will we?'

'Unless someone else has liberated it.'

'Right, Mr Dunnit,' said Shanti. 'You've caused a lot of aggravation and you've wasted a lot of police time. If you'll step inside the vehicle, we're going to need a full statement. You're going to have to confirm every detail of what you told us. I want to know precisely where you found the bike and anyone who can corroborate your story. If everything you say is true, it shouldn't take more than an hour or two.'

'Oh, come on,' wailed Dunnit. 'Ulalla Strump is playing tonight. She's wicked . . .'

## Chapter 24

# Moon of Doom

A monumental rainbow spanned the valley.

Caine showered, changed into clean clothes and dry boots, and found his way to the Hundred Monkeys Café, where he shared a light meal with Misty.

His sister was all set to see a band, followed by another night of dancing; but Caine made his apologies, kissed her fondly and set off up the hill, against the happy tide flowing to the stages.

On the way, he passed many tents that had been battered by the storm, and he stopped to help a young couple who were struggling to set up camp in a drier spot.

The prayer flags had withered to dripping ribbons, but the old white tent had stood up well, and now the rain had thinned to drizzle.

Behind Glastonbury Tor, the sun went down as slowly as an old man lowering himself into bed. In the hawthorn tree a blackbird shook its wet feathers and let loose an evening song of fluid purity above the thudding of the festival. Caine alone heard it, as he relit the fire and brewed chamomile tea. Then he crawled inside his canvas home and settled down to sleep.

Balancing her bag and a large portion of chips in one hand, and the umbrella in the other, Shanti exited the festival site and headed towards Unworthy Farm. In the fading light, the ancient stone of Kilton parish church shone like beaten bronze.

And all the time, she reflected on this strangest of cases. Tomorrow was Sunday. Then the whole tented metropolis would gather itself up and scatter to a hundred thousand different destinations. And with it, the murderer in their midst.

What a disappointment it had been earlier at the cabaret. She had been convinced that she had her man beneath her fingertips; certain that when she lifted that mask, Tyrone's sneering face would appear beneath the skull. Or one of the Flynn entourage, at least. But that annoying man Ben Dunnit was clearly of little consequence.

Of course the bike might be useful if they could find it. Benno had promised to send a couple of uniforms to search the car park. Dawn and her team would give it the once-over for fingerprints and DNA, along with the saturated remains of the costume. But all of that would take days or even weeks.

In the meantime, Shanti had arranged to meet Caine first thing in the morning. Her colleague was insistent about speaking to the barmaid with the piercings at the Five Heads; but as far as she was concerned, the trail of Medusa was not the top priority. Her focus remained stubbornly on Tyrone. He had made an enemy of her, and that was a mistake for any man.

The village was still gridlocked, and several exhausted uniforms were doing their best to keep things under control. Shanti knew they were under orders to be extra vigilant for anyone suspicious entering or leaving the area. As she walked along the main road, she witnessed a couple of vehicles being stopped and their drivers questioned. It had to be done, she supposed, but there seemed little chance of detaining anyone but a few drunk or drugged drivers.

Shaking off the cluster of ever-persistent reporters, she turned into Totterdown Hill and called her mum.

'Paul's fine,' Amma reassured her. 'He's sound asleep after all that football. He keeps seeing you on TV.'

'And did he say I looked like I'd slept in a hedge?'

'He said you looked like Superwoman.'

'Jeez, Mum.'

'And I said you looked beautiful, and how proud we both were.'

'To be honest, Mum, I've never felt less like Superwoman in my life.'

'How's my friend Vincent Caine?'

'Worse than useless.'

'Oh come on, Shanti, I'm sure you don't mean that. I like Vincent.'

'I know you do, Amma.'

'And are you any closer to catching Ethan's killer?'

'You know I can't talk about the case. If you want to help, tell me how I can get a decent night's sleep.'

'Have a hot bath. And take a couple of tablets, darling. It won't hurt for once.'

'Maybe you're right. I really need to switch off.'

'Look after yourself, Shanti.'

'I will, Mum. Love you.'

She slipped successfully into the house without meeting anyone, including the rat-faced terrier or his Punch-faced master. Creeping up the stairs, she paused on the landing, with one ear pressed against the door of the Lilac Suite. Not a sound. Unlocking the door quietly with the huge key, she entered cautiously. She spent a full five minutes examining every cupboard and cavity, including the dark recesses beneath the bed, and even under the bath. Finally she closed the curtains and jammed the chair beneath the door handle.

Boy, that bath felt good. Caine's bath oils were ... well, if not essential, then certainly beneficial. And what was the harm in a few sleeping tablets, so long as you didn't make it a habit? She swallowed one with water, then another two, to be on the safe side. Tomorrow night she'd be in her own bed. Monday at the latest. And arrest or no arrest, no one could say she hadn't tried her damnedest. At least Mum and Paul were proud of her.

The cotton sheets of the enormous bed were chilly as expected, but she was well insulated with a T-shirt under her pyjamas and a jumper on top. Lying back on the huge stack of pillows and skimming through the messages on her phone, she felt the relief of the medication seeping into her veins.

Nearly asleep, she pulled up some of the TV footage of the case, deliberately skimming past her own statements to the press. On YouTube she found something she hadn't seen before – the beginning of the Stigma gig, in which beautiful Ethan entered the Pyramid Stage with bare feet and floaty clothes. The footage must have been taken from a Steadicam on the stage itself, so she got some idea of what the vast audience looked like from up there – an endless vista of bulbous heads. How strange that was, all those skulls. All those brains. Like a hundred thousand turnips in a field. All those eyes focused on one man – Ethan Flynn . . . Or maybe she was feeling the effect of the tablets, which always made her woozy before they carried her down the long, soft stairway to sleep.

With the microphone in one hand and a mandolin dangling from the other, the pale prodigy began a mumbly speech, beginning with 'Fank you, Glastonbury.' He told them that Stigma had been in their teens the last time they'd played that stage. He informed the vast crowd that 'a lot of stuff has gone down since then'. In the ensuing years, he and Tyrone had lost their dad, Frankie Flynn – 'Fank you, Dad. Love you, man.' He reminded them that death – or rather 'def' – was all around. 'Def an' life are like twins, ain't they, Tyrone?' he said. He informed the adoring audience that this was why everyone needed to love one another. Finally he announced that something wonderful had happened recently – that someone special had come into his life and made him 'refink everyfing'.

The camera panned across to the far end of the stage, where Tyrone was visibly fuming with impatience and indignation.

'This one's for her,' concluded the pale prodigy, 'the one I love more than any uvver in the world, and no matter what happens to me, I always want her to remember that. Fank you. I love you all . . .'

As Shanti plunged into oblivion, the phone slid over the side of the giant four-poster. The last thought she had was that tonight was the night that Queenie had talked about. The third night on which Ethan would rise again.

In his sleeping bag close to Mother Earth, Caine could not sleep. This was unusual for him. But if he could not sleep, he could always meditate.

He rose and stepped outside, stretched a little, then settled himself cross-legged near the remains of the fire. A fresh breeze had blown away the storm and it was a perfect clear night. Across the valley, the festival lights sparkled, and high above his head, a huge moon peered down – so well defined that he could almost make out the craters of that astronomical body.

Now Caine understood the reason for his restlessness. The full moon had always unsettled him. Many times as a youngster he had found himself padding to the window as the rest of the house slept. Drawing back the curtains, child Vincent had stared up at that wise eye. He almost felt that they were acknowledging each other – the innocent boy and the ancient moon.

And later, as a young man, he had learned from his teacher, Tu, about the significance of the full moon to every Buddhist festival. He knew of the moon's importance in many cultures, and the way in which it shaped the tides of the sea and the female cycle. For pagans, the lunar peak was a time of madness and mischief. It was, after all, where the word 'lunatic' derived.

An hour passed, or more, then Caine rose, touched fingertips to forehead in the dedication of merit, and returned to his tent. He felt that tonight and the following day would be strange ones indeed.

In her dreams, Shanti pushed her fingertips deep into the eye sockets of Death and struggled to pull the mask free. Who was lying trapped beneath her knees? Was it Tyrone? Was it Ethan? With one last tug, she tore the mask away and stared into the black void below. Within the russet bowl of the skull, a mass of maggots seethed.

She struggled awake. The pills . . . those damn pills had her body pinned to the bed. She could not move her limbs. Her eyes were sealed. But to her horror, she heard something moving noisily in the room. A creature padding and pacing. If she could only wake . . . open her eyes . . . If she could only breathe . . .

Queenie had been right. He was here! Ethan had returned. Here he was, kneeling on her chest, pushing her deeper into this great house of a bed.

She heard him whisper, 'Find her for me. Find the one I love more than any uvver. Then you will understand. Fank you. Fank you so much . . .'

With one last superhuman effort, she inhaled a huge gasp of cold air and lurched upwards.

It was all a horrible nightmare. The room was cold and empty. The ancient window had blown open, and through the flapping curtains she saw a vast moon, which bathed the room in a silvery sheen.

'Holy crap!' she gasped, shaking her head to dispel the drug that had solidified her brain. Swearing never again to take those tablets, she swung her feet to the floor with the intention of closing the window.

As she did so, something caught her eye.

Something white and gleaming within the complex carvings of the bed.

The moonlight had illuminated a bright object hidden in the dark wooden canopy. It was a strange trick of the light; one of those ugly gargoyle faces appeared to possess a set of brilliant white teeth.

Shanti climbed shakily onto the bed and stepped across the vast trampoline. Now she could see it clearly. The polished face of a grimacing man, carved in the darkest of oak, with something small and white in its mouth . . .

Not teeth, but a wad of tightly folded paper. She tried to pull it out, but her legs were unsteady on the soft bed, and her fingers would not fit inside the narrow slot.

She lowered herself onto the cold floorboards, pausing to close the ill-fitting window. Then she turned on the light and rummaged in her wash bag until she found a pair of tweezers.

Returning to the bed, she was able to delicately prise the folded paper free, touching it only with the metal prongs. It was, after all, a potential piece of evidence.

Now fully alert, she laid the object carefully on the glass-topped dressing table. In her bag she found a packet of latex gloves, and after a long search, she located her phone where it had fallen on the floor. Under the bright light of the torch beam, she delicately unfolded the paper.

It was a heavily annotated musical score, with the heading: *Song for Eve*. The manuscript was dense with symbols and clefs and musical notes that meant nothing to Shanti. But amongst the horizontal lines were strange, enigmatic lyrics written in an elegant forward-sloping hand. She read the first verse aloud:

*Sleepy creature of the sacred dome*
*Spread your wings, it's time to fly from home*

What did it mean? Shanti took several photos, then laid the sheet of paper carefully inside a polythene bag.

It was many hours before she slept.

## Chapter 25

# The Tragedy

'Take your feet off the bed, Caine.'

He was staring with disbelief at the musical score inside the evidence bag. From outside, the timeless bells summoned Kilton's faithful to their knees.

'This is extraordinary, Shant! You've found Ethan's last song.'

'I *am* extraordinary, Caine . . . What are you doing here anyway?'

'Hmm? Oh, I waited outside the Five Heads as arranged. But you didn't show.'

'Yeah, I had a rough night.'

'I got a little worried when you didn't answer your phone.'

'That's deeply touching.'

'So I walked up the hill. Primrose said you'd be down for breakfast, but when you didn't appear, I thought I'd bring you some tea.'

'Well, I appreciate the thought. And what's that in your hot little hand?'

'Wild flowers. I picked them up Totterdown Hill. Thought they'd cheer you up. You've had a tough week.'

'Oh my God, Caine. That is unbelievably inappropriate.'

'I'm sorry?'

'I'm a serving officer. Your fellow DI. We are deep, very deep in a murder inquiry.'

'What's the harm in some flowers?'

'Oh, I don't even know where to begin . . . OK, I'm going to get up now. Would you please avert your eyes while I get out of bed? You might see something disturbing.'

'You always disturb me, Shanti.'

'Shut it, Caine. Focus on the song and nothing else.'

She rose from the bed and darted into the chilly bathroom, while Caine ran his finger across the manuscript, silently mouthing the words.

'So what do you think?' she called. 'Cryptic clue or more Ethan drivel?'

'I like it . . . *Between us lies the ever-breathing sea . . . Big waves crying our love can never be . . . Dum di dum di dum dee dee . . .* Reminds me of a young Neil Young.'

'A young kneel young?'

'I mean it's reminiscent of a song like "Helpless".'

'That's what you are, Caine. Completely helpless.'

'Listen to this: *Forever strangers, like daytime is to night . . . Yet I love you, like the darkness loves the light* . . . It's as if Ethan is inviting us to decipher a code.'

'I agree. Two words stand out.'

'Really?'

'Yes. Pretentious bollocks.'

'Well, the melody is lovely. Do you want me to sing it?'

She stared with horror from around the doorway. 'Christ, no. Anyway, it's all dots and squiggles. You can't read that stuff, can you?'

'A little. I learnt to read music when I was with Half Man Half Bull.'

'Everything about that sentence is wrong.'

'I'll tell you what – it's damned intriguing . . . *Sleepy creature of the sacred dome* . . . You can see why Vula thought it was about her.'

'But it wasn't. It was about Eve.'

'Whoever Eve may be.'

'But why did he hide it, Caine? I mean, I only discovered it because the moonlight fell directly on it. Otherwise it would have been there for ever.'

'I don't know. I suppose it fits with Ethan's profile – he always liked to appear spontaneous and mysterious.'

'Or else there are clues concealed within the lyrics. Go back to that line about the sacred dome. What's that about?'

'Let's brainstorm,' said Caine. 'I'll start. If you look out of the window, you'll see a sacred dome that Ethan loved.'

'Please can I work with someone normal?'

'I'm talking about Glastonbury Tor.'

Shanti emerged from the bathroom and wagged a toothbrush at him.

'No, you're miles off the mark. But fortunately I've cracked it . . . Oh man, how did I get to be so clever?'

'Go on then.'

'Right. Remember when we were at Villa del Flynn?'

'You were feeling a little delicate.'

'I was sharp enough, 'cos I noticed something you didn't. Ethan had a special relationship with his granny, didn't he?'

'He did.'

'And Nana Flynn passed on her musical skills. They adored each other. Isn't that correct?'

'So Queenie told us.'

'Well, can you remember where her ashes were laid to rest?'

'In a casket inside her caravan.'

'And where was that caravan?'

'In a dome.'

'Correct. You lose five points because you had help, but you got there in the end. It was a sacred dome, which Ethan helped to design.'

'I suppose it's a possibility.'

'A possibility? I bet you a jar of honey the old girl was called Eve.'

'Organic honey?'

'Made by Buddhist bees.'

'I don't know. But I've got a feeling this song will help to reveal the real Ethan. Leave it with me, Shant. I'll need time to ponder this.'

'Sure thing, Caine – you skip off to a woodland glade and spend the day in contemplation. But as far as I'm concerned, today is the final day of this godawful festival, and I'm planning to make an arrest . . . Sweet Jesus, I look rough.'

'You look great, Shanti. Glowing.'

'Well I feel rough.'

'Anyway, I'm convinced that Medusa was right – this case is about love.'

'Wrong again, Caine. This case is about resentment. Good old-fashioned sibling rivalry. Tyrone wanted to eliminate the brother who'd overshadowed him all his life. It's almost biblical.

In fact last night I was watching some footage of Stigma, and you could actually see him burning with resentment. Also, please don't forget that Tyrone sneaked into this very bedroom. It's obvious that he was searching for that song. I reckon he'd heard Queenie and maybe Vula saying that it was the greatest thing ever written, and he wanted to claim it as his own.'

'You're saying that Tyrone killed his brother for a song?'

'I'm saying it's breakfast time. Big sizzling sausages. Oh, and thanks for the thought, but why don't you give those flowers to Primrose? I'm sure she'd appreciate them.'

She was right. Primrose did appreciate the flowers. Visibly flushed, she placed them in a vase in the centre of the kitchen table, where Vowles and Gavin Blackmore were already seated.

Blackmore hastily drained his cup, mumbled an apology and exited the room as if his curls were on fire.

'You sit here, my dear,' said Vowles, in cap and woollen socks, with a fresh drip on his red beak and two boiled eggs before him. 'And will your young man be eating?'

'He's not so young, and he's certainly not mine,' said Shanti. 'Anyway, he's already eaten, haven't you, Caine?'

'Just a cup of tea then,' said Primrose, grinning toothily at Caine. 'You're welcome, I'm sure.'

From the moment she entered the kitchen, Shanti had been acutely aware of the hound from hell, curled on its bedraggled armchair, baring its foul teeth and snarling in its sleep. She backed nervously around the table and sat herself in front of the huge breakfast that Primrose had laid out. And as she scooped home-made marmalade onto home-made bread, she witnessed an extraordinary thing. A kind of miracle.

Stirring a modest spoonful of honey into his tea, her colleague, Vincent Caine went over to the armchair and actually sat himself in it, wiggling his slim buttocks right against the flanks of the satanic beast. Primrose and Vowles saw it too, and an identical expression of alarm flashed across their faces.

Shanti waited for the snarling. The panic. The tearing flesh. The screams. The blood. But as Boner opened one beady eye, Caine calmly lifted the little fellow and placed him squarely on his lap, where he began to massage and fondle his tawny ears. The tyke stared about in pop-eyed wonder, and then began to relax, as if heavily drugged.

'Never seen anything like it,' gasped Vowles.

'Must have magic fingers,' sighed Primrose.

After a few moments, Boner wriggled joyfully onto his back, inviting Caine to scratch his chubby belly.

'Poor Gavin rushed off without finishing his breakfast,' said Caine, completely oblivious to the slack-jawed expressions around him.

'As I explained to your friend,' said Primrose, 'Gavin is a little awkward in company. He has his reasons, but we prefer not to talk about them. Isn't that right, Vowles? Best to let sleeping dogs lie.'

As Boner sighed and French-kissed Caine's hand, the irony of the phrase hung heavy in the air.

'I don't mind talking about it,' said Vowles slowly.

'Oh. Are you sure that's wise, dear?' said Primrose.

'Gavin is my nephew, see. More than that, I were his guardian when he were a boy.'

'You did everything for him, Vowles,' said Primrose.

'Young Gavin had it all – the looks, the brains. He were the most popular boy in the village. Then he met Carole . . .'

'Carole?'

'Girl from Exeter College. Love at first sight, it were. They were a perfect match. Where's that photo, Primrose?

'Oh Vowles, I'm sure the gentleman doesn't want to see that . . .'

'I'd love to,' said Caine.

Primrose went over to a cluttered dresser and pulled out a framed photo from behind a stack of plates.

'You mean this one?' she said, handing over an image of four smiling adults and a baby.

'That's the fellow. See, that's me . . . and here's Primrose in her prime. What a beauty!'

'Oh Vowles.'

'You all look very happy,' said Caine. 'And that must be baby Seth in your arms, Primrose?'

'Ah yes. Seth was a late addition in our lives. Is that how we put it, Vowles?'

'An unexpected addition, Primrose.'

'See, me and Vowles are from a different generation. To be honest, we don't understand Seth's ways, and it grieves me to say we've grown apart in recent years.'

'Families are complicated,' replied Caine.

Vowles tapped the glass on the photo. 'But this is what I wanted to show you. That's Gav with Carole. They'd just graduated, see, and that's why they're so happy.'

'They make a fine couple,' agreed Caine.

'They were head over heels, ain't that right, Primrose?'

'Vowles, perhaps you'd better not—'

'Happy as Larry, they were. I 'member Gav sayin', "I could search my whole life, Uncle Vowles, but I'll never find a better match than Carole." He'd watched me an' Primrose, p'raps. I leased them a farm cottage at a modest rent, where Gav resides to this day. But they wanted a place of their own. They saved and bought a nice plot of land a couple o' miles outside Kilton. It were Gav's dream to build his own place and start a family, see. Then one dark winter night, it all went horribly wrong . . .'

'Vowles, I really don't think the gentleman wants to hear all this . . .'

'No, really, I'm fascinated,' said Caine. 'So long as it's not too distressing for you.'

'Gav announced they were gettin' married. They were goin' out to celebrate the engagement. He'd bought a ring and all that.'

'Beautiful it were,' sighed Primrose.

'They went to the pub an' had one or two. Then a few more. And a few more after that. Carole had an early start the next day, so she upped and left, silly girl. Didn't think of getting a cab . . .'

'Oh now, don't upset yourself, Vowles,' said Primrose.

'Got in her car and set off, on that dark, wet night. Gav needed to check on the animals, so he said he'd walk back later, ain't that right, Primrose?'

'You were there, Vowles. I was tucked up in bed.'

'I were there. Me an' the dog were out rattin'. It were me what found her.'

'I'm so sorry.'

'It were flooded everywhere. She'd come off the road and driven straight into the dyke. I saw the lights of her little white car still blinkin'. It were stickin' out the water . . . Forgive me . . . I'll be all right in a moment . . .'

'Please . . .'

'Thing is, I still can't get that picture out my mind. Driven straight into a drainage channel, she had. Terrible way to go. Course, I rushed over and tried with all my might to shift it. If I'd had a tractor, it might've helped, but I think she were already gone . . .'

'See, now you've stirred it all up again,' said Primrose.

'I waded up to my waist in freezin' water. An' . . . an' I hauled her out through the window. Lovely little thing. Barely weighed more than a child. No seat belt, and she'd slipped right under the water. Dead as a rabbit.'

'How dreadful. Poor Gavin,' said Caine.

'A change came over him that night. He became afeared of life . . . like a weasel in a hole. Very sociable he were before the tragedy, but now . . .'

'Barely a word.'

'Barely a word.'

Vowles tapped at his egg and sliced off the top with a teaspoon.

'That's why he's the way he is. And of course, he won't never drive again.'

'Really?' said Shanti, looking up from her breakfast. 'But I saw him on a quad bike.'

'Ah yes, young lady, but never on the road. It's a damn nuisance if you ask me. Won't even take a tractor down the lanes to trim the hedges.'

'And then Vowles took him under his wing, didn't you, dear?'

'It were the right thing to do. He had nowhere to go. His

whole future drowned that night. When he were fit to work, I gave him odd jobs on the farm, an' he's been here ever since. We've no complaints, Primrose an' me. He pays his rent and gets on with the job. But don't go to Gav if you're looking for jolly company.'

'Poor chap,' said Caine.

'Thought you were entitled to know. Don't take it personal.'

Shanti rose to her feet. 'Well, it's a very sad story. But I'm afraid we have work to do.'

'You any closer to catching the person who did that terrible thing to young Ethan?' asked Vowles.

'I'm afraid we're not able to disclose that. But I'm satisfied that justice will prevail.'

'I'm sure it will, young lady. I'm sure it will.'

'Are you ready, Caine?' asked Shanti.

Caine stood up and gently resettled the dog, which appeared bereft at the parting.

'Thanks for the tea,' he said. 'By the way, I couldn't help noticing a beautiful grave in the cemetery, covered with fresh flowers.'

'My poor dear mother,' choked Vowles. 'Passed away ten year ago. Don't matter how old you are, you'll always miss your mum.' The drip tumbled from his nose and into his boiled egg.

'You're welcome, I'm sure,' said Primrose frostily.

'What the hell was that all about?' said Shanti as they stepped into the yard.

'Only making conversation,' said Caine. 'You never know what you might pick up.'

'Caine, it's nearly ten o'clock. We have achieved precisely

nothing today, and you sit there with the hound from hell on your lap, sipping tea and listening to ghostly tales.'

'I've been up since dawn, Shanti. It was you who had a lie-in. Now, how about joining me in the pub?'

'So you can probe the barmaid?'

'I want to find out her connection with Medusa.'

'Lovely offer, but I'm off to arrest Tyrone Flynn.'

'Shanti, you've got nothing on Tyrone, except a personal grudge.'

'So what should I do? Go and dance to Safe Squad? Do my nails and hope something turns up?'

'You know what I always say – we need to embrace uncertainty.'

'Yeah, and you know what *I* always say? We're not joined at the hip. So why don't you go and sit on the doorstep and wait for that barmaid. Maybe you could pick her some flowers on the way.'

'But seriously, Shant, I think you need to be careful over there. Tyrone is a dangerous man – we've already seen that. And he's got some heavy minders. Couldn't you wait half an hour?'

'Now we're getting to the heart of it. What you really think is that I need a big strong man to protect me.'

'Not at all . . .'

'Do you know who was top of her year in martial arts?'

'You were.'

'And do you know who got top marks in advanced driving? And riot control? And life-saving? And . . . and I can look after myself, thank you very much. I'll see you later. Go easy on the cider.'

## *Chapter 26*

# The Tale of Molly Appleyard

Caine let himself into the yard at the back of the Five Heads and peered through the windows. There was still no one about. After a while he crossed the busy road and returned to the steep lane in front of the churchyard. Near the church steps he stood for a while watching the modest congregation emerge into the sunshine. Here the clanging bells were painful on the ears, merging incongruously with the first bands of the day down at the festival.

When the vicar had shaken the last hand and closed the church doors, Caine stepped into the cemetery and took a few moments to study the graves. Finally he wandered up and down the lane until he found the place that the fugitive, Ben Dunnit, had described – a tiny opening in the shrubbery. He wriggled through and surveyed the green interior, thick with ivy, brambles and discarded fertiliser sacks. Everything was still saturated from the rain, but he noticed a subtle trail where the weeds had been trampled, and a flat area where the bicycle had probably lain.

Five minutes later, he re-emerged and wandered back to the pub, which was now unlocked. The lounge bar was empty except for the barmaid in the red leather jacket, who was vacuuming noisily behind the bar. All the chairs had been turned upside down on the tabletops.

'Good morning,' said Caine.

She jumped and turned off the machine.

'Couldn't keep away then,' she said, leaning on the beer taps. 'Would you like me to pull something for you?'

'Something non-alcoholic this time,' said Caine. 'An apple juice, please. And would you mind if I asked you a few questions?'

'Depends what they are. J2O or local?'

'Local please. Do you know Medusa Cole?'

She added ice and a lemon slice and handed over the glass.

'You're a cop, aren't you? Medusa said you'd been snooping about. You don't look like one, if I may say so. Don't they normally have big helmets?'

'I'm a detective – DI Vince Caine. We're looking into . . .'

'. . . the death of Ethan Flynn. She said. And yes, me and Medusa are best mates. She comes over all the time.'

'Sorry, could I ask your name?'

'Molly. Molly Appleyard. Pleased to meet you, DI Vince Caine.'

'You both live in Kilton, Molly?'

'We do. We went to school together and we shared everything, from first cigarettes to first boyfriends. We were the village bad girls, if you know what I mean.'

'Right. And do you go to the festival together?'

'In our teens we never missed it. Highlight of the year it used to be. You get free tickets if you live in the village, you know. Oh yeah, we saw Beyoncé, Björk, Amy Winehouse, Skunk Anansie – they were well good.'

'Nineteen ninety-nine, wasn't it?'

'You were there?'

'I'll never forget it,' said Caine.

'Skunk Anansie were the last headline of the twentieth century.'

'I suppose they were. But what about you, Molly? You don't go to the festival any more?'

'Does it look like I have the time? Besides, in my opinion it ain't what it used to be.'

'But you like Stigma?'

'They're all right. To be honest, I'm a single mum with a three-year-old and a one-year-old. Any spare time I have is spent on my little hobby.'

'Oh yes. What's that?'

'Motorbikes, Vince. Dirt bikes in particular. You never feel more alive than with the wind in your hair and something throbbing between your legs. You ever done it?'

'Not really. I rode a few bikes when I was young . . .'

'You should try it. There are some great trails round here.'

'Maybe I will. So, you knew about Medusa's commission for Stigma?'

'Tell the truth, I got a bit shagged off hearing about it.'

'It sounds like anyone in the pub could have heard about it, and seen photos of the costumes.'

'That's probably true. Look, do you mind if I carry on? Only we're a bit short-staffed today, and it may not look like it now, but Sunday lunchtimes are manic during the festival.'

'Go ahead. Let me help.'

They began returning the chairs to the floor and setting out fresh beer mats.

'If every cop was like you, the world would be a happier place. I expect you're married?'

'Molly, can you think of any customers who showed a particular interest in those costumes?'

'I'd have to think about that . . .'

'I'm going to give you a contact number.'

'Sweet.'

'Call me if you remember anything unusual.'

'Don't you worry, I will. Now, was that everything, DI Caine?'

'Not quite. We found a bicycle and I want to return it to its owner.'

'They keep you busy, don't they? Murder squad and lost property too.'

'All part of the job.'

'See, lots of people have pushbikes round here. Look at the traffic outside and you'll understand why. It takes half an hour to drive from one end of the village to the other. I'm all right, though. I get about on my Yammy. It's out the back now.'

'So you can't think of anyone who has lost or misplaced a pushbike in recent days?'

'I could ask around.'

'It's an old bike. Black, with mudguards. No lock, but it has an old-school dynamo light on the front. And a pannier . . . but only on one side.'

'Ah yes, I know that bike. It's often parked out front.'

'Really? Do you know who it belongs to?'

'Maybe I do. Maybe I don't. I'll give you a call, shall I? After work, perhaps . . .'

'Why don't you tell me now, Molly?'

## *Chapter 27*

# The Pool of Envy

Queenie Flynn opened the imposing front door in her widow's weeds.

It was shocking to see how exhausted she looked. As if she had visibly aged since Shanti's previous visit. Beneath her sad eyes, dark fleshy rings were pushing through the make-up; and she seemed shorter too, if that were possible – or perhaps it was just that her self-possessed stance had wilted.

'I've got a bone to pick with you, young lady,' she said.

'I'm sorry?'

'Tyrone tells me that you're staying in Ethan's room at Unworthy Farm. Is that correct?'

'I . . . well, yes. I've been renting it this week.'

'And you thought that was appropriate?'

'I'm sorry if you don't think so. But I had to stay somewhere, Mrs Flynn. And as your lads cleared everything out without consent, the room was vacant.'

'Well I don't want to argue with you. Lord knows there's enough anger at the moment. Now what was it you wanted?'

'I was hoping you'd answer a few more questions.'

'On a Sunday?'

'I'm truly sorry, Mrs Flynn, but I must stress the urgency of this investigation. As you know, today is the final day of the festival, and if we don't make some kind of breakthrough, everything will become more difficult.'

'Are you saying you've made no progress at all?'

'I certainly wouldn't say that,' said Shanti. 'We've established several good leads, which is why I'm here. But time is of the essence.'

'Well you'd better come in. But you may as well know that things have been unsettled here.'

'It's a terrible time for the family, I understand that.'

'There's more to it than that,' Queenie said as Shanti stepped past the marble columns and into the hallway, which was dominated by a large jar of peacock feathers. 'I'm in the conservatory, where we sat before,' she added. 'It's where I like to remember Ethan.'

They walked along the dog-leg corridors and through the glass-domed room, where Shanti paused to contemplate the vintage caravan on the plinth. From some distant part of the villa, she thought she heard raised voices.

The French doors of the conservatory were open and one of the brawny Flynn menfolk was cleaning the pool with a long-handled net.

Queenie sat herself tidily on the white leather sofa and gestured towards an armchair, where Shanti set down her bag and pulled out a notepad.

'You didn't bring your nice colleague?' said Queenie.

'DI Caine is involved with other inquiries.'

'A very polite young man. A good listener, too, which is a rare quality. I'll call for coffee if you want, but I'm hoping this won't take too long . . .'

'Let's get straight to business,' said Shanti. 'This may seem like an odd question, but could you tell me your mother's first name, Queenie? Ethan's grandmother, I mean.'

'You're right. It's a very odd question. I can't see what possible relevance it has . . . But you've just said it.'

'I'm sorry?'

'My mother's name was Queenie too. All the oldest girls are Queenie in our family, and always have been.'

'Oh.'

'You seem surprised.'

'Ethan didn't have, you know, a pet name for her?'

'He called her Nan.'

'Not Eve.'

'Now why would he call her Eve?'

'Just a possibility. The name doesn't mean anything to you?'

'Well, Eve was the first woman, wasn't she? She liked an apple or two . . . Ah! I think I might know where this is leading. It was in that song, wasn't it? That beautiful song I overheard. The lyrics were all about someone called Eve . . . *don't you grieve, darling Eve* . . . something like that.'

'That's correct.'

'But how would you know that? Have you heard the song?'

'I'm sorry, but at this stage I'm not at liberty to disclose that information.'

'And are you at liberty to disclose whether he came to you?'

'Whether who came to me?'

'Ethan. I felt he was afoot last night.'

'As you know, I'm not a believer, Mrs Flynn. But I will say that Ethan has been heavily present in my mind. And I do feel that solving this case will bring peace and closure to a lot of people. Ethan too, if it helps you to think that way.'

'Right, I'll tell you something I probably shouldn't. Tyrone has been turning the house upside down searching for that manuscript . . . I'm telling you this in confidence.'

'Absolutely.'

'I told him it wasn't his to take. But you know what brothers are like. They'll fight beyond the grave.'

'Mrs Flynn, can I ask you very directly: do you think Tyrone might have had something to do with his brother's death?'

There was a long pause. The man at the poolside finished his work, laid down the net, nodded at Queenie and went on his way. As the waters settled, Queenie glanced about to make sure they were alone. Then she answered quietly.

'I should be outraged at that suggestion. But I'd be lying if I said I hadn't considered it myself. Tyrone is so bitter. And he has hurt one or two people in the past.'

'I know that.'

'He scares me sometimes, I must admit. But no. I don't think he'd go that far. I think he knows that killing Ethan would kill his mammy too.'

'Perhaps there'll be an opportunity for me to talk with Tyrone later?'

'Oh, I don't think so. Tyrone's got a lot on his plate right now.'

'Of course, but—'

'And you swear you won't mention what I said? I'm sure there's nothing in it.'

'I won't say a thing, Mrs Flynn. But you can see why we need to question him. What is it he's so tied up with, if you don't mind me asking?'

'It's personal. A family matter. Nothing to do with Ethan.'

As she spoke, the peaceful atmosphere was shattered by those same blood-curdling shrieks, and the two peacocks came frantically cascading across the poolside, their beaks wide in alarm, feathers outspread in a fabulous fan of fear. A moment later, a half-open suitcase hurtled through the air and landed in the centre of the pool, so that the contents floated in every direction. Shanti saw capsized stilettos, drifting items of clothing, bobbing books, and pieces of jewellery, which slipped slowly to the bottom.

'You whore! You fookin' whore!' yelled Tyrone.

'Oh Lord, here we go!' said Queenie.

As Shanti watched in horror, a scene reminiscent of the *Expulsion from the Garden of Eden* took place in front of her. First Tyrone emerged, hauling cases, coats and boxes, which he flung towards the outer doors at the far end of the pool area. Then Ophelia appeared, so delicate of limb and yet so heavily pregnant she could barely walk. As before, her face was streaming with tears, but this time there was a defiance to her.

'Well now you know, you dreadful, dreadful little man!'

'I knew it all along, bitch. I've been watching you tie yourself in knots with your lies.'

'When did you know?'

'Three weeks or more. I'm not fookin' blind.'

He went back to gather more of Ophelia's possessions, which he tossed outside. But by now Shanti had grabbed her bag and was tearing around the poolside to where the altercation was taking place.

'Tyrone Flynn, let me warn you—'

'Ah, Jesus, here she is again, Miss Stick-Her-Fookin'-Nose-Where-It-Don't-Belong.'

'Tyrone,' yelled Queenie, rushing to join them. 'That's enough of that language in this house. The things you're saying to Ophelia are not acceptable.'

'But Mammy, she's a whore, a fookin' whore. There's no other word for it.'

'One more time, Tyrone, and the both of you will be out. Then maybe I'll get some peace to grieve.'

'Tell her. Tell her, you bitch . . .'

Ophelia pulled herself up to her full majestic ballet dancer's height, which was taller than everyone else present.

'I'm not ashamed of anything. Whatever I did, I was driven to by you, you utter beast.'

'Right! You've asked for it this time . . .'

'Tyrone Flynn, this is a formal warning,' said Shanti firmly. 'If I witness aggression or violence of any kind, then—'

'You mean violence like this?'

He seized Ophelia by the hair with his right hand, and raised his left fist.

'No. I mean violence like this . . .'

In one fluid movement, Shanti executed a classic ashi guruma, in which she seized Tyrone by the collar of his over-tight T-shirt, placed her right leg behind his shin, and then, using the rotation of arms and body, hurled him in a swinging motion into the water, where he landed with a mighty splash and promptly sank like a stone.

'Crikey!' said Ophelia.

'Oh Lord!' said Queenie. 'He can't swim. He'll drown . . .'

Shanti was not about to dive in after him, but she seized the net and poked it vaguely in his direction. In blind panic, he grabbed it and hauled himself to the surface, gasping for air in huge terrified gulps.

'Stop panicking, Tyrone,' she said. 'Put your hands on the edge and calm down.'

'I can't . . . I can't . . .'

'Now pull yourself along to the ladder. And for God's sake, calm down.'

He fumbled along the edge of the pool until he reached the aluminium ladder, where Shanti reached out to help him. As his foot found the step and his hand found the rail, she reached down and neatly clipped one end of the handcuffs to his wrist and the other to the aluminium tube.

'What? What the fook . . .?'

'You're fine there, Tyrone. Now be quiet for a moment. It isn't all about you, you know.'

Ophelia was grinning broadly. 'I say, that's damned impressive. Where did you learn that?'

'Are you OK, Ophelia? How's the baby?'

'Fine. I'm fine . . . we're both fine, thank you.'

'I'm glad.'

'Mammy,' wailed Tyrone. 'The baby, it's—'

'Yes,' said Ophelia. 'Ethan was the father of my child. He and I were lovers for ages. Far longer than you knew.'

Queenie buried her face in her hands. 'No!' she wailed. 'It can't be true.'

'It's what I've been tellin' you all along, Mam. She's a whore. And that bastard Ethan had it coming.'

'I will not have you speak ill of the dead . . .'

'It's hard to believe that utterly divine man was related to a Neanderthal like you,' sobbed Ophelia. 'He was . . . he was everything you will never be: cultured, caring, talented . . .'

'Look, will you unlock these fookin' things?' roared Tyrone.

'When I'm good and ready,' said Shanti, punching a couple of buttons on her phone.

'Benno, can I get some support at Villa del Flynn? Soon as you're able, there's a good chap.'

'Are you in immediate danger, boss?'

'Nothing I can't handle, but don't hang about.'

Still cuffed to the rail, Tyrone had managed to haul himself onto the pool side, where he lay squirming in a furious puddle of pulsating muscle and sodden clothing, yelling at the top of his voice: 'BOYS! BOYS! WILL YOU GET THE FOOK DOWN HERE?'

A moment later, Shanti heard the sound of clattering feet from far-flung corridors. Then three doorways opened simultaneously to reveal a mob of Flynns – the uncles, the nephews, the cousins.

'It was her,' moaned Tyrone, gesticulating at Shanti. 'The bitch tried to drown me.'

'Let's hope she's a good swimmer,' said one of the heavies, approaching her menacingly.

Shanti squared up to face him. 'Right, here's your warning – I'm a senior police officer. There's backup on the way, and if any one of you comes within a metre of me or Ophelia, you will be going down for a long, long time.'

'You think you scare us?' said the big man. 'We eat cops for breakfast.'

As one, they rushed her. Shanti ducked. Retreated. Fumbled vainly for pepper spray.

'Bloody hell!' called Ophelia.

Shanti felt many powerful arms grab her, but even as she shouted and struggled, she realised that she stood no chance. How would Mum feel, or Paul, when they saw her battered, bruised body swathed in plaster and bandages?

Then above the yells and oaths and threats came a shrill command.

'Nathan! Wayne! Daniel! Michael! Damon! Craig! Now you listen to me, and you listen good.' The small but solid form of Queenie Flynn confronted them, hands on hips. 'You turn around now and go back to your quarters. Then you sit and reflect. And think about this: every penny you have comes from me. This is my home you live in. It was me who turned those songs into gold, was it not?'

'It was, Queenie.'

'Without me, you'd be nothing. Nothing, do you hear? There's been enough violence and enough loss of life. The choice is simple. You behave in a decent Christian way, or you pack your bags and leave along with Ophelia. Is that clear?'

'Yes, Queenie.'

'Sorry, Queenie.'

They turned and filed out sheepishly.

'And as for you,' she said, looking down at her bedraggled son, 'if what you say about Ethan and *her* is true, there's no excusing it. It's against the laws of God and nature. But maybe you should take your share of the blame. I've seen the way you treat her. All that aggression – where did it come from, son? You never learnt that from me, nor your father, bless his immortal soul. It's not surprising she turned to a gentler man.'

She turned and walked away.

By the time Shanti had scooped Ophelia's possessions from the water and carried them together with her other belongings to the turning circle at the top of the drive, Benno and his team had arrived. Two in a squad car. Two in a van. With the blues and twos wailing.

'Sorry, boss. Traffic's a bit heavy.'

'Unfortunately you missed the climax, Benno, but you're just in time for the credits. You'll find Tyrone Flynn cuffed to a handrail by the swimming pool. He says he's a bit chilly.'

'Has he confessed?'

'As good as. I think his exact words were "that bastard Ethan had it coming".'

'I'm not sure if that's technically a confession.'

'Right, Benno, this is a little delicate . . .' They stepped discreetly out of earshot. 'See the pregnant lady? That's Tyrone's wife, Ophelia. Only she's carrying Ethan's baby.'

'Ouch.'

'It seems Tyrone has known about it for some time. So if we're looking for a classic motive, there it is. Add to that the grinding humiliation of a super-talented brother who overshadowed him in every way, and it's not surprising he felt a little emasculated.'

'Got you, boss.'

'But for the time being, I suggest we hold him for assault . . . or at least obstructing an officer in the execution of her duties. Then if you'd like to give him a gentle grilling, we'll see if he's ready to sing. Obviously he didn't work alone. He'd have needed help with the technical stuff. We've eliminated Sparky Mudget, right?'

'Wouldn't hurt a fly. Got a watertight alibi too – he was with his team the entire evening. Turns out the Spark1Up team double-check each other's work.'

'OK, then I guess we're looking for one of the Flynn family with technical knowledge.'

'I'll see what I can find out.'

'We'll also need a detailed search of Tyrone's rooms.'

'I'm on it, boss. By the way, where's Caine?'

'Oh yes, I'd forgotten about Caine. There was some talk of a glass of cider and returning a lost bike. Good old-fashioned community policing, Benno. Where would we be without it?'

As Tyrone was escorted kicking and raging towards the back of the van, he turned and glowered at Shanti and Ophelia.

'I'll fookin' sue you . . . both of you! You're ruined, you slags.'

'Don't worry,' said Shanti. 'It's natural for men who are frightened of women to behave in that way. Fortunately there won't be many women where he's going.'

When the van had departed down the curving drive of Villa del Flynn, they stood waiting for Ophelia's taxi.

'I know what you're thinking,' she sniffed. 'Why did I marry him in the first place?'

'I did wonder.'

'I know it's hard to believe, but Tyrone can charm the pants off you when he wants to. When we first met, he seemed so self-assured. He flattered me and . . . yes, he was wealthy too.'

'I was unhappily married myself, Ophelia, so I understand all of that . . . well, maybe not the wealthy part.'

'Besides, I loved Stigma's music. But here's the thing – Tyrone deceived me. He turned everything back to front. He painted a picture of himself as the talented one. He claimed that Ethan had always been in his shadow, and that he had generously helped him. He used to boast that it was him who had written all the songs, but he let Ethan take the glory because he felt sorry for him. Whereas the exact opposite was true. Tyrone was often credited for those songs, but that was simply Ethan's benevolence. After we were married, I began to realise that it was Ethan who created everything. He *was* Stigma. Tyrone contributed nothing.'

'Maybe we can afford to be a little charitable, Ophelia. I've always thought it was the contrast between their personalities that made the music unique. Ethan's soulful lyricism, Tyrone's thumping bass. Sort of yin and yang, if you know what I mean. Tender love songs, but with that heavy bass groove.'

'Crikey. You've really studied this.'

'Just part of the job. Did Tyrone ever talk about killing Ethan?'

'Absolutely. Almost all the time. But then he talked about killing everyone – me included.'

'And me too, no doubt. But you never heard him discussing specific plans? Tampering with the stage electrics, for example?'

'Honestly, I spent as little time with the man as I could. And every possible moment with Ethan. The one thing I know is that since Ethan's death, Tyrone has been completely obsessed with finding a particular song. It's been driving him nuts. I thought it was rather amusing to see him getting so steamed up . . . and I hope he never does find it, because it doesn't belong to him.'

'I probably shouldn't do this, Ophelia, but I think it's only fair to tell you that I have found that song. If it belongs to anyone, it's you and your child.'

'Crikey, did you really? Look, that's awfully kind, but I don't want it.'

'It could be worth a lot of money.'

'I don't care about money. Ethan provided well for our future. It was typical of him.'

'Well, if you change your mind . . .'

'Here comes my taxi. Listen, thank you for everything, Inspector. You know, the more I think about it, the more I believe that song belongs to everyone who loved Ethan. I'd like to give it freely to the world. Would you see to that for me? It's what he would have wanted.'

'And what about you?'

'I'm going to try to build a life for our child and me. I know Ethan would want that too.'

'I'm sure he would. Do you have somewhere to stay?'

'I'm very fortunate – Mummy has a house in Hampshire. And Daddy has property in Notting Hill. They'll look after me. They always do.'

'I'm glad you've got support. I'm afraid there will be more questions, but they can probably wait until after the birth. When's it due?'

'Tuesday officially, though I felt a few twinges today. Do you have children, Inspector?'

'A boy. Paul. He's nearly nine. Quite a handful, but I love him to bits.'

'That's wonderful. Ours will be a little girl.'

'Nice. And do you have a name for her?'

'Eve. We thought we'd call her Eve.'

## *Chapter 28*

# A Half-Built House

It had been many years since Caine had ridden a bike. The Yamaha WR250R that Molly lent him took a bit of getting used to.

'It's an awesome machine,' she had said. 'Great on or off road. That engine can take a right thrashing.'

Caine took it steady down the narrow gap between the two rows of traffic, but after a few miles he began to get the hang of it, and as the traffic thinned, he opened the throttle, feeling the thrill of the g-force in his body, and the wind whipping his shirt.

Deep inside the helmet, behind the snarling engine, a song obsessed him, and those enigmatic lyrics repeated endlessly:

*Sleepy creature of the sacred dome*
*Spread your wings, it's time to fly from home*
*Between us lies the ever-breathing sea*
*Big waves crying – our love can never be*

As he reached the outskirts of the village, he entered a flood plain where cows grazed mournfully on reedy islands surrounded by sluggish dykes. On the other side of the road he noticed something of interest. He slowed, crossed the carriageway and drove the bike onto the grassy verge, then killed the engine and unbuckled the helmet.

A road sign was mounted on the bank above a murky channel. It read: *KILTON WELCOMES CAREFUL DRIVERS*. But what made it unusual was a huge bunch of oversized metal roses, twisted artfully around the pole. Each giant thorn and petal had been studded with red solar lights, like tears of blood. It was a forlorn tribute to the victim of a road accident.

Caine was about to resume his journey when the phone began to ring in his shoulder bag. By the time he had located it, the ringing had stopped. And when he finally got through to Shanti, she sounded more than a little pleased with herself.

'Sorry, Caine, were you levitating?'

'Feet firmly on the ground, Shanti. Is everything OK?'

'All done and dusted. I've had a busy morning, but Tyrone's in custody and I've even identified the mysterious Eve ... It wasn't Ethan's granny, as you so foolishly suggested.'

'Eve is Ophelia's baby. Am I right?'

'Damn you, Caine. But you'll never guess the father ...'

'I've been wondering if it was Ethan.'

'Double damn you. Anyway, I've been looking at those pretentious lyrics, and I must admit they make a little more sense now. The sacred dome and all that.'

'Yeah, it's spooky when you think about it – a love song from a dead father to his unborn daughter ... *Between us lies the ever-breathing sea ...*'

'What's the ever-breathing sea?'

'Life, I suppose.'

'Right.'

'I've had the tune in my head all day. It's hauntingly beautiful.'

'I need you to promise you won't sing it to me. Now or at any time.'

'Scout's honour.'

'Anyway, one way or another, the case is falling neatly into place. I'm finishing up at Villa del Flynn, then I'll head back to Unworthy for my Sunday roast, which I think I deserve. Primrose is doing roast parsnips, which are a bit of a favourite. Where are you?'

'Oh, I'm tidying up a few loose ends in Kilton. Shouldn't take long.'

'Well, I feel I've been a bit mean to you this week, so I've got a special treat lined up for tonight . . . You're welcome. Laters.'

'Shant . . .? Shanti . . .?'

Caine remounted, replaced the helmet and booted up the engine. After a couple of miles he came to a well-hidden turning on the right, where he swung the bike along a heavily potholed single-track lane – all just as Molly had described.

'The place you're looking for is at the top of the track amongst the trees,' she had said. 'It's a magical spot. I know it pretty well 'cos there's a cross-country bike trail up that way.'

'That's very helpful, Molly.'

'My pleasure. I can't guarantee he'll be there today, but it's where he hangs out whenever he has a spare moment. Not that you'd know it from the progress he's made.'

Caine bounced along the rutted track for half a mile, noticing how nimbly the bike handled the uneven surface. At last he reached a grassy glade surrounded by birch trees, again exactly as Molly described. And suddenly, there it was – the unfinished frame of a house on a little hill.

It was clear that the building project had been long abandoned. The A-shaped roof trusses, which crowned a rectangle of block walls, were stained with moss and algae. Caine saw eyeless window frames. A rusting cement mixer. A lonely wheelbarrow.

He silenced the engine and parked the Yamaha on its stand alongside a red quad bike.

In the centre of the skeletal house stood a stack of cement blocks. And on top of the blocks sat a solitary figure with a cloud of blonde curls.

'Molly?' he said.

As Caine's head popped free of the tight helmet, he saw Blackmore lurch in surprise.

'It's all right, Gavin. Molly lent me the bike. She said I might find you here.'

Caine strapped the helmet to the bike and walked up the slope. Now that his ears were free of the roar, a comfortable silence descended like a blanket. And one by one, the birds resumed their chatter in the trees.

At the top of the half-built steps, he paused by the empty door frame.

'May I come in?'

'There's nothing to stop you. Everyone else comes in. Kids from the village and all manner of wildlife.'

'It's your place, Gavin. I wouldn't come in without asking.'

'You're police, aren't you?' Blackmore said.

Caine stepped across the cement floor, where large puddles reflected drifting clouds.

'Sunday's my day off,' he said, taking a seat beside the mournful man. 'And I'll let you in on a secret – I'm only half a cop anyway.'

'What's that mean?'

'It means I sometimes wish I could do something different with my time. Something practical, like you're doing here.'

'I haven't lifted a brick in years.'

Caine opened his bag, pulled out a flask and set two mugs on the blocks between them.

'Would you like some tea?'

'No, ta. You're all right.'

'I'll pour one anyway in case you change your mind. It's certainly a lovely spot, Gavin.'

'It's where I come to think.'

'I get that. And I'm sorry to disturb you.'

'What you doing here then?'

'I think we've found something of yours and I want to give it back.'

Gavin recoiled. 'What've you found?'

'I'll tell you in a minute. There's no hurry. First I want to ask you something. On the way over, I noticed something . . . something beautiful and a little sad. Was that Carole's memorial? The metal roses by the roadside? I'm sorry, I don't want to upset you.'

'How do you know about all that?' he said, tears leaping to his eyes.

'Primrose and Vowles told me. They showed me a photo of you all together. She was a beauty, Gavin.'

A fat tear rolled down Blackmore's cheek. 'This was gonna be our home.'

'I know,' said Caine gently. And handed him some tea.

The slogan on Caine's mug said: *Buddhist of the Year.*

The slogan on Gavin's mug said: *Three things cannot be long hidden – the sun, the moon and the truth.*

Sipping his tea, Caine remembered another forest, long ago and far away. Old man Tu had talked about the contrasting ways in which people experienced silence. 'For one person, silence may be like the company of an old friend. For another, it is a painful eternity. Maybe they feel lonely. Anxious. Afraid. It's the same forest. It's the same silence. Only the mind is different. Only the conscience.'

So it was that Caine sat peaceably and waited, while Blackmore shuffled and squirmed and suffered.

Eventually he said, 'Look, why are we sitting here? You're not saying anything. It's doing my head in.'

'Just enjoying the moment. Was that a woodpecker? A flash of red and green. I suppose it's a perfect habitat.'

'What is it you want from me?'

'Vowles told me he was your guardian. He said he looked after you when you were young.'

Blackmore bristled. 'Looked after me? Controlled me, more like!'

'In what way, Gavin?'

'No. I've said too much already.'

Once again silence fell. Once again Blackmore shifted. Anxious. Agitated. Tortured. And once again Caine waited.

'I lived all my childhood under his roof. On his farm. Under his rules.'

'But you went away to study.'

'That's true. When I was eighteen, I got a place at Exeter College. It was a new world. I saw what other people my age were doing. I learned a trade. And best of all, I met Carole. We went travelling together, all over the world; I saw places I'd never dreamed of.'

With the words, the tears flowed freely. Caine laid a hand softly on his arm.

'Where did you go?'

'New Zealand, Australia, Indonesia, you name it . . .'

'Thailand?'

'Yes, there too. When we came back, my eyes had been opened. We saved up and bought this plot of land. We wanted a family . . .' He dissolved into sobs.

'Vowles told me what happened to Carole. I'm truly sorry.'

'Did he? Did he really? And what did he say?'

'He told me about the night you got engaged. He said that Carole got in her car but she'd had too much to drink. He said that she drove into the dyke, and he tried to rescue her but it was too late.'

Gavin leapt to his feet. 'He's wrong to blame Carole!'

'So tell me what happened.'

He began pacing about the open-air house.

'Can't say.'

'Why not?'

''Cos you're police.'

'But I'm also a human being. I want to help.'

'So you promise not to tell?'

'I can't make that promise, Gavin. But a wiser person than me said, "The truth will set you free."'

'Maybe. And maybe it'll put me in a prison cell. But I don't care any more. I can't stand it any longer. I'll go crazy if I do. It was . . . it was me at the wheel that night. We'd both drunk too much, but I felt I could handle anything. I'd never felt so sure of myself as I did that night, once she said she'd marry me. I said I'd drive her back to her mum and dad's. I was a good driver. I was sure I'd be OK. And it wasn't far. It was me who lost control of the car, and me who drove into the flooded dyke . . .'

Once the silent man began to talk, he couldn't stop.

'I reckon I was knocked unconscious . . . I can't remember. It was the water that woke me. Icy it was. My legs were numb. I looked for her on the passenger seat but all I saw was the top of her hair. It was too late. She'd slipped under and drowned. I killed her.'

'So Vowles was never there?'

'Oh, he was there. He was out ratting with the dog and he pulled me from the wreckage. I was devastated. Ranting and raving on the roadside. I wanted to call the police, but Vowles stopped me. He said I was a bloody fool. He said the first thing they'd do was breathalyse me, and I'd spend years of my life rotting in jail for what I'd done. He convinced me there was another way. He said we should drag her into the driver's seat, make it look like she was alone at the wheel. It was the hardest thing I've ever done. We floated her poor dead body to the other side. Even forced her hands onto the wheel. I should never have agreed. And I've regretted it every minute since. That's why I come up here. To sit and think what might have been.'

'My heart goes out to you, Gavin,' said Caine, screwing the lid on the flask and putting it back in the bag with the mugs.

'Afterwards, Vowles had even more of a hold over me. He gave me work, but I was always in his debt. I had to pay him rent and he never, ever let up about what I had done. If I dared to speak up, he'd pretend he was going to call the police and tell Carole's family what I'd done.'

'But didn't you realise that Vowles was culpable too?'

'What's that mean?'

'It means that he lied to the police. He broke the law too. He covered up a death.'

Gavin stared up through the cage of his roof at the trees. And then it was as if something snapped.

'All those years!' he raged. 'All those fucking years!'

'You were young. He was your guardian. Don't be too hard on yourself. He exploited you.'

'I thought losing Carole was the worst thing that could ever happen. Who knew there could be so many layers of hell?'

Gavin paced up and down, clawing at his curls. Then suddenly he stopped and stared wide-eyed at Caine.

'You said you'd found something of mine and you wanted to give it back.'

'We found your bike. The black one with the pannier.'

His face twisted and turned through a multiplicity of emotions. Confusion. Comprehension. Disbelief. Fear. And then . . . rage.

'I'm . . . going . . . to . . . get . . . him . . .' he muttered through gritted teeth.

Before Caine could rise from the blocks, Blackmore had dived through the non-existent wall, hurtled down the slope, leapt onto his quad bike and fired up the engine. In seconds, he was a red roar of rage, racing through the trees towards the open fields beyond.

Caine bounded after him, plunging down the slope and mounting the Yamaha, which he kicked into action. Revving the throttle, he accelerated at such speed that the front wheel rose from the ground, sending an arcing fan of mud in his wake.

Gavin was almost out of the forest, driving recklessly on a well-used dirt trail, which snaked up and down through thick pools of mud, over roots and fallen branches. He thundered through an open gate into a field, where the machine accelerated over dense grass.

The quad bike was made for this terrain, and Blackmore was an experienced driver. On Molly's bike, Caine slithered and teetered precariously, almost falling as he took the bends. As he entered the field, he felt the wheels lurch and spin beneath him, and it took all his concentration to stay upright.

Blackmore was already a quarter of a mile ahead, standing half upright on the speeding vehicle. Without the helmet, Caine felt dangerously vulnerable, but there was no time to think. No time to pause. All he could do was follow the aggressive red dot in the distance as it climbed the sloping field to another gateway.

This gate was closed, but it took Gavin only seconds to dismount and haul it aside before hurtling into the next field, where a flock of sheep scattered before his raging wheels.

With hair flying, Caine gave chase as fast as the motorbike would allow, which was considerably faster than his nerves could stand. He glanced at the speedometer and saw the needle push past 40 . . . 45 . . . to 50 mph. As he reached the top of the field, he found himself standing fully upright, and from this vantage point he could see the quad bike rocketing towards a cluster of buildings in the distance.

'Unworthy Farm,' he muttered.

He slowed for a second, just long enough to wipe the spatters of mud from his eyes, and then he was off again, but as he entered the next field, the petrified sheep rushed towards him in blind panic. Suddenly there was a bustling confusion of leaping livestock and hot steel in the narrow gateway. As Caine swerved to avoid the struggling mass, he slammed on the brakes and his body parted company with the seat before soaring majestically over the handlebars. The woolly backs of the bleating flock broke his fall as the riderless bike careered into a ditch, and Vincent Caine found himself crowd-surfing sheep.

## *Chapter 29*

# The Savage Noose

In the dining room at Unworthy Farm, Shanti savoured the aroma of roast beef and gravy. The huge table was only a quarter full, as many of the stars had already performed and departed.

'You got a motherfuckin' nerve coming here,' said Sista Tremble at her side.

'Are those roast potatoes?' asked Shanti.

'Didn't you hear what I said?'

'Yes, I heard you. And I've got three pieces of good news for you, Sista.'

'Oh yeah?'

'If you pass the potatoes, I'll tell you. And the parsnips too. So, in order of excitement, I can confirm that the Pyramid Stage has been signed off. At this very moment, Sparky Mudget and the festival team are setting up for your gig tonight.'

'OK, that's good. That's two exciting things, so you get the potatoes.'

'Thank you. And the parsnips?'

'You said three things . . .'

'I did. Even though you were spectacularly rude to me in the execution of my duties, I think you are a truly great artist.'

'I appreciate that and I apologise for what I said. I had a bad headache that day. I have no idea what they put in the wine in this place.'

'I had a headache too. I accept your apology. Now, what do you make of this?' Shanti handed over a slip of paper.

Amongst the celebrities around the table there was considerable interest in what Sista was staring at.

'Ho-oly fuckin' motherfuck! Is this what I think it is?'

'It's Ethan's last work, "Song for Eve". Eve is his baby daughter, who is due any day now.'

'Why, this is beyond extraordinary! I'm sorry, what was your name?'

'Shanti Joyce. DI Shanti Joyce.'

'Well, DI Shanti Joyce, I will never forget this moment. *Spread your wings, it's time to fly from home* . . . That is truly beautiful.'

'If you can do something with it, Sista, I think Ethan would be very happy. The song was his parting gift to the world.'

Shanti turned her full attention to the steaming plate before her. But as she was about to take the first bite of crisp potato and succulent beef, a roaring like a jet plane shattered the silence outside.

'What the motherfuck . . .?' yelled Sista.

'Oh my heart!' groaned Marcel Snapper.

Shanti rushed to the window in time to see a quad bike spiralling to a halt and Gavin Blackmore sprinting towards the kitchen door, yanking a length of electric cable from his pocket.

He had mud all over his clothes. And murder all over his face.

'Holy smoke!' said Shanti, throwing down her serviette and tearing from the room.

As she hurtled along the flagstone corridors, the farmhouse echoed with Boner's howls.

Kicking open the door, she burst into the kitchen, where Gavin was efficiently throttling Vowles with the cable as Primrose hauled at his arm and Boner fastened himself to his leg.

'I'm . . . going . . . to . . . kill . . . you . . .' declared the farm-hand.

'After everything he's done for you, Gavin Blackmore!' screeched Primrose.

'Your husband ruined my life!' he yelled, hauling the cable ever tighter.

Apart from the snowy eyebrows, Vowles had turned the hue of a varicose vein. His mouth was a devilish cartoon of horror and fear. His tiny eyes bulged.

Shanti dived past the kitchen table, where stacks of bowls and tubs of Unworthy Ices sat ready for transportation to the dining room. She seized Gavin's wiry arms and after a consider-able struggle managed to fling him backwards against the Aga, with the dog still clamped firmly to one leg.

'Gavin Blackmore,' she panted, 'I'm arresting you for actual bodily harm and . . . and other things too. You don't have to say anything, but anything you do say . . .'

Vowles had collapsed choking onto the table, where Primrose was frantically unravelling the cable from his throat. Once he was free, he collapsed backwards into his chair and gasped, 'W-w-water . . .!'

Shanti thought about the handcuffs in her bag in the dining room, but made a swift judgement that they would not be necessary. Blackmore, who had finally freed himself from the dog, looked absolutely depleted.

'He made me do it,' he sobbed.

'Do what, Gavin?' asked Shanti.

'Everything. So many bad things. I told everything to your partner.'

'You told Caine?'

'Gavin's not in his right mind,' said Primrose. 'Never been right since the tragedy, has he, Vowles? After all we've done for him. It's a disgrace.' She handed her husband a tumbler of water – 'You're welcome, I'm sure.'

'Right, everybody calm down,' ordered Shanti. 'I'm going to call an ambulance and a couple more officers.'

'There's no need for that!' croaked Vowles like a parched man in a desert. 'I'm all right now. You call a psychiatrist – that's what we need round 'ere. Should be in a straitjacket, he should.'

As she escorted Gavin to a chair a safe distance from Vowles, Shanti heard the rumble of an approaching motorbike in the yard. After a moment the door was flung open and Caine burst into the room.

'Damn it, Caine. Can't you stay clean for a single day?'

'Shanti, are you OK?'

'I'm fine. A little confused.'

As Boner leapt joyfully into Caine's arms, Shanti advised Vowles and Blackmore that as she was about to question them formally, she would need to deliver a formal caution.

At that moment, Seth Vowles shuffled in wearing a faded

Arctic Monkeys T-shirt and a baggy tracksuit, rubbing the sleep from his eyes.

'What's for breakfast?' he said.

Primrose exploded. 'Breakfast! We're halfway through lunch, and your father's been near murdered while you were out for the count. See that trolley? You go through and see if our guests have finished. Clear the dinner plates and make yourself useful. It's time things changed around here.'

Shocked at his mother's reaction, the skinny boy with the tousled red Mohican did what he was told.

'Perhaps you'd better sit down too, Primrose,' said Caine. 'I'll make us all some tea, if you don't mind. And Gavin, I wonder if you'd kindly tell my colleague what you told me.'

'I . . . I don't know where to begin . . .'

'Why don't you start with your engagement to Carole? I believe it was a dark and stormy night . . .'

# *Chapter 30*

# A Kitchen Confessional

'Everythin' he says is a lie,' said Vowles. 'All I ever done is help him.'

'So you weren't present when Carole died?' asked Caine

'Oh, I were present. I hauled Gavin out the car, otherwise we'd have had two bodies that night.'

'But you realise this contradicts what you told us only this morning? You clearly stated that you discovered Carole alone in the car.'

'You must have disremembered.'

'So it wasn't your idea to drag Carole into the driver's seat?'

'Never.'

'You liar,' said Gavin. 'You planned the whole thing – though you made me carry it out. And you've used it to control me ever since.'

'Oh Gavin. How can you say that?' wailed Primrose. 'Vowles has been like a father to you.'

Blackmore stared at her in disbelief.

'Look, this is all terrible,' said Shanti. 'But these are historic issues. I'll obviously ask my colleagues on the local force to look into your story, but my job is to gather information about the death of Ethan Flynn.'

'I think you'll find that the two matters are connected,' said Caine.

Four pairs of eyes turned to him.

'Gavin, I'd like to ask you something,' said Caine. 'You were a student at Exeter College, isn't that correct? A higher apprenticeship, if I'm not mistaken, which combines an academic element with practical training.'

'Caine,' groaned Shanti. 'In what way is this relevant?'

'What subject did you study, Gavin?' continued Caine.

A long silence.

'OK, well maybe I should answer that for you. All it took was one call to the college to find out. Your subject was electrical engineering, isn't that correct?'

Blackmore hung his head.

'Jeez!' gasped Shanti. 'Are you suggesting . . .?'

'I think it's better if it comes from Gavin,' said Caine.

'I don't know where this is leading,' said Vowles. 'But five minutes ago this feller tried to choke the life out of me with a length of cable. You saw it with yer own eyes. So why don't you do what you're paid to do and take him away, an' leave me an' Primrose in peace?'

'Because I believe you were involved, Mr Vowles,' said Caine.

'Nonsense. You're all mad.'

'Today is the tenth anniversary of your mother's death, isn't that right?'

'What of it? You leave my mother out o' this.'

'I'm sorry, Caine,' said Shanti. 'I'm really struggling . . .'

'The thing is, Shanti, ten years ago to the day, Stigma headlined on the Pyramid Stage. The Flynn twins were only nineteen – that's right, isn't it, Mr Vowles?'

'What do I know?'

'Tell me about that night.'

'My old mother had a heart attack. That's the long and short of it.'

Gavin Blackmore's face was sickly pale. 'He knows, Vowles. Can't you see that? He's cleverer than the three of us put together.'

'Three of us?' squawked Primrose. 'Don't go blaming me for nothing. All I do is cook and clean. I done my share for you too, young Blackmore.'

'I've got one thing to say,' said Vowles. 'If you're trying to accuse me of murdering Ethan Flynn, then you're as mad as Blackmore. You sit 'ere in my kitchen . . . in the Vowles kitchen, what has been in this family for centuries, an' you accuse me of some sort o' dastardly deed. Well, 'ere's some information for you, young man. Jes' so's you know, I ain't never been on that festival site in all my days. An' I don't want to neither. So don't you dare go accusin' me of what happened to that lad. I were down the Five 'Eads when it 'appened, an' there's twenty or more can testify—'

'He's doing it again,' said Blackmore. 'He's making me responsible for his crimes.'

'You mind yer mouth, young Blackmore. It was you that killed Carole. All I ever tried to do was save your neck. I kept your secret all these years, but now it's out an' I can't protect you no more.'

'All right, Mr Vowles,' said Caine. 'It doesn't look like we're going to get much cooperation from you, so I'm going to talk to Gavin for a while. Gavin, I think you realise that I know what happened. It's all over, my friend. But if you work with us, then I will make sure that it goes on record that you are a man of honour, who was pressurised into taking part in certain events—'

'Don't you bloody dare, Blackmore.'

'No. That's enough, Uncle,' said Blackmore, placing both hands squarely on the table and staring directly at Vowles. 'This man, Vincent Caine, said something to me earlier. He said "the truth will set you free". Well, you know what? I can feel that already. At long last I can hear voices other than yours. I can hear Carole begging me to tread the right path. You bullied me and I felt I had no choice. But now I do. Even if I spend the rest of my days behind bars, at least I'll be free of you.'

'Could someone please explain?' said Shanti.

'It all started with the farm,' said Caine. 'As Mr Vowles keeps pointing out, his family have lived here for generations. They were all successful, weren't they, Vowles? Until you took the helm.'

''Ang on. Jes' you 'ang on. That's not my fault. I did my best. You blame the supermarkets for that. They shaft you, they do. Then that damned festival come along. Everything were fine till then.'

'Oh Vowles, you're saying too much,' said Primrose.

'Your mother had a special place in Kilton, didn't she?' said Caine.

'She did. She were respected.'

'I'm sure she was. But she was also the founder of KATFAT.'

'KATFAT?' said Shanti.

'Kilton Against The Festival And That,' said Caine.

'My mother was an upstanding woman. That festival is a vipers' pit – a den of Sodom. It ruins lives, you know?'

'I understand. Change is always hard,' said Caine. 'However, the festival has brought pleasure to many millions, and perhaps it hasn't been all bad for the village. After all, you have a house full of wealthy guests.'

'Degenerates! Every last one o' them.'

'Vowles! Enough!' hissed Primrose.

'You loved your mother,' continued Caine. 'I appreciate that. So it's understandable that you felt the festival contributed to her ill health.'

'Contributed! It bloody killed her.'

'How so?'

'The night she were taken ill . . .'

'Ten years ago to the day.'

'. . . that band . . . that . . . Stigma were playin'. She got herself more an' more worked up. All that racket! That infernal din! I pleaded with her. "Mother, it ain't worth it," I said.'

'I gave her cotton wool,' whispered Primrose. 'So she could stuff her ears.'

'But it weren't no use. When she collapsed, I called the ambulance an' . . . an' . . .'

'Don't get yourself upset now, dear.'

'It got caught up in the damn traffic. There was no chance o' them getting' through. I held her in my arms until . . .'

'Your mother was old,' said Gavin. 'My Carole was in her prime.'

'And that's what turned you, wasn't it, Vowles?' said Caine.

'I'm saying nothin'.'

'Then I'll finish it,' said Gavin. 'He had a grudge the size of the Tor against the festival and against Stigma in particular, ain't that right, Uncle? It was that song, "While My Guitar Gently Kills", that they played that night. You heard it everywhere back then.'

'And it became the soundtrack to your loss?' mused Caine.

'No comment.'

'One festival night,' continued Gavin, 'we were sitting in here – me, Vowles and Primrose—'

'Don't you bring me into this,' said Primrose icily.

'It was like every sound from the festival and the bedrooms was driving you mad, wasn't it, Uncle?'

'Lies. All lies.'

'*Thud! Thud! Thud!* it went. Do you remember? *Thud! Thud! Thud!* That night, you vowed to undermine and destroy Glastonbury Festival. And it grew, didn't it, Uncle? It became an obsession . . . a mania, you might say! So when you heard that Stigma had re-formed and that they'd been booked to perform on the tenth anniversary of your mother's death, that's when you thought of murder.'

'You're mad. Madder than I thought.'

'Thing is, I have an excellent memory, Uncle Vowles. I recall every last word. You said, "Gavin, you're a clever young chap . . . speaking hypothetically now, would it be possible to electrocute a musician on stage?"'

'I never said that.'

'Oh, but you did. And I remember my answer. I said, "Hypothetically, yes." But I told you about all the checks and balances that would be in place to stop that happening. And how did you reply, Uncle?'

'As I never said none of it, I don't s'pose I replied at all.'

'You said, "Ah, but hypothetically speaking, a clever young chap with a qualification in electrical engineering could find a way around those checks and balances?" And I thought it was just a game. So I said, "Hypothetically, yes, Uncle. But you'd still need to make sure the current wasn't impeded." "Oh," you said. "And how would that work?" You remember this game, Uncle?'

'Not a word of it.'

'I said, "Well, hypothetically, water helps a current to flow." And the idea hatched, didn't it, Uncle? And then, as the months drew on, I began to realise it wasn't a game at all. I told you I could never do such a thing. And what did you say?'

Vowles stared at the swirling wood grain of the tabletop.

'Well,' continued Gavin, 'first you said what you always say, that if I didn't cooperate, you would tell everyone that I'd killed Carole in such a terrible way. And I said, "Do it, then. I've nothing else to lose." That was the stick, Uncle. Then you tried the carrot. You asked me when I'd been happiest, and I said, "You know when it was – when I was travelling with Carole." That's when you said you'd buy me air tickets and hand back my passport if I just did this one thing.'

'Is this really true?' asked Shanti. 'It sounds like—'

'Like slavery?' said Blackmore. 'That's exactly what it was. One way or another, I found myself trapped into planning this terrible, terrible thing. And it all fell into place, didn't it, Uncle? Those nights in the pub when Medusa Cole was going on about the costumes—'

'It was you who broke into her shop?' asked Shanti in disbelief.

'Uncle Vowles couldn't get in on account of his gammy leg. But he gave me a push up, didn't you?'

'Never been near the place.'

'I was shitting myself,' admitted Blackmore. 'But I thought it was my only way out. I did my homework – watched endless YouTube videos of bands playing; worked out how I might deliver a shock big enough to bring one of them down. I didn't plan to kill him. I swear it. Just enough to get Vowles off my back so I could leave for ever.'

'And last Wednesday . . .?'

'I put the costume in my pannier and cycled down to the turnstiles, just as we'd planned. I couldn't take the bike on site, I knew that, so I carried the costume in a white carrier bag, along with a few tools and cable.'

'And as a villager, you had a pass to the festival,' said Shanti. 'But how did you get backstage? That VIP area is guarded round the clock.'

'You tell her, Uncle.'

'Tell her what? There's nothing to tell. It's all fantasy.'

'Seth had a backstage pass,' said Gavin. 'Everyone in the football team got one in exchange for grunt labour. Vowles slipped it back the next day, and Seth never even noticed, the dozy idiot.'

'So then you walked backstage . . .?' said Caine.

'I was bricking it. I put the costume on first, in one of the toilets. I was convinced I'd get caught, and almost hoping I would. But when I walked up to the VIP area dressed as Death, the security team must have thought I was one of the dancers, 'cos they just waved me through. I knew there was a ten-minute slot when the Pyramid was empty – I'd done my homework – so it was now or never. I walked up onto that stage, in front of all those thousands of people. It felt unreal. Like a dream, or a nightmare. It was dark at the back of the stage. I set to work on the amp that was connected to Excalibur, rejigging it so it would deliver two hundred and forty volts direct to the guitar. I even brought a bottle so I could squirt water on the floor. Added a little washing-up liquid to make it more conductive. It came from over there . . .' He nodded at the detergent bottle on the windowsill behind the sink.

'You really thought of everything, didn't you, Gavin?' said Shanti.

'I had to. I thought I'd never be free if I didn't.'

'So what happened afterwards?' asked Caine softly.

Gavin's face was so pale it appeared translucent. 'I couldn't get down those steps fast enough.'

'Which was when Misty spotted him,' muttered Shanti to Caine.

'I rushed straight back to that toilet and removed the mask and the costume. I rolled them up and shoved them in the bag with the tools. I thought about dumping it in a bin on site – there were plenty there – but I figured everyone would be looking out for that costume and it would have my DNA all over it – I was that sweaty, you see. So I took it with me, intending to set fire to the bloody thing. I got off the site all right. Picked up my bike, shoved the bag in the pannier and set off up the lane. Then suddenly there were police cars everywhere. I panicked and pushed the bike into the bushes. I meant to go back and get it, but the area was always crawling with police.'

'You're a bloody idiot is what you are,' spat Vowles.

'But I swear to you, I never thought Ethan would die. I'd

done so much homework. A shock like that should have stunned him. Knocked him flat, maybe … but … but … ' The tears streamed down his handsome face. 'It was Vowles who broke the news of his death. He'd seen it on the TV in the pub. He was mad with happiness.'

'Now you gone too far … '

'I was horrified at what I'd done. I begged him for my passport and the tickets, but he said it would be too obvious if I left straight away. You lied to me yet again,' snapped Gavin, and he lurched across the table, sending his uncle cowering into the corner and the dog into a snarling frenzy.

As Caine peeled them apart, Shanti made a call to Benno.

## *Chapter 31*

# I Scream Sunday

Two hours later, as Dawn Knightly's white-suited SOCO team swarmed over Unworthy Farm like bees around a hive, Shanti and Caine emerged into the sunshine from the unlovely Vowles bungalow.

An initial search had revealed little of interest, except Blackmore's passport concealed at the back of a drawer, and the sad tip of Seth's Mohican, protruding from the bed where he had returned to hibernation.

Caine marvelled at the way Shanti took control. She was like a movie director, calmly coordinating a dozen details.

A group of investigators had been dispatched to search the worker's cottage that Gavin rented from his uncle on the outskirts of the farm.

A team of dog handlers began to work their way through the barns and outbuildings. One of them had undertaken the tricky task of relocating Boner to a local kennel.

Shanti, who had already cleared her belongings from the

Lilac Suite, instructed a couple of uniforms to remove any vehicles not directly relevant to the proceedings. This included Shanti's own car, which they moved to the emergency vehicle area on the festival site.

Near the front door, in a state of manic hypertension, Primrose Vowles was seeing off the last of her illustrious boarders. Their drivers, agents and minders had arrived to collect them like wealthy parents at a boarding school.

'The hell I'm gonna pay for extra electricity,' Sista Tremble roared. 'If this place wasn't so goddam cold, I wouldn't need no heaters. Do you have any idea who I am?'

'Oh, everyone knows who you are,' said Primrose coldly. 'Sister Snooty Fat-Arse Tremble. But I'm not trembling no more. No. And I'll never launder your oversized underclothing again.'

It seemed that the latest developments had reached the pricked ears of the press. Near the back gate, which opened onto the yard, Dunster and Spalding – now restored to full uniform – were remonstrating with a pack of excitable newshounds, who had ducked beneath the tape at the foot of Totterdown Hill.

As the stable door from the kitchen opened, a dozen cameras swung towards Gavin Blackmore, who was being led to a waiting van. Beneath his cherubic curls, he wore an expression of benevolent calm.

As he passed, he raised his handcuffed palms, as if in prayer, and nodded respectfully at Caine.

In a considerably more agitated state, Vowles was also led outside in handcuffs. The pair of officers who accompanied him to the squad car towered over the irate man.

'Don't you hear it?' he yelled. "That infernal music! *Thud! Thud! Thud!* It's enough to drive anyone out of their mind!'

He was right. Behind the turmoil in the yard was the persistent throb of the festival. For the first time all week, Shanti realised that she had become habituated to the din, and it troubled her no more.

'Where do you want him, boss?' asked Benno.

'Sit him in the back of the car to cool off. He'll be fine so long as someone stays with him. In fact I'd like to keep both Vowles and Primrose on the premises until we've completed the searches.'

Caine handed Shanti a coffee, and they stood with their backs against the stuccoed walls of the bungalow, which pulsated with blue lights.

She should be happy. The cards had been kind. The riddle of Ethan's death had been solved. His killers had been apprehended. And yet Shanti Joyce felt frustrated.

'I think you can begin to relax now,' said Caine. 'You caught your killer. From the first moment, you vowed to crack this case before the end of the festival, and it looks like you've succeeded.'

'That's just it, Caine. People keep congratulating me, but I was barking up the wrong tree. It was you who solved it.'

'We're a team, Shant. We work together like—'

'Like the Flynn twins?'

'Which reminds me – maybe it's time to let Tyrone go. I know what you think of him, but he's not a murderer.'

'Already done. He's been released with a caution, although I've made it clear he's not to harass Ophelia.'

'Something else is troubling you . . .'

'You're right. I'm worried. I'm not sure if we've got enough to nail Vowles. Gavin's confession is convincing, but it's still his word against his uncle's.'

'But of course there's no way Gavin could have operated alone. And more importantly, Vowles has motive, whereas Gavin has none.'

'I know all of that, but I wonder if it will satisfy the CPS. Realistically we haven't got a scrap of hard evidence against him.'

In the back of the police car, Vowles continued to berate the unfortunate officers, who were powerless to do anything but soak it up.

'It's that arrogance and self-righteousness that gets me. He is genuinely convinced of his own innocence. And the trouble is, people like that can be terribly convincing in court.'

'And of course Primrose will back him to the bitter end. They're virtually conjoined.'

'Supposing he gets away with it, Caine? I've seen it happen before.'

'Yet more injustice for Gavin.'

'Now hold on a minute – I agree that Vowles was the mastermind, but Blackmore is a calculating killer. How can you talk about injustice?'

'It was coercion, Shant. Gavin was vulnerable and Vowles worked on him, day after day, year after year.'

'If you say so. But frankly, no one could coerce me into murdering a superstar in front of a hundred and fifty thousand fans.'

Benno came rushing towards them across the yard. His normally composed face appeared ashen.

'What's up, Benno?'

'My God, boss! It's . . . It's . . . You'd better come and look. I've never seen one of these before . . .'

They followed the burly sergeant to a dilapidated milking

parlour at the far end of the yard. The large hasp and padlock had been levered from the door frame. Dawn Knightly and two of her team were waiting in the cool interior, their masked faces expressionless beneath the fluorescent lights.

On the steel-topped surface of two large tables, a range of kitchen utensils were laid out, alongside tubs of nuts and chocolate chips and stacks of empty Tupperware boxes. Leaking sacks of sugar were piled on pallets on the floor, and around the walls were various items of industrial kitchen equipment – mixers and rows of slightly rusty freezer cabinets.

'Unworthy Ices,' said Shanti. 'They're pretty good actually. I'd recommend the soft-scoop peach and bilberry.'

Dawn didn't reply. Instead, she guided the DIs across the uneven floor and paused in front of a large chest freezer. Still she did not speak, but her eyes spoke volumes. With a blue-gloved hand, she reverentially raised the lid.

Shanti and Caine peered inside the illuminated interior.

'Damn it, Dawn!' said Shanti. 'That's not even funny.'

Within the cabinet was a macabre display. Wedged between bags of frozen fruit lay the glacial forms of two or more humans. One was a New Romantic, his permed hair, powder-white make-up and mascaraed eyelashes encrusted with frost. Jammed tight beside him lay a deeply chilled female rocker in frosted miniskirt and leather jacket.

'I ate that ice cream,' said Shanti.

'May they be free from suffering,' whispered Caine.

'That's not all,' said Dawn. 'Look here ... and here too ...' She marched around the room, throwing open freezer cabinets. Every one of them was crammed with ice cream, fruit, and ice-bound corpses, each dressed in snow-dusted clothing of various genres – a punk here, a metalhead there. The pitiful creatures buried deep at the bottom of the cabinets appeared to have withered into stiff-limbed ice-encrusted carcasses.

When they discovered a rapper, his icy head clad in a reversed baseball cap, his frigid hand raised sideways as if clutching a mic, it dawned on Shanti that this place was a storehouse for glacial Glastonbury performers.

'Sergeant Bennett.'

'Yes, boss.'

'Would you be kind enough to bring Primrose and Mr Vowles over here? I think they may have a few questions to answer.'

She stood stick thin in her apron, with wild hair and wild teeth, beneath the flickering lights of her milking parlour.

'Primrose Vowles, I am arresting you on suspicion of the murder of these . . . unfortunate persons . . .'

'Best keep the lids closed,' she said. 'The chill gets right into your bones.'

'You do not have to say anything, but anything you do say . . .'

'I don't know why you're making such a fuss. They're only minor celebrities.'

'I'm sorry?'

'Only minor celebrities. There's no A-listers in there, so don't waste your time looking.'

'You . . . you murdered these people?'

'That's a strong word.'

'Well, what word would you use?'

'Cold storage.'

'But . . . I mean, when did this occur?'

'Not all at once. One at a time, over many years. And some years we didn't freeze anyone, did we, Vowles?'

The tiny man appeared in the doorway, framed by the towering cops. His cap was pulled down to just above his snow-white eyebrows; a drip trembled on his burgundy nose.

'They're treatin' me like a common criminal, Primrose. Don't tell 'em nothin'. Just say "no comment" like they do on TV.'

'I rather think it's too late for that, Mr Vowles,' said Caine.

'I'm assuming these people were house guests at Unworthy?' said Shanti. 'But what I can't understand is *why?* Why would you do this, Primrose?'

'Minor misdemeanours,' she explained. 'Late payment of rent. Cracked sinks. Blocked toilets. Sneaking guests into bedrooms, that sort of thing.'

'Or bloody awful music,' muttered Vowles.

'Right, I'm going to ask you to tell me whether Gavin Blackmore was involved in any way whatsoever with these deaths.'

'Oh, I'd never allow Gav in here,' said Primrose. 'Nor Seth. No one except me and Vowles. It was our little hobby. That's what we call it, isn't it, dear?'

'No comment.'

'I often think that's why we've been together so long,' said Primrose sentimentally. 'Shared interests, see. When you've been married a very long time you become . . .'

'. . . like one,' said Vowles.

'We even . . .'

'. . . finish each other's sentences.'

'You'll be finishing some very long sentences if I have my way,' murmured Shanti.

'But Primrose,' said Caine, 'didn't you ever worry that this was . . . *wrong*?'

'Wrong, no,' said Primrose. 'We worried about power cuts and that. But Vowles had the foresight to set up a generator, didn't you, dear? In the early days we used to worry about getting found out, but you'd be surprised how careless folk are about minor celebrities. They fall off the radar all the time, those minor stars. Drugs or drink, or they just get burnt out. It's almost as if folk *want* them to disappear. Then they become legends, see, and I suppose the families and the record labels carry on taking their royalties, so everyone's a winner . . . Look I'm sure you don't want them to defrost . . .'

'Close the lids, would you, Dawn?' said Shanti.

'But Ethan Flynn was a step too far,' said Primrose. 'I told Vowles at the time, didn't I, dear? But you were always ambitious.'

Shanti turned to Vowles. 'So you admit that you conspired with Gavin Blackmore to murder Ethan Flynn?'

It was as if the congenial, Punch-like mask had slipped, revealing something devilish beneath.

'All right, damn you. I did. An' I relished every bloody second.'

'Mr Vowles, please listen carefully to what I am about to say. I am formally charging you with conspiracy to murder Ethan Flynn on the Pyramid Stage on the evening of Wednesday the twenty-sixth of June. In addition, you and Primrose are both charged with the multiple killings of other unnamed persons, on or near Unworthy Farm, Kilton, Somerset. Anything you say—'

'An' I'll tell you another bloody thing,' interrupted Vowles. 'See this nose? Don't say you ain't noticed, young lady. I seen you stare. Yes, there's a drip on the end. It's a Vowles thing. My father 'ad a drippy nose, an' his father before him. Working on the Levels, that's what does it.'

'I fail to see—'

'I dripped into the ice cream. Ha ha! That's right. I never told you, Primrose, 'cos you were always on about 'ealth an' safety. But it were my little pleasure. I'd come in 'ere with Boner and we'd drip into the ice cream.'

'Oh Vowles . . .'

'They deserve it, Primrose. They're degenerates, the lot of 'em. I'd deep-freeze every last one o' the buggers if I could.'

The small man was led away, stiff-legged and ranting.

'I've been in the force a long time,' said Shanti as she clipped the handcuffs to Primrose's wrists. 'I've witnessed some shocking things. But I have to say this beats them all. Nonetheless, it is not my job to cast judgement. You have at least cooperated in your statement . . .'

'You're welcome, I'm sure,' said Primrose frostily.

## *Chapter 32*

# Life's Longing

'And that, DI Caine, is the embodiment of a cold-hearted killer.'

They were walking down Totterdown Hill, with Caine wheeling the mud-coated Yamaha at her side.

'I've got something to tell you,' he said.

'Go on.'

'I think this will be my last case.'

'Are you absolutely kidding me? You cracked this, Caine. You did it. I let my emotions run away with me, and that was a fatal mistake.'

'You did?'

'You know what I mean. I'm talking about Tyrone. I took against him from the start.'

'You and the rest of the world. Everyone thought he was guilty.'

'But not you. The trouble is, it became personal, because he reminded me—'

'Of your ex-husband. I know. I'm sorry, Shanti.'

'Whatever. Anyway, I took my eye off the ball, while you did your thing. Slow and steady, like some kind of native tracker.'

'You're very kind, but I assure you I'm a hundred times more emotional than you. Maybe it's time I opened my heart to you, Shanti . . . I want to tell you that I . . .'

A swarm of journalists came buzzing towards them.

'DI Joyce? DI Caine? How many arrests have you made?'

'Got a statement for us?'

'Right, ladies and gentlemen, we're not in a position to go into detail, but I can confirm that three persons are in custody.'

'Is that the farmer – Vowles, isn't it?'

'And his wife?'

'Who's the third?'

'As I said, it's a little early for details. What I can tell you is that without my colleague here, we would still be in the dark about the tragic circumstances of Ethan Flynn's death.'

'Is it true you were involved in a high-speed cross-country chase, Inspector Caine?'

'Well, I rode through a sheep field . . .'

'Yes, it's true,' said Shanti. 'DI Caine put his life in jeopardy.'

'But the fugitive eluded me,' said Caine. 'So in fact it was DI Joyce who apprehended all three suspects.'

'Do you have a comment about Tyrone Flynn?'

'Did you know he will be seeking damages for false arrest?'

'Have you heard his statement, DI Joyce?'

'We've been rather busy this afternoon, haven't we, Caine? No time for TV.'

'Here, I can get it on the iPad. I think our viewers would like to hear your response.'

There was a moment of confusion, then Shanti found herself

watching a screen on which Tyrone was standing beside his lawyer and a few Flynn heavyweights on the steps of a police station.

'First thing I wanna say is that I was falsely imprisoned by some fook . . . by the cops. My lawyers will be claiming damages against those fookers . . . against the police. Everyone who knows me knows I fookin' loved my brother . . . Sorry . . . Yeah, it cuts deep. But instead of leaving my family to grieve, the feds have harassed and falsely accused us from the start. But you know what? I'm used to this shit, man. None of it surprises me. Do you know where the name Stigma comes from . . .'

As Tyrone continued with his diatribe, Shanti felt another twist of loathing.

'What's your response, DI Joyce?'

'Do you have a comment for Tyrone?'

On the screen, Tyrone was displaying his *ETHAN* tattoo for all the world to see.

'Right,' said Shanti. 'On Wednesday night, I was called in to lead this investigation. It is now Sunday afternoon, and in that short period my team and I have identified and detained three potentially dangerous suspects, in the most difficult circumstances imaginable. In order to achieve that, we needed to explore every avenue. We do that as fairly and impartially as we can. If that process caused offence, then I apologise. But my overwhelming concern was to identify a murderer before anyone else came to harm. We'll be giving a full statement at a later stage.'

'What about you, DI Caine?'

'How would you sum up the case?'

The scrum had reached the bottom of Totterdown Hill, near

the back of the Five Heads. Caine kicked out the foot stand and leaned on the bike.

'I think this case was about love,' he said.

'Love? How could it be about love?'

'What's love got to do with it?'

'Can you hold that pose while we get a few shots, DI Caine?'

Molly Appleyard materialised from behind the pub wall. 'Right, fuck off you lot,' she told the journalists. 'I've been telling you all week not to hang about here.'

They dispersed reluctantly.

'And what have you done to my bike?' she demanded. 'I said you could take it for a short spin. Look at the state of it! Look at the state of *you*!'

'Molly, I'm so sorry. I got into . . . a situation.'

'Right, well here's another situation. Here's a bucket. And here's a cloth. And a brush. And a hose, look. So you get stuck in now, and don't say another word till my Yammy is gleaming. Is that fair?'

She marched through the back door and banged it behind her.

'Damn it, Caine,' said Shanti. 'We've got plans for tonight, remember?'

'You haven't told me what we're doing.'

'Can't you guess? I'm taking you to watch my mate Sista on the Pyramid.'

'OK. And after that?'

'After that, you and I are going to shake hands. Then you'll go back to your lonely man-cabin, and I'll head home to my cosy little bed in Yeovil, where I will sleep for a month.'

'Shanti, there's no way you can do that.'

'Of course I can. Benno and the team will finish up here.'

'I don't mean that. I mean you won't get home tonight. I've been to this festival loads of times, and trust me, when the headline act finishes on a Sunday, a hundred and fifty thousand people head for their cars. You'll be stuck half the night.'

'I'll use the blues and twos.'

'You wouldn't.'

'I would.'

'That won't work anyway. Remember what happened when Vowles called the paramedics for his mother. The ambulance was gridlocked. No. If you really want to get home, you need to leave now.'

'And miss Sista Tremble? You must be joking. We're like besties.'

'Then you'll have to stay till morning.'

'Stay? Stay where? In case you hadn't noticed, Unworthy Farm is a major crime scene. Anyway, I detest that place. It's like the bloody Antarctic. And the bed is haunted too.'

'Right, can I make a suggestion?'

'Possibly.'

'I promised Misty I would cook dinner for her tonight. Something special to celebrate the success of her gig. But it's only fair that I clean Molly's bike. So why don't you go ahead to my tent? You think you can find it?'

'Possibly.'

'And tell Misty that I'm on my way. It will be a pleasure to cook for the two of you. You'd like that, wouldn't you?'

'Possibly.'

'Then we'll all go and watch Sista Tremble. And after that . . .'

'After that, Caine?'

'After that, you can have my tent to yourself.'

'And where will you sleep, Buddha-pest?'

'Under the stars. It's going to be a beautiful night. It'll make a perfect end to the festival. Say yes, Shanti.'

'Possibly, Caine.'

The beautiful girl lay sleeping outside Caine's tent in the late-afternoon glow, her flame-haired head propped against a backpack, her guitar at her side. Shanti studied her for a while. Although Misty's complexion was fairer, there was an unmistakable resemblance to her half-brother.

'Hello,' she said, opening one eye and smiling. 'Is Vince with you?'

'He said to tell you to wait. He won't be long.'

Misty appeared to have the same ability as Caine to sit elegantly cross-legged without support. Shanti had never learned to sit without a chair, and she lounged uncomfortably on the grass.

'So what heroics have you two been up to?' said Misty. 'The whole festival is buzzing. Is it true you made an arrest?'

Shanti felt exhausted.

'Yes. Several arrests. No doubt you'll hear the details soon enough. Not so many heroics from me, but in case you hadn't realised, your brother is a first-class DI. Best I've ever worked with. I don't say it to him because I don't want his head to get any bigger than it is.'

'Oh. I don't think Vince would ever get big-headed.'

'This is called kidding, Misty. You know that concept? Or as they say in the canteen, banter.'

'Oh yes, isn't that what people do when they're embarrassed to say what they really feel?'

'Jeez, there's no doubt about it – you definitely are his sister.'

'To be honest, Shanti, I worry about Vince. He's too sensitive for this job. He should probably have been an artist like Mum.'

'Your mother is an artist?'

'Didn't Vince tell you? I think he was actually named after van Gogh.'

'Caine never tells me a thing. So, to get this straight – you have the same mother, but different fathers?'

'Yes. Several years before I was born, Mum separated from Vince's dad and remarried. My dad is a wonderful man.'

'Tell me if this is none of my business, but I get the impression that there's some history between Caine – I mean Vincent – and his dad.

'Yes, I think there is.'

'He doesn't seem to want to talk about it with me.'

'No, he's never talked to me about it either. I used to ask Mum, but she didn't want to go there.'

'But you've met his father?'

'Only a few times. He's an unusual man. Very good-looking. Olive skin, with brushed-back silver hair. And the same Malteser eyes as Vince.'

'Yes, I've seen a photo.'

'I believe he has Persian heritage, the old man. But there's definitely something secretive about him. He's like a closed door. And then there's Vince's brother, of course.'

'What? Caine has a brother?'

'Oh dear. You swear you won't tell him I told you?'

'I'd really like to hear about this, Misty.'

'Look, I don't want to offend you, Shanti, but I have to go.' She rose to her feet and hauled her pack onto her back.

'Oh, OK. But why don't you hang around for a bit? I think Caine was planning to cook for you.'

'I know. But I think he'd be happy to share a meal with you. In any case, someone's giving me a lift, so I really need to shoot. Please tell Vince I love him and give him a kiss from me. A big one. You promise?'

'Sure. And listen, Misty, I'm not very good at compliments, but your singing is out of this world. I was really moved, and believe me, I don't do moved. You've got something very special, I'm sure you know that.'

'That means a lot, Shanti. And I hope you don't mind me saying that you and Caine are made for each other.'

'Ah, now wait a minute. We're colleagues. It couldn't work any other way. Besides, we're very different, you know. Like chalk and cheese.'

'But you know he's in love with you?'

'He's what? What did you say?'

'Bye, Shanti. Let me give you a hug. Thank you for getting justice for Ethan.'

Then the girl with the guitar was gone.

It was the smell that woke her – a delicious aroma of sautéed vegetables and herbs. Shanti pulled back the tent flaps and crawled outside, where Caine was tending the fire and stirring several simmering pans.

'Oh, I'm sorry, Caine. I was so tired.'

'Why are you apologising? I told you – the tent is for you.'

'It's very cosy in there. I hope you don't mind, I borrowed this shirt.'

'It suits you. Help yourself to anything else you need. Did you see Misty?'

'She said she had to go. I'm supposed to give you a big kiss.'

'Go on then.'

'What are you making, Caine?'

'I call it fried end-of-festival thing.'

'It sounds wonderful. So long as there's no ice cream. Tragically, I'll never eat ice cream again.'

'It's a shame Misty isn't here to share it.'

'It was you who told me that she lives up to her name. She has a tendency to evaporate.'

'I know I'm too protective. I still think of her as a little kid. Did you ever read *The Prophet*?'

'Accountancy book?'

'Kahlil Gibran. It's beautiful, Shant. There's a line about parenting that applies equally to eight-year-old boys and little sisters – *Your children are not your children, they are the sons and daughters of Life's longing for itself.*'

'Talking of bullshit, what was it you said to those reporters? That this case is about love?'

'Yeah, Medusa was right, wasn't she? The whole thing is about love.'

'I wouldn't say so. No.'

'Look at all the love for Ethan. I've never seen such an outpouring.'

'Well, yes, but . . .'

'Then there's Ethan's love for Eve, which goes beyond life itself.'

'And what about Drippynose Vowles? He didn't love anyone.'

'He loved his mother. He loved Primrose. And he loved Unworthy Farm.'

'Well I'm touched by your naïvety, but I maintain that Primrose has a choc ice for a heart.'

'Which reminds me – Benno had an email from the Harley Street doctor. It turns out Ethan was suffering from something called dilated cardiomyopathy.'

'Translation?'

'His heart struggled to pump blood round the body. Maybe that's why he was always tired. The consultant said that many people live with it, if they have the right treatment, but there's a small group who are prone to life-threatening abnormal heart rhythm, which can cause sudden cardiac arrest. Ethan was one of them.'

'So are you saying it was the disease that killed him, not the shock? Because we don't want some smart-arse barrister pulling the case apart.'

'That current could have killed anyone. But his condition certainly didn't help.'

Caine served the food onto their plates.

'Oh my God, I'm having a mouthgasm. Where did you learn to do this?'

'Years of solitary living.'

'Well I've got a solution for that . . .'

'Oh Shanti, that would be—'

'Boner, Caine. You could look after him. You're made for each other. There's plenty of room in the cabin, and that dog truly loves you.'

'Ah. No thanks. I'm sure Seth will care for him.'

'Oh yes, Seth. Do you think he knew about the goings-on at Unworthy Farm?'

'I think he slept through everything. From what I gather, he may inherit the place one day. Let's hope he makes a better job of it than his parents.'

'There's still an unanswered question. A deep one . . . mysterious and enigmatic.'

'Really?'

'Who was the Unworthy Wanker?'

'Perhaps not everything in life has an answer, Shanti.'

She looked out across the valley, where a raggle-taggle army were folding their tents and packing their belongings, and felt the weight of responsibility drift from her shoulders. Everything was fine. In fact when you stopped to notice, life was absurdly beautiful.

Like Medusa said, all you needed to do was stop fighting.

As the burning ball of the sun descended behind Glastonbury Tor, they found a place to sit on the densely crowded hillside, with a perfect view of the Pyramid Stage, which thrust like an intergalactic chariot into the sky.

Caine set out blankets and retrieved the flask from his shoulder bag. 'Thought you'd like a nip of something stronger,' he said.

'Ha, look, Caine!' laughed Shanti. 'I'd recognise those cheeks anywhere.'

With pale buttocks upended to the teasing crowd, Sparky Mudget was kneeling before an amplifier, as if in worship.

When the Spark1Up team, in black jeans and T-shirts, had departed, the stage fell into ten minutes of brooding darkness, in which Shanti felt excitement mounting and spreading through the ever-increasing multitude.

At last a single spotlight glided across the boards and a vast roar exploded as the elegant form of Vula Plenty filled the enormous screens on either side of the stage. It was strange to see her simultaneously so huge and so tiny, dressed in lavish harem pants, an elaborately patterned headscarf, huge hoop earrings and a silver embroidered waistcoat.

Before she had uttered a word in those familiar bourbon and honey tones, she was weeping with emotion.

'What a week, my friends! What a festival. But I know you haven't come to see me ... Thank you, thank you, you are too kind. All I want to say is that love conquers all. In a moment it will be my privilege to introduce the undisputed queen of soul, but a quick reminder that this concert will be broadcast live on the BBC, and on a special edition of my own humble radio show, *Vula Has Plenty For You*. Thank you. Thank you ... Ladies and gentlemen, please give all the love you hold in your hearts for the wonderful, the astonishing, the incredible ... SISTA TREMBLE!'

Shanti felt a physical quake of excitement surge through her body, magnified a hundred thousand times for every person in that endless arena, in which the ceiling was an infinite sparkling galaxy.

As Caine poured another cup of whatever deliciously potent brew he carried, she texted Paul and Amma, who would be watching at home.

*Love u both so much. Home 2morrow my darlings xxx*

Then she was swept to her feet by a rising tide of people, and there in the very centre of the Pyramid was her table companion, Sista Tremble. Now she understood why Sista had been created so large in every way – because she was built for this stage. Here she appeared perfectly proportioned and magnificent, dressed in a flowing red ball gown, cut so low that her breasts surfaced like twin planets.

Shanti and Caine clinked cups and toasted everything that was good in the world. And then Sista addressed the crowd.

'Our hearts ache, my sisters and brothers. But the pain we feel reminds us that we *have* hearts. As my friend Vula Plenty has said, love conquers all. All is love. And speaking of love, something magical has come into my possession . . . I ain't done this before – performed without a whole lotta rehearsal. But I think this song is worth that risk. That's because what I am about to perform, for the very first time in public, is Ethan Flynn's final song. This is my tribute to him, my friends. Yeah. I thank you. Before I begin, I wanna give a personal shout-out to my very dear friend who shared this wondrous gift with me and made this possible. Is she here? Is she amongst you? Ladies and gentlemen, please give all your love to my sister Shanti Joyce . . .'

Shanti leapt about on the grass, waving her arms, as people around her took photos and selfies.

'That's me, Caine. Holy moly! She said my name!'

As Sista was addressing the crowd, her band and a full-sized orchestra had quietly taken their places behind her. Now a troupe of dancers and backing singers emerged from stage right and left. Amongst them were the Tarot dancers – including a beaming Fabrizio – dressed more traditionally on this occasion, in skin-tight leotards that gleamed on every muscle and appendage.

Sista Tremble swayed towards a vast golden piano, where she sat, adjusted her microphone and began to play the hauntingly beautiful tune devised by that enigmatic genius Ethan Flynn. As the violins started to build, Sista leaned in to the microphone and whispered, 'Brothers and sisters, I give you ... "Song for Eve" ...

*Sleepy creature of the sacred dome*
*Spread your wings, it's time to fly from home ...*

Amongst the enchanted crowd, Shanti and Caine swayed and danced, swept away by Sista's mighty voice, which soared across the valleys of Worthy Farm.

And far away in a private hospital in Hampshire, a woman named Ophelia cried, 'Crikey!' and writhed in labour as her dancer's body split, and she was delivered of a child. A child named Eve, who gazed into her mother's smiling face with unbounded intelligence and compassion in her emerald eyes.

Later, in Caine's tent, a little drunk, a little foolish, Shanti pulled off her clothes in the candlelit interior and burrowed deep into the warm bed, which smelt deliciously of man. Which smelt of Caine.

'What are you doing out there?' she called.

'Fixing up a bed, Shanti. It's a wonderful night. You get to sleep.'

'Damn it, Caine ... OK, I can't do this ...'

'Can't do what?'

'Can't take your bed while you sleep outside.'

'Honestly, it's fine. The stars are amazing. I think that's Venus over there.'

'Realistically ... I mean, there might be room for both of us. Come and try it, Caine. I'll move over. Does this thing ...?'

The sleeping bag unzipped effortlessly into one large duvet.

'Ah, Shanti, I don't want to—'

'It's your tent, Caine. I'm cruel, but not that cruel.'

'But what about the line?'

'What line, funny man?'

'The line of duty. The thin blue line between us.'

She thumped him hard on his muscular arm and tried not to notice as Caine removed his clothes, folding them neatly in a pile, then, dressed in nothing more than beauty and snugly fitting briefs, slipped in beside her.

She lay on her back in the flickering glow, her feet throbbing from miles and miles of walking, as a cosy warmth permeated the makeshift bed. She felt absurdly conscious of the proximity of their bodies.

'Why is it so warm, Caine? I mean, we are actually outside, in a tent in a field, but it's like a furnace compared to Unworthy Farm.'

'Body heat, Shant.'

They lay for a long time. Each wondering if the other was asleep.

'What time does the music stop?' she asked.

'Oh, the bands have finished. But I'm afraid the drums and guitars will go on for a while.'

'Go and arrest them, Caine.'

'It's just people. Just sounds. Shall I play some music on my phone?'

'What kind of music?' she asked warily.

'A surprise. I think you'll like this . . .'

He tweaked the volume and the tent was filled with an excruciating disharmony.

'Oh my God, Caine! What is that? It's utterly horrific. Like musical waterboarding.'

'Half Man Half Bull. I admit, it doesn't sound great – it's an old recording, I suppose.'

'Listen, Caine. Nothing personal, but it's time someone broke it to you – I'm afraid you didn't inherit your sister's musical gene. Maybe you should stick with cooking ... or police work. You're good at that.'

'OK, I'll find something else to listen to ... Ah! This is nice. Vula's radio show. I think we can ... yes ... we can listen again. Here we go. Tonight's Sista Tremble concert.'

'Now you're talking.'

Caine propped the iPhone near the shrine, as Vula's sultry tones introduced a special live performance from the Glastonbury Festival, deep in the Somerset countryside.

It seemed that Caine's tent, like everything else at Glastonbury, had been pitched on a slope, because no matter how she tried, Shanti found herself drifting towards him.

'What are you thinking, Caine?' she whispered.

'You never answered my question.'

'I didn't hear a question.'

'I asked if you ever thought about that night. By the bay near my cabin.'

'All the time,' she sighed.

'Here it comes, Shant. Listen. "Song for Eve". You like it?'

'I'll show you what I like ... Kiss me, Caine. Just kiss me.'

# Song for Eve

Sleepy creature of the sacred dome
Spread your wings, it's time to fly from home

*Chorus: Look down*

Between us lies the ever-breathing sea
Big waves crying – our love can never be

*Chorus: Look down*

So c-cold, my chamber underground
I am lost. But darling you are found

*Chorus: Look down*

Forever strangers, like daytime is to night
Yet I love you, like the darkness loves the light

*Chorus: Look down*

They say 'We're north and south. Our lives are poles apart'
I say 'We turn together on the compass of my heart'

*Chorus: Look down*

So whenever you need me, sleepy little bud
You'll find me spinning, singing . . . I'm swimming in your blood, girl

*Chorus: It's time to leave, darling Eve*
*Don't you grieve, darling Eve*
*Stay naïve, darling Eve*
*Just believe, darling Eve*

*(REPEAT TO FADE)*